NATION

RALPH COTTON'S

BLOWBACK

TREASURE COAST

BOOK III: THE GUN CULTURE SERIES

COTTON-BRANCH PUBLISHING

BLOWBACK
TREASURE COAST

BOOK THREE OF THE
GUN CULTURE SERIES

BY RALPH COTTON

He may be reached at **www.ralphcotton.com**

Cover photo by Mary Lynn Cotton

Interior art from 123RF.com
Author's photo, p. 317, by Shay Morton

Cover design & book layout by Laura Ashton
laura@gitflorida.com

ISBN: 979-8695678505

Printed in the United States of America

COTTON-BRANCH PUBLISHING

Some Reviews from Books I and II of the Gun Culture Series

Patrick Naville, Bestselling author of Pipeline

Book I: Ralph Cotton has consistently been an outstanding writer in the Western genre, but I believe he's hit upon a whole new talent for modern day literary fiction. This was one of those books that you hate to put down because you're afraid something will happen and you'll miss it! It's fast-paced, the characters are well developed and story hooks you from the first page. Ralph describes the seedy side of the Florida drug underworld and does so in such a way that you hope you never cross paths with any of these people. The bad guys are as nasty as they come! Ralph throws some plot twists in there that the reader never sees coming. I won't give the ending away other than to say, you WILL be surprised! Great job, Mr. Cotton! I look forward to the next one in the Gun Culture Series. Keep 'em coming!

Cheryl, Amazon Reviewer

Book I: Mr. Cotton's first book in his new Gun Culture series: *Friend Of A Friend* does not disappoint! His gift for capturing the subtle and not-so-subtle nuances of his characters -- from seedy, psycho criminals to everyday heroes is flawless. There is a realism and a familiarity of his characters that draws the reader in from page one. His ability to weave riveting plot twists is one of the reasons I have trouble putting his books down when I know I should be turning out the light to get to sleep! I'm anxiously awaiting the arrival of *Book 2* in the Gun Culture series: *Season of the Wind.*

Casper Parks

Book I: Great story line, looking forward to more in this new series. *Friend of a Friend* does an excellent job of setting the stage for up coming books in the series. Ralph's writing style carried very well into this genre. With roughly 70 books in print, glad to see he isn't slowing down.

Some Reviews from Books I and II
of the Gun Culture Series

T. Rice

Book I: I have read many of his westerns and really enjoyed them. Was a bit skeptical about reading this type of book, but I really enjoyed it and will buy the next one. His characters are always interesting and usually twisted in unexpected ways. What happens next is pretty unpredictable. The plot moves right along with many unusual results from what you think is coming. A fun read.

Carolina Mud Duck

Book I: Best. Dialog. Ever.

Book II: After 'Friend of a Friend', I had high expectations for this book. Once again, Ralph Cotton does not disappoint! Rich dialog and a meticulous attention to detail made this a "cover-to-cover' read for me!!!

Harald G. Hall

Book II: Great story to read.all the action you want.lots of twists and turns.

FloridaGal

Book I: Mr. Cotton's stories never disappoint, I look forward to the next in his Gun Culture series. Anyone on the gulf coast will recognize the locations and the outrageous characters. Nobody does it better!

Bob H

Book II: Another bestseller by R.C.

I just finished Ralph Cotton's new book and am ready for the next one. Lucky for me there are others books of his that I can read while I wait for the next book. I would recommend this book to everyone.

For Mary Lynn ... *of course*

PART I

CHAPTER 1

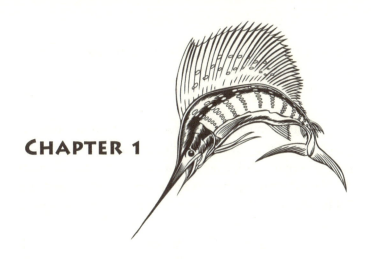

Fifteen stories up, on the balcony of the Oceana Princess II Complex overlooking the beach, Harold Wright sat in a wrought iron deck chair with a flat briefcase lying on his shaky knees. He was nervous—*far too nervous to be around these people,* he told himself. But there was nothing he could do about it now. Lately, being in business with Victor Trio and Ian Lambert, AKA: *the Lamb,* gave Harold a jittery sick feeling down low in his stomach. He looked back and forth between the two men.

Jesus! What was he doing here? *Okay,* it was his name, Harold Wright, on the business cards: *Wright Way Venture Capital, Harold Wright, Owner.* It would also be his name on the engraved brass door plate, if they ever had a real office door they could hang it on, which they didn't have so far, doing business as they were from Victor's residential condo. But they might have, someday soon once they leased office space somewhere and moved out of here. *Jesus!* None of this made him feel any better right now.

He'd taken two valiums the Lamb handed him earlier, but that hadn't helped either. All the valium did was put a fuzzy glow around everything and make things seem to move a little slower.

In the sharp sunlight, Harold looked at big Victor Trio.

Victor leaned back, three-hundred-plus pounds of gristle and fat against the balcony rail and blew a long puff of cigar smoke up and away on a coastal breeze. As Harold stared at him, Victor spoke to this newcomer, Eddie Vango, who'd shown up only moments ago and stood facing Trio from a few feet away.

Victor said to this Vango, "So, what's Stanley think, that I'm trying to stiff him or something, sending you down here?"

Eddie Vango smiled, an easy sort of smile that didn't give much away. He looked around from Victor Trio to Ian Lambert, who stood a few feet away on the other side of him. Lambert stared at him real hard through coppery, bloodshot eyes. *Interrupt our meeting this way* …. Across the balcony, Victor's bodyguard, Bones, an ancient Cuban, sat staring through his blackout shades. A semi-automatic shotgun rested on his knobby knee. Eddie Vango shrugged, looking back at Trio.

"Let me be clear," said Vango, "I'm not a debt collector. If I was, and Stanley thought you were stiffing him, I wouldn't come knocking on your door, would I?" He spread his hands. Up one side of Vango's loose white shirt, a flashy green and gold deco palm tree pressed against his chest and fluttered in the warm breeze. "Stanley wants his money. Think of me as an extra—sort of a personal *VIP service,* come all the way down here to pick it up from you."

"Yeah? A *VIP service?"* Victor stuck his black

cigar back in his mouth and glanced at the Lamb. Harold Wright watched, trying to swallow a dry lump that had settled into his throat, his valium losing its kick, off and on. He didn't know how much longer he could be around people like this—people who acted like this, who talked this way, people with nicknames that sounded childlike, yet sinister, dangerous. Victor once told him that back in the day he'd been known as *Victor the Bull*. Thinking back, that was the day Harold should have left, just dropped whatever was in his hands at that second and made a run for the door. Should have but didn't. The money was too good.

Victor tried to out stare Eddie Vango for a second, but Vango didn't appear the least bit put off. Seeing it, Victor turned, shook his head, laid his hands along the steel balcony rail and spoke back over his shoulder to Harold Wright.

"Little Harold, give this monkey thirty bucks, get him out of here before he upsets me." Sunlight shot off his diamond ring like some mini laser beam. The breeze nipped at his wide shirt collar.

Of course, Harold Wright knew that bucks meant thousands in these guys' language, and at that moment he had less than forty dollars and change on him. He squirmed a little under his briefcase, looked at this Eddie Vango, and said, "I'm afraid we'll have to make other arrangements, Mr. Vango. Thirty thousand is a rather large amount to be carrying around." He smiled, but Vango saw a nervous twitch in there.

"Make that thirty-*eight,* bucks," Vango said, smiling back at Harold Wright, Harold squirming some more, thinking, *geez,* how'd he become the responsible party all of a sudden?

"The hell you talking about?" Victor Trio snapped back around from the rail. He shot Vango a look full of daggers and acid. "Where'd you come up with this thirty-*eight* figure?"

Again, Harold Wright saw Eddie Vango's easy smile as he reminded Victor of an eight-thousand *vig and penalty* that had accumulated. He went on, coolly telling Victor he should have taken care of the gambling debt sooner, beat all the extra charges. But Harold Wright only heard part of it because he'd turned, half-startled, toward Ian Lambert who'd just kicked a deck chair out of his way and moved toward Eddie Vango, bristling.

"You got some balls," Lambert hissed, "come barging in here over some two-bit—" But Lambert stopped short, less than a foot back, when Victor raised a hand, stopping him.

"Hold it, Lamb," Victor said, seeing that this Eddie Vango hadn't backed an inch –wasn't going to, it appeared. He just stood there smiling, both hands deep in his trouser pockets. This guy was cool. *You had to give him that,* Wright thought.

"Come on, Victor!" the Lamb shouted. "Say the word. I'll put this *punk* in the wind, see how he flies." He gestured a big red hand out past the balcony rail, him and Vango standing face to face, inches apart. Vango still wore the loose easy smile, but his eyes looked different now. They'd turned flat, resolved, like at any second now he might coolly, calmly, take *the Lamb* apart. Dismantle him where he stood.

But then Vango cut his gaze away from Lambert, real slow, craned up a little on the balls of his feet and gazed out over the rail. He looked a long way down at the beach, at waves rolling in, at tiny people moving around down there, half-naked.

"Ouch ...," he said. Then he smiled again, looking back, straight into the Lamb's boiling eyes.

Lambert almost lunged at him; but Trio stopped him again.

"I said, *hold it!"* he said, glaring at *the Lamb.* "This is between me and Stanley the Pole."

Stanley the Pole ...? My God! That's a new one, Harold Wright thought, watching. *Jesus, these guys ...!*

Lambert still boiled, but he took a step back. In the far corner, Bones had raised an inch from his chair. Now he eased back down as tempers settled. Harold Wright sat biting at the inside of his lip, struggling to keep his nerves at bay.

"What can I tell you, Mister Trio," Vango said, "nobody in their *right mind* would've taken Baltimore and six." He shrugged, chuckled a little. "Now, if everybody's through scaring me," —he gave Lambert a hard-challenging stare, then turned back to Trio— "pay up and we'll forget all this. Stanley's still your friend, but a debt's a debt. Everybody pays the Pole. You know that."

A tense silence moved through, a coastal breeze whispering across them, warm and steadily.

Harold Wright sweated, his valium—or whatever it was—only working on and off, for now it had gone completely flat. He glanced from one to the other in this gathering of madmen: Victor, formerly called *the Bull,* his three-hundred-plus pounds of bulk standing on stick legs; Ian *the Lamb,* tall, raw-boned, Scots-Irish head breaker, red-gray hair curling every which way; Bones, an ancient Cuban bodyguard, looking like a skeleton, with sunlight sizzling on his blackout shades. All of this was feeling like some bad dream. And in their midst now, this Eddie Vango, confident, half-smiling, his feet planted shoulder-width apart, like some young Sinatra ready to break into *That's Life*. After a long tight second, Victor Trio chuckled, flashed Lambert a glance, and rolled a big thumb at Vango. "You believe this guy? He tells me, '*Nobody in their right mind takes Baltimore and six.*'" He looked away, shook his head again. "Little Harold, bring Mr. Vango over to your place tonight, give him *thirty-eight bucks.*" Victor gazed out across the ocean, chuckling in a low growling wheeze. "Christ all-mighty, *Baltimore and six.* I must've been out of my frigging mind ...."

Now, with Eddie Vango gone and the door closed behind him, the Lamb eased back another step, red heat lifting from his pockmarked face. Harold Wright sat staring, going over what had just happened, some of it real, some of it ... he wasn't sure. Even the parts that were real he couldn't fully believe. He tried to recount the entire scenario to himself, seeming to have gone blank for a moment as it actually happened.

Their meeting had been going on, if you could call it a meeting. This Eddie Vango fellow had shown up out of nowhere, telling Victor Trio he'd came here to collect a gambling debt for some bookie named Stanley the Pole, (one more peculiar nickname) and he wants it right now. Like today! First thing Trio does is try to hard-stare Bones for letting this guy in. Bones only shrugged; he didn't care.

"Let's not dick each other around," Vango had told Victor right off, getting his full attention. Harold clenched up; nobody spoke that way to these guys. Maybe he should talk with this Vango tonight when Vango came by his house for the money, see if Vango had any advice for him. He sure needed to talk to somebody.

When Trio told Harold to bring him over to his place and give him thirty-eight bucks, Harold had shakily come up with a business card, scribbled his home address on the back of it, and gave it to Eddie Vango. "I'll expect you around ten?"

"Owner, Financial Adviser, and Accountant, huh?" Eddie Vango glanced at the card, smiled. "Yeah, ten o'clock then." He snapped the corner of the card with his thumb and slipped it into his shirt pocket behind the fluttering deco palm tree. Still smiling, he'd gazed out across the ocean, taking his time now, closing his eyes against the warm breeze. "Nice weather, huh?"

Victor and the Lamb looked at one another—the *nerve* of this guy—until Victor finally said, "Anything *else* I can do for you today, *Mr.* Vango?"

Vango said, "Yeah. You guys live down here year 'round, maybe you can tell me something?"

"What's that?" Victor drew on his cigar and let a gray stream go off on the breeze.

"I'm only here a couple of days. I'm wondering ... what's the best sunblock for this time of year?" He rubbed his left hand up and down his right forearm— again the smile—his right hand still down deep in his pocket. "I'm asking for a friend."

The Lamb was through with this guy. "Get your ass out of here," he growled, stepping away, knowing the guy was only breaking their balls now that he had delivered the message.

Victor gave Vango a flat stare. Yeah, this Vango guy is cool. Like he'd said, he was no debt collector. Victor believed him. Stanley the Pole was known to hire the best. And Vango had been right, everybody paid the Pole. Victor let the sunblock remark go. But Lambert picked it up and said, "You want to get rid of a sunburn? Get a bottle of scotch and lay all day on the beach with it. More sun will sweat it out—toughen up your system." His voice was a little slurred by alcohol. Vango just gave him a look.

Trio cut in. "Mr. Vango, we get this debt settled, you tell Stanley not to quit taking my action, huh? We go back a ways, Stanley and me. You let him know we're okay, right?"

"Sure." Vango shrugged again. "Like I said, He's still your friend, Mr. Trio." –Vango giving Trio a little respect now that they were straightening things out. "He wanted his money. He didn't hear from you ... what's he going to think?" Vango took a step away, waited as Bones the bodyguard got up to follow him to the door. Then he lifted his right hand from his pocket for the first time since he'd arrived. The weight of a pistol pressed down slightly in his pocket behind the pleated summer gabardines. He spread both hands now—a young Sinatra making a breezy exit—and said, "Gentlemen, it's been a pleasure."

Ian Lambert tossed back a shot of scotch and let out a whiskey hiss, clenching his teeth. "Van-go, huh? Like the guy who painted the pictures and stuff?"

"Yeah, except I got two good ears."

Lambert didn't get the part about two good ears.

"I'll remember you, Mister Eddie Van-go."

Vango sucked at a tooth, a wicked little curve coming into his smile. "You do that ... and I'll remember you, Mister *Sheep.* " He poked a finger at him.

"It's *Lamb,* you punk! Nobody calls me a *Sheep.* Now, you get out of here!" His face swelled red again, neck tendons standing out tight.

"Yeah, I got it." Vango tossed it off and said, "Lamb, *Sheep,* whatever." And he left.

Harold Wright, flashing back on it, wondered if he was still hanging onto any level of semi-sane reality, sitting here watching dangerous madmen make fun of each other's names? The valiums were coming on stronger, as was often the case when the Lamb came up with some pills for him.

On the way across the living room to the door, Vango whispered over his shoulder to Bones who had stood up and walked along a half-step behind him. "Bones, are these guys for real?"

"Yeah, they're for real." Bones followed him only a foot behind.

"Geez ... Then you might should have told this chump nobody was taking Baltimore and six last year."

"I wasn't here last year," Bones replied under his breath.

Eddie gave him a slight nod and asked, "What's this guy Harold on?"

"Valium, they're telling him," Bones said. "Who knows?"

"Yeah, who knows," Vango said. "Suppose I want to reach you. I can still find you at Teensi's?"

"Yeah, for now," said the old Cuban. "Drop by. We'll catch up."

"Will do," Vango said. "I might want some good advice down here."

Neither of them spoke again until they reached the door and Vango reached out and turned the knob. Then as Vango tilted a glance to him, Bones said in a whisper that sounded like the quiet hiss of a snake, "Good advice? Go home soon, Eddie, you won't like this heat."

CHAPTER 2

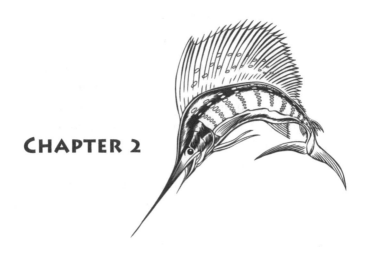

Out front of the Oceana Princess II Complex, Eddie Vango had taken notice of a white service style van that had been sitting there when he had first walked inside. A simple plastic sign on the side of the van announced: J W Home Cleaning Co. By The Room Or By The Hour. On his way out the van was still sitting there, its engine running, no one in the driver's seat.

There was something else—something that wasn't right about the van. He couldn't say what, but it would come to him. Without looking more closely, he walked three rows past the van and got into a dark green Pontiac that sat with its engine also running.

"So? How'd it go up there?" his backup man, Lew Stucky, asked. Stucky sat behind the Pontiac's steering wheel, beads of sweat standing on his red forehead with the AC blowing full blast.

"Everything's cool," Vango said. "These guys are friendly enough."

"Good. So, you got Stanley's money then?" Stucky fanned his loose, sweaty shirt against his broad chest.

"Tonight," Vango said, gazing ahead through the

windshield.

"Tonight? Man! I knew I shoulda gone up and cracked this guy's head. Didn't ya push him for it?"

"No," Vango smiled. "That's not how Stanley wants it handled. He wants to keep the guy's action. Evidently the guy spends big. Let's get you back to your room. You don't look so good."

"Forget how I look. I think cracking the guy's nut *is* the way to handle it," Lew Stucky said, bumping the shift lever into drive. "You been up there all this time, the guy jerking ya around, I'm down here burning the hell up. You and Stanley are worried about this chump because he's connected, is what I think."

"You're wrong, Lew. This Trio's not connected to Trafficante's people down here. Trafficante leaves this Treasure Coast wide open—the rest of the state is his. These guys are just a couple of indy operators."

"Yeah? Even more reason you shoulda straightened the guy out," Stucky insisted. "Let everybody know you don't dick Chicago around."

Vango let out a breath. Nobody could tell Lew Stucky anything. He wasn't going to try.

They'd pulled away from the curb, and as they passed the Home Cleaning van, Vango glanced over at it. *Bingo!* Now it came to him what was wrong. There was no phone number on the sign or the side of the van. *Good catch* ..., he told himself. He settled back in the seat.

"It wasn't the right time or place to straighten anybody out," he said to Stucky. "These guys are bugged."

"How ya know that?" Stucky glanced at him and gunned the Pontiac over into the far lane.

He didn't feel like explaining about the white van, so he said, "Anytime you're talking to these big independent blow dealers, always figure somebody's listening."

"Yeah right, like you're telling me something I don't already know?" They swung around the corner onto Ocean Drive, heading South to the island drawbridge. "I think these guys shook ya up, is what I think."

Vango gazed off, rolled his eyes, and made a sucking sound through his teeth.

"Bet you didn't mention about the sunblock like I ask ya to, either."

"Lew, do you realize how weak that sounds, asking these guys about *sunblock?*"

"Screw them. I'm burning like a freaking grilled pork chop!" A second passed. "So, you didn't ask?"

"Sure, I told you I would," Vango said, thinking it over. *A pork chop ...?* "I asked them. But I don't believe what they told me." He glanced at Stucky, seeing his glowing red forearms, and smiled.

"Yeah, what's that?" Stucky staring ahead, sweat beads filling up and running down his sunburned face.

"This guy Lambert says the best thing for sunburn this time of year is to get back out in the sun with a bottle of scotch for a few hours and let the sun sweat it out of you." He shrugged and added, "Sounds crazy, don't you think?"

"Sweat it out, huh?" Stucky stared ahead, considering it.

"Forget it though," said Vango. "The guy doesn't know what he's talking about. You don't *sweat out* a sunburn."

"See, you been here two days, you already think you know more than the locals?"

"If it was me, I'd forget the scotch. I'd get soaked in vinegar and stay in the shade." Vango shrugged again. "That's what I'd do."

"And go around smelling like a pickle for the next week? No thanks, smart guy."

"Then do what you think," Vango said. "No way I'd get back out in this hot sun with a sunburn, no matter who told me to."

"Scotch. Wonder why scotch?" Stucky tilted his head, still considering it, and drove on …

When the Lamb closed the door behind Little Harold, he rolled his eyes toward the ceiling, *Jesus ….* He smiled, then walked back out on the balcony rubbing his hands together.

Victor clamped his teeth down on the cigar and puffed it. "So, what do ya think?"

"Scared out of his mind, is what I think," the Lamb said, stepping up beside him, staring out at the silver-gray swells on the horizon. "You wanta know the truth, I figure he's good for maybe another week before he starts wanting to confess his sins to somebody."

"Yeah, me too, about a week. Less than that if you run out of the crap you've got him living on." Victor took the cigar from his lips and let out a long sigh. "So, that's another thing we gotta deal with."

"Yeah, but don't worry, I've got him on a string. I told him, if you make a move on him, I'll come take him away." The Lamb smiled, held his face to the breeze, feeling the sun warm on his face.

"I wanted him to pick up some of that *private* blow for us, coming in through Jamaica, but maybe it's not a good idea. Get rid of him, *tonight.* Give him a few hours, let him get good and high. Then drive him over to Crazy Terry's tonight and send him out on an airboat ride."

"What about his wife? Think he tells her everything?"

"Yeah," said Trio. "What he doesn't tell her she figures on her own—a sharp lady like her. You never met her, have ya?"

"Naw. Harold always keeps her out of sight whenever I'm around. He must figure I'll go up her skirt or something." Lambert chuckled. "You told me she's a knockout."

"Yeah, she's a knockout," Victor said, "but whack her too, just in case." He thought for a second, then added. "Make sure he pays this punk, Vango, the thirty-eight bucks first, so's Stanley the Pole don't drop my action."

"Yeah," said the Lamb, "no problem." He looked Victor in the eyes. "I know you want me to get the key he's wearing, huh?"

Victor stared back at him. "Yeah, the key, and the box. Be sure and get them both. We got to gather our stuff in closer to us. Things have been getting too loose."

A silence passed. Then the Lamb said, "You feel like running over to Spano's? Get something to eat? They're making that yellow fin pizza, you know, with the pineapples and that."

"Yeah, why not?" Victor turned and walked his big chunky body back inside the apartment. Bones stood up, followed him in, then sat down in the chair in a corner and laid the shotgun back over his knee. The Lamb stood in the middle of the room with his hands in his pockets, rocking on his heels while Victor stopped and looked all around the room. "So … where's my jacket?"

The Lamb looked around with him, shrugged, and looked at Bones. Victor flagged his hands at his sides a little, and said, glancing at Bones, "Maybe I wore it to the can and left it there?"

Bones' head nodded once real slow, as if giving permission, and Victor walked into the bathroom, found his sports jacket and lifted it off the hook on the wall. "I don't like the Pole sending down this guy, Vango, to stretch me for that thirty-eight bucks," he said.

"Yeah, some nerve." The Lamb had moved over behind him right outside the bathroom door, listening, watching Victor check himself in the mirror, getting his thin linen jacket straight. A corner of the jacket's rear vent pleat turned under, so Lambert reached inside the door, smoothed it down and stepped back. "There," he said.

"So, be sure you get him paid off tonight and get him out of here. He strikes me as the kind won't go along with nothing. You've seen those kind." Victor reached down, picked up a hairbrush and ran it back along one side of his head. He stopped and looked at the Lamb in the mirror.

"Aw—yeah, hard to deal with." Lambert answered, grinning, nodding, glancing over at Bones, then back to Victor in the mirror. "But forget about him. I'll take care of him."

"Right, by *paying* him," Victor said, running the brush back again, smoothing his hand along behind it.

"I'm telling ya, we got to be careful with this guy."

"Why's that? He's not a made man, or he wouldn't be working for Stanley the Pole."

"Naw, it don't matter that he's a made man or not—"

"Yeah, but if he's a made man we couldn't lay a finger on him," said Lambert. "Ain't that what you always say?"

"You ain't letting me finish," Victor said, laying the brush down, something coming across his mind. He stopped, trying to figure something out, thinking, *When I came in here earlier, I'd taken out a cigar first ...*

"Nothing to finish," the Lamb said. "I get it. If this Vango gets in our hair, I'll take care of him. Same way I'll take care of Little Harold and his wife."

"Yeah, those two got to go—" Victor stopped and thought about something again. When he'd come into the can earlier, he took a cigar out of his jacket pocket. *Right! And the jacket was, where ...?* He looked all around, *again.*

"Yeah, that poor Harold. He really thinks you're some kind of big-shot ... a member of some Mafia family or something."

Victor looked at him in the mirror, chuckled and wheezed down under his breath, and said: "You mean I ain't?" *Let's see now. My jacket had been laying across the arm of the ... uh-oh!* He glanced around the bathroom, the shiny tiles, no carpet, no wallpaper, no cloth furniture here. Nothing that would stain! *Oh no ...!*

"Naw, I been watching, checking you out, Victor. You're nothing, letting a punk like this Vango come in and bump ya around for a gambling debt?" Lambert laughed a little. "You've had people fooled, but not me, not anymore."

Victor heard the click of metal across metal and looked wide-eyed into the mirror.

"Bones! Bones!" He yelled, just starting to duck away when the Lamb's first shot hit him in the neck and slammed him against the lavatory. He staggered sideways, *"Booones!"* His blood spattered on the tile wall when the next shot hit him. Shot after shot, the silenced 9mm bucked in Lambert's hand as he walked Victor backwards to the open shower door.

The sound was more like that of a high-powered BB gun than a pistol shooting high grain steel jackets, the action of the slide making more noise than the shot itself. As Victor swayed backwards through the open shower door and slid down the tile wall, the Lamb stepped in close and put the seventh-round right above his ear from a foot away, holding his palm above the pistol shielding his face from the blowback. Then he reached in, yanked the thin gold chain with the key on it from Victor's neck and dropped it in his pocket.

He stepped back, took the silencer off, dropped it into his other pocket and pitched the pistol inside the shower. Snapping the surgical glove from his right hand, he ripped it with his teeth, then flushed it down the toilet.

"So, what do you think?" He asked Bones as he stepped out of the bathroom, looking himself up and down for any blood spots or bone fragments.

"About what?" Bones didn't move a muscle. He sat staring through the black shades, the shotgun still across his knee, only with his finger across the trigger now, and the safety off.

"You got this taken care of?" The Lamb nodded toward the bathroom.

"Yeah." There was no breath in Bones' voice. His words were barely more audible than the rustle of curtains in the breeze.

"Got a good saw?"

"Yeah."

"Got a trunk, some suitcases?"

"Yeah."

"Some plastic?"

"Yeah."

"Take care of that mirror?"

"Sure, everything. Leave it to me." Bones nodded, once, real slow.

"Okay." The Lamb nodded, adjusted his trousers up under his shirt, and pulled out three flat, bound stacks of new one hundred-dollar bills. "So … you want it all in cash, or you want some in product when we get it?"

"I don't want no product." Bones sat still as stone. His thin lips hardly moved when he spoke. His gaunt face revealed no more than the black lens hiding his eyes.

"What? You don't want to invest with me?"

Bones shook his head real slow. "You gonna see to it this Vango from Chicago gets paid? You don't want to screw over the Pole."

The Lamb smiled. "You kidding me? That was Victor's debt."

"You didn't listen, did ya?" Bones replied.

"Listen? To what?"

"To what Victor was telling you right before you clipped him."

"Forget about Victor Trio. You want in on this or

not? Cash now, or some of the action down the road?"

Bones shook his head again.

"I told you, give me cash," he said. "I don't want this action down the road."

CHAPTER 3

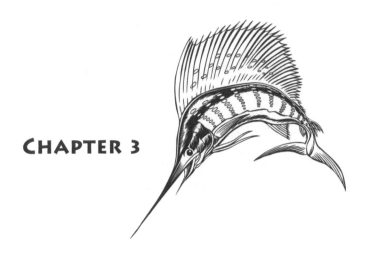

Around four that afternoon, after listening to Lew Stucky's voice for as long as he could stand it, Vango went out strolling along the beach. At a Seven-Eleven type beach store with used surf boards lined up for sale, he bought a large bottle of white vinegar and strolled back to the Surfside Motel. When he walked through the connecting door to Lew Stucky's adjoining room, he saw Stucky's glowing red toes outside on the balcony, hanging over the edge of a lounge chair.

Poor Bastard .... He walked out on the small balcony and draped a couple of soft white towels across Lew Stucky's blazing red chest. Stucky lay snoring-drunk in the harsh evening sun. Vango picked up the empty Dewar's scotch bottle from a balcony table and sat the vinegar bottle down in its place. He shook his head. Back inside his own room, he sat on the side of his bed and called Stanley the Pole to let him know where things stood.

"I don't like it, you going there tonight alone," Stanley said after Vango had filled him in. "You be sure to take Lew with you next time."

"I can handle this myself, Stanley." Vango cleared his throat. "Fact is, Lew ain't feeling so good."

"What's wrong with him?"

"It's his first trip south this time of year, you know. He got out yesterday and got himself burned."

"This time of year? Are you kidding me? Tell him I said he's *going* tonight, and that's an order! That's why I sent him, to back you up, 'case these guys get frisky. Whether you like Lew or not, he's good backup."

"Nothing against Lew, but you should see him, Stanley. He looks really bad. Compared himself to a grilled *pork chop.*" Vango smiled to himself. "Poor bastard. He laid back out in the sun again today, and *Man!* He looks like a big neon tomato."

"Again today? That idiot! Doesn't he know better than that?"

Vango shrugged. "I told him not to, but you know Lew. This Lambert guy says it's the best thing to do, so he did it."

"The Lamb? He listens to what *Ian Lambert* tells him? You don't turn your back on the Lamb, you got that? One reason I sent Lew along is because of the Lamb. The Lamb is from here in Chicago, ya know. Nobody here will give him the time of day."

"You told me that. Don't worry, the Lamb's got nothing to do with this. I'll take care of this without any problems, so you don't lose Victor's action. That's the way you want it, right?"

"Not if it gets your face shot off. You take Lew with ya tonight."

"I will, Stan. But with that van watching everybody, I don't want Lew going nuts over the least little thing, start shooting or something? Besides, I'm only meeting with their financial adviser tonight. What can go wrong?"

"With these guys, anything can be a set-up," Stanley said. "I like Trio's money, but with the Lamb around ...? I don't trust that snake."

"Neither do I. But let me just get in there, close this thing out real quiet like for you and come home."

A silence. Then the Pole said: "Okay, do what you got to, get my thirty-bucks, then get out of there. Drug dealers always got the law circling over them." He paused, then let go a breath. "Sunburn, huh?"

"Man. I've never *seen* one this bad," said Vango. "I was hoping you'd tell me to send him home on a *jet.*

"If he gets any worse," said Stanley, "you do *just that.* I don't want him out there screwing something up because he feels bad. Take charge of this for me, Eddie. All right?"

"I'm on it, Stanley," Vango said. "You'll hear from me."

While Vango and Stanley the Pole had talked on the phone, Lambert was calling Harold Wright at his home. The Lamb was already making his takeover. He had shaken down Victor's apartment, found the fireproof safe box stashed behind a wall mirror in the bedroom, and taken out close to three hundred thousand cash.

Not a bad piece of walk-around money, but what he really needed wasn't there. He needed the bank box that Harold Wright kept for Victor, the one with the keys to all the Wright Way safety deposit boxes. There could be a couple of million operating capital in it—*enough get-out-of-town money to really get-out-of-town.* If he wanted to, he grinned. What he needed most were the deposit box keys.

The boxes were full of cash, and with on-demand bearer bonds, which was the same thing, even better, he told himself. How much cash? How much in bearer bonds? He didn't know—but a lot. Lately the money had gotten so huge and hard to keep track of, him and Victor had left all the *head-work* up to Harold.

All you could do with money this large was keep it moving and make everybody around you think you still knew the total. Lambert chuckled a little thinking about it. The other thing he needed? He needed the names of the middlemen connections, the guys who kept the dope moving. He also needed the shipping order number for the huge shipment coming in from Jamaica any day.

Victor Trio thought he'd kept his connections a secret. But the Lamb figured it out. Now it was all his. That afternoon he'd made a few calls, let a few heavy buyers know that the product was coming, and that Victor had turned the whole product operation over to *him* and skipped the country. Trio had already paid Bones five thousand to pick up the twenty-eight keys of blow. The dope itself would be paid for in bearer bond—by mail once Lambert knew the meeting arrangements.

Five bucks. He couldn't believe it. *Five bucks*, to handle twenty-eight keys of blow! And to think that at one time old guys like Bones ruled the streets. He smiled. *But that was yesterday, and yesterday's gone.*

Nobody would question Bones picking up product, he'd done it so many times before. It might take them a while for everybody to figure out Victor Trio was dead, but what would they care? The money would be in their hands as usual. Bones was the only one who knew what he'd done, but he'd never open his mouth. Besides, Bones would soon be on his way back to Havana, going to spend what time he had left watching baseball and sipping wine.

If his suppliers ever asked what happened to Victor Trio? He'd split-up with the guy, because to tell the truth, he didn't think the guy could be trusted anymore. Come to find out, Victor didn't have all the protection he'd said he had. But if they wanted to keep dealing with *the Lamb* ... well, look what he could do for them here. He smiled to himself.

Victor had been right about one thing though. Harold Wright and his wife had to go down. The Lamb didn't want any partners or any loose ends. Tonight, once he got all the savings deposit box keys, he would collect up the whole bank and Victor's connections. What more did he need?

"Yes?" Harold's voice came on the phone, sounding woozy and worried already. That helped.

"It's me," the Lamb said. He waited a second, then he spoke in a quick, hushed tone, adding tension to his voice. "Remember what we talked about this morning? How if something ever went wrong, you'd hear it from me?"

"Yes, but— But what's going wrong?"

"Nothing you've done, Harold. But that doesn't matter. Victor's worried about ya. You know too much. You're in some big trouble. Are you alone there? Okay to talk?"

"Well ... *yes* ... that is, my wife's been shopping down in Miami the past few days, but I expect her back anytime."

Lambert could hear the effects of quaaludes and vodka in Harold's voice.

"Thank God for that," he said, sounding concerned. "We better bring her with us." He let Harold hear him take a deep breath, and sigh. "Listen to me, Harold. Go, right now, and pack a bag for yourself and her." *Yeah—* he liked that part—*go pack a bag, like this was all on the up and up.* "Take enough to last you both awhile—a few days, maybe, until I can straighten things out. And be sure to bring our box of keys, okay?"

"Certainly, I'll bring it. But, you mean, we have to hide out? How long? What about my wife? She's not going to like this."

"She ain't going to like *dying* any better, tell her. I got to get the two of you out of here tonight. Every second counts, so get a move on. We got a long drive ahead of us."

"Jesus." His voice quivered. "Where are we going?"

"Don't worry about it. I got a friend named Tony, owns an airboat rental deep in the glades. We'll take one of those babies out, and I guarantee Victor will never find either of you. All right?"

"Out to where?"

"Never mind to where. Are you with me here?"

He swallowed. "Yes. But what about this Vango fellow coming by to get the thirty-eight thousand? Should I—"

"Forget him, you'll be gone before he gets there. Now, are we straight on this?"

"Yes, I'm with you. And—and Ian?"

"Yeah, what?" The Lamb glanced at his watch as

he spoke.

"I just want to—to thank you. Thank you for helping us, Leslie and me."

"Hey, that's what friends are for, pal. Now get a move on, or I'll shoot you myself, you lug, ya." He chuckled. Harold let out a nervous little laugh himself. They both hung up the phone.

Man … Lambert smiled and fingered the silencer in his trouser pocket. This was going to be almost *too* easy.

When Eddie Vango finished talking to Stanley the Pole and hung up the phone, he took a shower, slipped on a pair of khaki slacks and a polo shirt, and shoved a 9mm semi-automatic down in his waist. He smoothed his shirt over the pistol and left the room. Outside, he walked right past the Pontiac with the keys to it in his pocket, crossed the street, hailed a taxi, and had the driver take him to a car rental halfway across town.

He rented a plain white Corsica on an anonymous credit card and cruised around in the beach area until he crossed the draw bridge from the island into downtown Jensen Beach. There, he stopped at an alfresco seafood joint for an early dinner of clams in white wine sauce. Afterwards, he sipped chilled white wine and smoked a cigar, watching long shadows stretch out and darken the city streets.

When he'd settled his check, tacking on a twenty percent tip, he asked the waiter for directions to the address Harold Wright had scribbled on the back of his business card.

"Ah, yes," the waiter said recognizing the waterfront

community, "very nice there." He'd spread a wide smile.

Vango saw what the waiter meant when he'd left the downtown beach area and cruised south on a two lane alongside a large lagoon until it gave way to gated landscaped yards with towering palms and cultivated stone walls spilling over with mature vines and tumbling mounds of bougainvillea. The clock in the Corsica's dash read a few minutes past eight. He was early. But, he figured, since Harold Wright had said *ten o'clock,* maybe he'd get there ahead of time and scope things out a little—maybe even show up unexpected around nine and check the guy's reaction—just come strolling up, *Yo, how's it going, Harold?*

Stanley was right, you couldn't trust these guys; but Vango figured you could trust anybody so long as you kept them off balance—kept them in a *trusting* position.

On his third pass, he pulled the Corsica into a narrow sandy street and into a pull-off that lay alongside a five-foot stone wall bordering the Wright's yard, partially hiding the Corsica. The pull-off itself lay almost entirely hidden by a surge of palmetto, more drooping vines and more plush red bougainvillea crawling up the palm trunks and hanging down from atop the stone wall.

Vango stepped out, closed the car door without a sound, parted a tangle of foliage, and swung himself up atop the five-foot wall.

He eased down into another tangle of vines and foliage and had started to step out, across the yard to the house, when he saw the white streak of headlights reach into the yard from the driveway. *Close call.* Dropping straight down in the foliage, Vango waited and watched as the big black Mercedes with dark tinted windows slipped along the driveway, soft yellow ground lights reflecting up off its sides until it stopped up near the house.

The rear door opened on the driver's side, and Ian Lambert stepped out and closed it, glancing all around the dark yard from within the light of a large smoked glass chandelier hanging from the porch ceiling. Before the car door closed, Vango caught a glimpse of two more men in the back seat. He waited.

While he waited, a big, hairy, orange-striped cat slid up against his ankle and rubbed back and forth. He eased it away with the back of his hand, but it came back *right* with his hand, and he eased it away again … then again. Finally, he drew back a hand to swat it. "Get outa here!" He spoke in a harsh whisper, but the cat would have none of it. It swayed back an inch, raising its back straight up, and hissed at him across bared glistening teeth.

"All right, my fault. Easy," Vango whispered, glancing across at the Mercedes. Harold Wright came out of the house carrying a tan leather bag, followed by Lambert, carrying a huge shiny metal box. Harold's face looked drained and tormented, the light from the porch losing him as he rounded the Mercedes. The Lamb stayed close, and when Harold swung the rear door open and saw the other two men, he jerked back a step. But the Lamb's hand came out his pocket with a pistol and jammed it into Harold's ribs, forcing him in, then hefting the metal box in behind him.

The travel bag fell from Harold's hand; the Lamb kicked it away, climbed in and closed the door. The car sat still for a second, then the rear door on the other side swung open and an older man stepped out. Vango heard

Harold Wright's voice pleading, sobbing: "No please, no—" Then it was cut short by the closing of the car door. Vango got the picture. Harold was going down for the count. He watched as the car backed around and headed back out along the driveway.

The man stood alone in the glow of the porch light for a second, adjusting a pistol down in the back of his waist. Then he stepped over, picked up Harold's suitcase, and walked into the house. *Waiting for somebody …?* Sure he was. But Vango had no idea who, or why. All he knew was that the thirty-eight bucks—thirty for the Pole, eight for himself—he'd come to collect had just breezed off down the driveway.

Well …," he whispered, glancing at the cat, reaching down where it stood rubbing once more against his leg. *Back at square one,* he thought, picking the big cat up and feeling it purr against his chest as he ran a hand along its back.

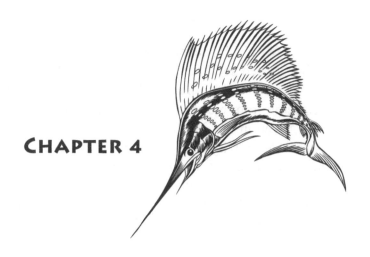

CHAPTER 4

Around ten o'clock, getting dark, Leslie Wright swung the silver-gray Mercedes convertible into the driveway and stopped up close to the garage doors. She clicked open the door with a built-in remote in her dash and pulled the car inside next to Harold Wright's Buick Park Avenue. Entering the house with a large shopping bag she'd taken from the seat beside her, she stopped just inside the glass foyer doors leading in from the garage, waiting there, listening to the silence of the big sprawling house. *No light? No TV, no music?*

The house lay quiet and dark except for the glow of a night-light from the kitchen, and she walked toward it taking off her earrings, saying, "Harold? Harold? Are you in there?"

But the man sitting at the table facing her in the dim-lit kitchen was not Harold Wright. This was a younger man, younger than Harold, closer to her own age? Handsome, early thirties, casually dressed, she saw the gun come up from his lap as he raised halfway from the chair. She glanced at the tan leather travel bag near his feet. She looked around the kitchen.

41

"Mrs. Wright?" The man asked.

She stopped short for a second, then said, "Yes, I am." Her voice sounded hushed, her eyes taking in the gun, glancing from him to the other man sitting across the table. Even in the dim light she could see that this man was older, a wiry little man with frizzy gray hair, holding a white hand towel to his right cheek. His left cheek had three long bloody cuts down it.

"Where's Harold?" She called back over her shoulder into the dark house without turning around. "Harold?"

Vango stood the rest of the way up from his chair, checking her reaction. Cool, this one. No panic. Her voice stayed low and level, her eyes darting for a second, then settling on his. Even in the dim light he could see her eyes clearly. From the floor up, this was one a straight-up beauty! Nice eyes, pale blue, translucent, one of them partially hidden behind a drift of smoky ash-blonde hair. *Jesus!* A real looker, he noted. *Be careful,* he cautioned himself. *No problem ....*

Vango smiled, gesturing the 9mm Targa pistol he'd taken from this guy, toward the floor beside her as he stepped over and switched on the overhead track lights. "Want to put the bag down, Mrs. Wright?"

She did, straight down at her feet, her eyes going to the other man's face, then to the open bottle of merlot standing in the center of the table between two half-filled glasses. Vango caught the look in her eyes, and said, "Hope you don't mind, we helped ourselves to a bottle."

"Of course not." She tossed her words away. She looked much too gorgeous and far too sexy for Harold. Everything about her, her skin, her body, her demeanor, said she spent her time bathing in soft large piles of money. "Now, where is Harold?"

Her voice had turned crisp, but there was no fear in there.

"We'll get to that," Vango said. With his free hand, he reached out and gestured her over to a chair at the table. He checked her out as she stepped around, then stopped without sitting.

"Who *are* you people?" she asked.

"Oh, excuse me," Vango said, jiggling the pistol toward the other man. "This is Delbert Moss. It's Moss? Right?"

"Yes, it's Moss," the man said, moving the towel from his right cheek to his left, both cheeks equally cut and bloody.

"Delbert's been telling me about his tattoos, about all the jails he's been in," Vango said. "I found him here waiting for you and took this pistol from him." He wagged the Targa. "My guess is he was going to make you go somewhere with him. Right, Delbert?"

"Yeah." The man's eyes turned down, embarrassed, a schoolboy caught looking up his teacher's dress. His arms and hands were riddled with cheap tattoos. Crosses, hearts, blue jays, dice, a nude woman and numerous jail-house phrases all fading on weathered skin. A badly worn Betty Boop stood beneath a wide umbrella on his forearm. A dagger stood with drops of blue blood hanging from it on his other forearm.

Vango looked at Leslie Wright. She stood staring at Delbert Moss, raising a hand to her hip, adjusting a gold bracelet as she did it.

"Oh? What happened to your face, Mr. Moss?"

Delbert couldn't remember a time anybody called him *Mister* unless he was in serious trouble. He swallowed, nodded toward Vango and glanced back up at her. "He threw a big cat in my face."

"A big *cat?*" She stared from one to the other. Vango shrugged.

"I didn't want to hit him, knock him out. So, I sort of pitched your cat on him. Turns out, Delbert here has been in jail in places I've never even *heard of,* right Delbert?" Vango stifled a short chuckle.

"You got that right," said Delbert. "I can do more time than anybody you know."

"Really?" A pause. Then Leslie Wright stared at Vango in an air of resolve. *"FYI*, we don't *own* a cat."

"Well, you do now. He's somewhere around here, a big orange-striped bruiser. He won't come out." Vango glanced around the floor, then back to her, gesturing. "Please have a seat, Mrs. Wright."

"Where. Is. Harold?" Her voice demanded in a level clipped tone.

"It's a long story. But I'm pretty sure your husband's dead, Mrs. Wright." He let out a breath. "There, I said it. Now, you want to take a seat?"

"Oh Christ." She sighed and eased down, shaking her head with an I-told-him-so expression. "I'm not surprised. He never listened to me. Him with his new friends." She reached a hand over to her wrist and adjusted the bracelet again.

Vango and Delbert Moss looked at each other. Leslie Wright said to Delbert Moss: "And I suppose *you* killed him?"

"Me?" Moss's eyes went wide. "Hunh-uh! That's

one thing I ain't never done. All's I did was waited here for you. This is more like breaking and entering—with the door already open, you can't even really call it *breaking*. You plead this thing down a little and most it comes to is—"

"Easy, easy, Delbert," Vango said, cutting him off. "What'd I tell ya before? We're not police here, right? Just chill down."

"Sorry," Delbert said, lowering the towel and taking a sip of wine. "But I told ya what happened to me in Minneapolis, Hennepin County jail? What a *you-know-what* hole that was. Pardon me for saying."

Vango smiled, noting the man at least knew how to watch his language. "That was another time, another place."

"I just don't want to get stuck with somebody else's rap again," Moss said.

Leslie Wright stared from one to the other, a couple of guys who'd been sitting here in the dark, armed, in the kitchen, enjoying a nice merlot, one telling the other about all of his past criminal convictions.

Delbert added: "I especially don't want to end up in *Dade* County lock-up, getting blamed for something the Lamb done. That place's an oven on weekends."

"Ian Lambert." Leslie Wright perked forward. "I should have known he was involved in this. That bastard! I knew he'd hurt Harold someday." She placed a hand down on the tabletop for balance. "Do you work for him?"

"No, ma'am," Vango said. "I came here to pick up a gambling debt on Victor Trio from your husband. Ian Lambert got here first. I saw him leave with your husband. Harold didn't look real happy."

"Oh," she said, and she looked down at her hand on the table. After a pause, she shook her head slowly and nodded toward her shopping bag sitting on the floor, her purse lying atop the bag's contents. She said in a firm yet quiet tone. "I have some cigarettes in my purse in there. Can I get them?" She added, "And please stop calling me *Ma'am.*" She started to rise, but Vango raised a hand.

He said: "Please, Mrs. Wright. Allow me to get them for you."

He lifted her purse from the shopping bag, opened it, noticed a small caliber Beretta automatic, palmed it, and dropped it in his back pocket. He brought the purse back to the table, took out a pack of Virginia Slims and a Bic lighter, and shook a cigarette to attention in the flip-top pack. She took it between her fingers and looked up at him as he held the lighter out and clicked it on. She paused with the cigarette up close to her lips.

"The pistol happens to be a gift from a personal friend," she said. "I'd like it back, please?"

"No problem." Vango smiled. "But I'll just hold onto it while we talk."

"Thanks." She took a draw, let it go, and settled back. "Are you the fellow who came by Victor's earlier asking for thirty-eight thousand dollars? Something about Baltimore losing by more than six points to—"

"Yes, that's me," he said, cutting her off. "Your husband told you that, huh?" He gestured with the gun to the bottle of merlot, and Delbert Moss filled the glasses.

"Yes, he mentioned it when I called him earlier."

"On the phone?"

"Yes, on my hand phone. It's in my purse."

Vango reached into her purse, fished his hand past an open package of condoms, and brought out the thin gray phone and laid it on the table.

"Care for some wine, Mrs. Wright?"

"Yes, thank you, just a smidge, please." She held up her thumb and finger, indicating what she estimated to be the size of a *smidge*.

Delbert half-filled her a glass of merlot and sat it in front of her. As she gestured Delbert to pour just a *smidge* more, Eddie Vango watched and said, "So, your husband talked a lot about his business with you?"

She shrugged, drew on the Virginia Slim. "Not a lot, but some, I suppose. He told me you were at Victor's. He said you handled Victor Trio and his playmate, the Lamb, without any problem. Harold seemed impressed." She paused for a second, then said: "You're a bookie, I presume?"

"No, just running an errand for a friend. But that's not important. What's important is that you're going to have to get out of town, real quick. If you don't, it's even money you're going to end up as dead as your husband."

"Poor Harold …." She let go a thin stream of smoke. Then she tilted her head and asked with a curious expression. "What *exactly* are you waiting for here?"

Vango had been checking her out, her voice, her eyes, her cool, calm manner. She hadn't mentioned calling the police. Hadn't seemed real upset about her husband probably laying somewhere dead by now—in no hurry to run and hide from the Lamb, it appeared.

"I'm waiting. I'm figuring the Lamb's going to call pretty soon to see what's taking Delbert so long," Vango said. "I'm going to tell him either bring me the money I came here to collect, *tonight,* or I'm going to get *seriously* upset with him." He gestured the pistol toward Delbert Moss. "Delbert's waiting for me to cut him loose, so he can split town once the Lamb finds out he didn't do what he was supposed to."

"Yeah, he'll *kill* me for sure," Delbert said, throwing back a sip from his glass, shrugging. "Just my luck. Finally get a job …"

Vango tapped the pistol toward Leslie Wright.

"And you?" he said. "You can do what ya want, now that I've warned you."

"Why *did* you warn me?"

He shrugged. "Why not? Call it my good deed for the decade. I figure now you know what's going on, you'll do what you figure is best for you."

"Yes," she said. "I can handle it from here. So, if I simply thank you and ask you to leave …?"

"Sorry. Can't do it just yet. Not until I let Lambert know where I stand on this." He nodded at the tan leather travel bag. "I'm prepared to camp out here."

"Oh?" She stared at Vango for a second—"Well."— then she stood up slipped off her shoes and added, "In that case, I could use some coffee. Anybody care for some Mocha Amaretto?" She gestured a hand toward the bag of coffee sitting beside the coffee grinder.

Delbert and Vango looked at each other as she stepped over to the sink counter where she bent down and rummaged through a lazy Susan cabinet. Vango smiled, watching her search for coffee filters.

"Yeah, thanks. Maybe slice an orange to go with it?" He laid the Targa automatic back on his lap, watching her. "Mind if I use your phone?"

"Help yourself." She stood. Having finally found the coffee filters, she smoothed down her skirt and reached for the glass coffee pot.

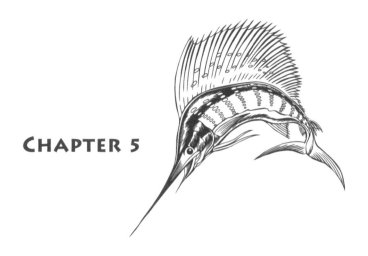

CHAPTER 5

Vango called Lew Stucky's room at the Surfside Motel. When Stucky didn't answer after the seventh or eighth ring, he clicked the phone off, laid it down, and tapped his fingertips on the tabletop, asking Delbert: "What about Peoria, Illinois, Delbert? Ever do any time there?"

"Better believe it. *Twice,*" said Delbert Moss, raising two fingers. It was crazy, Delbert Moss knew, but he liked being here. He liked talking to this guy and this beautiful woman while he chain-smoked Camel cigarettes. In a nice big house like this, he enjoyed sitting at the table, sipping wine that wasn't wrapped in a paper bag, now some first-class coffee he'd never heard of—not some instant crap from a glass jar. This was something he wished he'd done more of in his life.

This guy, Vango, had a nice way about him. Okay, he *had* thrown the cat in his face. But he could've shot him. He could've turned him over to the law. Instead, Vango had gotten him a warm wet towel for his scratched-up face, seated him at the table and after a while told him, *"You go along with me on this, Delbert, I'll give ya a couple hundred traveling money."* You couldn't beat *that,* Delbert thought. After all, he would have to leave; he didn't have any money. This Ian Lambert would kill him, he was pretty sure.

Before the woman showed up, he'd enjoyed telling this Vango guy about all the jails he'd been in. The guy had seemed genuinely interested—most people on the outside couldn't care less. In the joint there were always people to sit around and swap jail talk with, but not out here. Out here, nobody listened. Except this guy, and this woman now that she was here.

He'd just told them all about Peoria, then about the federal pen up in Terre Haute and some of the guys there, most particularly about a fellow called Pop Decker who filled a sock with pilfered kitchen utensils from the kitchen and used it on cons any time he had a score to settle. *Pop the Sock* .... Moss thought about him as he finished a slice of orange, laid the peeling beside his coffee cup, and had started to tell them about Moundsville up in West Virginia; but Vango raised a hand stopping him.

"How long have you worked for the Lamb?" Vango asked.

Delbert drew on a Camel. "A couple of weeks, is all. Friend of mine, Benton Byrd, set me up with the guy—told Lambert about all the time I pulled. Met Byrd up in Illinois; he was doing two to five on a gun charge a few years back. He knows I'm not a trigger man like he is. But he told me to just keep quiet a while, he'd get me out of this end of the business and maybe just deliver dope or something. When we were both in Illinois, Byrd used to work in the laundry. Every Saturday night he sponsored a race, you know, rat race, spider race, whatever he could come up with. During the week I'd take care of his animals for him. We got to be friends."

Delbert liked the way Vango sat smiling, nodding, listening to him, and the way this woman leaned forward with her chin in her hand, like she was fascinated by his stories. He'd told them how the three dots tattooed on the web between his thumb and finger stood for murder robbery and rape, except in his case he'd only earned the robbery part—but who knew the difference unless he told them.

He'd lit a fresh Camel off the one he just smoked and had started to tell them about the time everybody in Soledad got stomach poisoning on some raisin jack wine, when the phone rang on the wall above the counter.

"Okay, Delbert," Vango said, standing, moving over to the house phone, "I push this button, you answer. If it's Lambert, I'll take over once you fill him in." Leslie Wright stood and moved over beside him. Delbert nodded and folded his hands on the table. "Here goes," said Vango on the second ring. He pushed the speaker button and nodded to Delbert.

"Hello," Delbert Moss said in a flat tone. Vango and Leslie Wright sat listening to the speaker in silence.

"That you, Moss?" Lambert asked.

"Yeah, it's me, Mr. Lamb," Delbert said, raising his voice from the table six feet away.

"So? What's the deal there? Did the woman get home yet?" Lambert sounded a little extra cautious over the phone.

"Nope, not yet. I'm still waiting." Delbert took a draw on his short Camel, the pack lying close to his other hand.

"What the hell—?" A silence, then the Lamb said

in a testy, but controlled voice, "She was supposed to be getting home anytime."

"Well, she's not," Delbert said, grinning a little across white, government-maintained dental work.

Vango shot Leslie Wright a smile, nodding.

"Okay," the Lamb said. "When she shows up, just hold her there, okay?"

"Sure," Delbert said. "Anything else?"

"Yeah, a guy might be coming there anytime to collect a gambling debt. Don't even answer the door. He'll go away."

"Is this guy's name Vango?" Delbert squinted, grinned, showing good federal penitentiary dental work.

Lambert said, "Yeah, but how'd you know—"

"He's already here," Delbert said. "We've been having a drink."

"What the—?" The Lamb fell silent, then said in a lowered guarded voice. "Listen to me, Delbert, this is real important. Just answer yes or no. Is he anywhere close to ya, right now, within arm's reach?"

"Yep, sure is." Delbert smiled back and forth between Vango and Leslie Wright, Lambert not knowing these two were listening.

"Good," said the Lamb. "I want ya to take your pistol and smack him in the eye with it as hard as you can. Really cold-cock him, ya hear?"

"I hear."

A few seconds passed. "Well? I didn't hear nothing. Did ya do it?" The Lamb was getting a little testy.

"Nope, can't do it," Delbert said.

"What do ya mean, you can't do—?"

"Because *he's got* my pistol," said Moss.

"What do you mean? You stupid mother—!"

"Whoa, easy, Mr. Sheep," Vango said, stepping in closer to the speaker. "You'll give yourself a heart attack."

Another pause, then the Lamb said: "What are you doing there, Eddie Van-go?"

"I came to pick up the *forty* bucks. Remember? Where is it?"

"Forty bucks?" said Lambert.

"Yeah, it's forty now. You tell Victor Trio the meter keeps running until he pays his tab."

"You're messing around where you don't belong, Van-go. You want your money, you better get the hell out of there. This is starting to really piss me off."

"Yeah, me too. So, you better start taking the forty bucks more serious. I'm not leaving without it. I'll just wait here, maybe tell the woman you're on your way back, gonna stick a gun in her ribs like you did her husband."

"What're you talking about?" The Lamb's voice turned a little unsteady for a second.

"I was there," said Vango. "I caught it all, the gun in the ribs, Harold begging in the car. Real cold stuff. What's worse is there's a security camera under the porch roof— it's all on tape. See what I mean about taking my forty bucks more serious? I tell the lady Harold's dead, show her the tape, and tell her you're on your way back here. I doubt if she's gonna stick around waiting to see ya."

A silence, then, "Okay, Vango. Listen to me. Let's both keep our heads. I'm gonna bring you the forty bucks. But you got to keep your mouth shut to the woman. Deal?"

"Depends. How long we talking about, you getting here?" Vango glanced back and forth at Delbert and Leslie Wright.

"I can be there inside an hour," the Lamb said. "Meanwhile, she shows up, I give you another five bucks to make sure she doesn't get away."

"Doesn't *get away?* I don't know," Vango said, giving Leslie Wright a little wink. "You make it sound like I'm being an accessory to something. If I'm gonna hold her for *five,* why don't I just go ahead and cap her for *ten?"* Leslie Wright started to move in terror, but Vango patted her hand on the table, keeping her near, reassuring her.

"No, no! Listen," said Lambert. "Make sure nothing happens to her, you hear me? It's important that nothing happens to her. She's got something of mine, you understand?"

"I understand," Vango said. "But if you ain't here with my forty bucks inside an hour, I'll leave her a note telling her what I saw, and I'm out of here. Tomorrow morning I'll be at Victor's door to collect my forty-*five* bucks."

"Forget Victor. I'm on my way to pay you," the Lamb said. Just keep everything cope until I get there!"

Vango punched the button on the speaker, cutting it off, then looked at Leslie Wright. "You ever seen anybody this stupid? What have you got that's so important to him?"

"I don't think I have any more to say to you, Mr. Vango," she said, tilting her head a bit. "If you'd be so kind now as to give me back my pistol, and leave …?"

"Whatever happened to gratitude?" Vango shook

his head, speaking to Delbert Moss.

"He's right," Delbert said. "If he hadn't been here—"

"And you," she said, pointing a perfectly sculptured silver-gray nail at Delbert, cutting him off. "You need to go somewhere and get help from a team of highly skilled professionals."

"Professional what?" Moss raised his brow.

She swung back to Vango. "Do you really think the Lamb is coming here to *pay* you? After *telling* him what you heard and saw? And FYI, there is no camera under the porch ceiling."

"I know." He grinned. "But it gives the Lamb one more thing to worry about. He's planning on coming here to shoot holes in me, Mrs. Wright. Since I won't be here, he'll start sweating, come looking for me. That'll give me an edge. Then I'll corner him and get the money he owes." He spread his hands. "Meanwhile, I take you somewhere safe. Simple, huh?"

"Oh, yes, *very.*" She pressed a palm to her forehead. "Look, I appreciate what you did. But I've got it from here."

"I'm supposed to just let you face this guy alone?" Vango asked, taking her small Beretta pistol from his pocket and handing to her.

"Thank you. Yes—" She took the pistol, stepped over to the tan leather travel bag, picked it up by its shoulder and pitched it to him. He caught it, staring at her, bemused.

"I'll be fine on my own," she said. "Take your *camping* bag and your friend and leave, please."

Delbert stood up, nodding toward the bag, starting

to say something about it, but Vango cut him off with a raised hand. "Come on, Delbert, she's right. It's her business. Let's go. We know when we're not wanted."

Delbert Moss looked confused, but only for a second. Seeing Eddie Vango turn toward the hallway leading to the front door, Moss drained his wine glass quickly, set it on the table and started following him.

They walked through the front door and started down the fifty-foot walkway to the street where Vango left the Corsica. Looking back, Delbert saw Leslie Wright standing in the open front door watching them.

"We can't leave her here, can we," he said, "with Lambert on his way?"

"We're not leaving her, Delbert," Eddie said turning left on the sandy street, heading toward the Corsica twenty-five yards away, alongside the stone wall.

"Not to doubt you, Eddie," Delbert said, seeing Leslie close the front door and lower the porch light. "It sure looks to me like we're leaving her."

"She's not going to let us leave her, Delbert. Not with Ian Lambert coming down on her."

"I don't know, Eddie," Delbert persisted. "Every time I've left somebody, it looked about like this."

"We're not leaving. She'll stop us first." Vango walked on toward the Corsica, farther out of the streetlights. Ahead in the shadowy darkness, between them and the Corsica, the sound of four silenced gunshots whistled past them. Two of the shots thumped into a Sable Palm standing two feet from Vango's arm.

"Whoa, Eddie!" Delbert gave him a strong shove.

The two turned, running back to the house.

"Inside of an *hour* he said!" Vango called sidelong to Delbert, the silenced gunshots popping around them. Behind them a car engine started. Ahead of them the Wright's front porch light came back on, bright again. "Get in there, Delbert!" Vango shouted at him as they ran. "Get that light off and get inside."

"What about you?" Delbert asked. A car sped toward them from behind as they ran.

"Don't worry about me. Get inside, lock the door! Get her gun!" Vango shouted. Seeing Delbert running toward her, Leslie Wright swung the door open farther and watched him run past her. She closed the door to just a wide crack, ran her hand down the wall switch and dimmed the porch lights. She saw the car zip by and heard its brakes screech two driveways down the street.

"Where's Eddie? Is he shot?" she shouted at Moss, staring hard out into the darkness, searching the shadowed foliage.

"I don't know. I don't think so," Delbert said, breathing hard. "I … I need your pistol. Things might start getting hairy!"

"Start getting *hairy* …?" The woman said. "Delbert, they are *shooting* at us—" Her words cut short as two loud un-silenced gun shots exploded from the direction where the car's brakes had screeched loudly a moment ago.

"Oh man," said Delbert, "that's the way Eddie was headed! I hope they didn't shoot him." He reached his hand out toward Leslie Wright. "Give me your gun."

Leslie had stuck the little Beretta down the waist of her skirt. She took it out and started to hand it to Delbert when a man's voice came from the doorway of the unlit dining room.

"Drop it, Lady!" Seeing Delbert Moss close beside her, he said, "Moss, stay where you're at." Then he gave a dark chuckle and added, "Did you lose your mind, throwing in with these people?"

"I don't know," Delbert said, "maybe. You going to kill us, Tony?"

"What do you think?" He jiggled the gun he held pointed at them. "Over his shoulder he said to another man standing back in the dining room darkness. "What do you think, Randall? Are we going to kill them?"

"Duh ..., yes?" said the man behind him as he stepped into the light, a big .45 cal. hanging loosely in his hand. "You really screwed yourself, Delbert. Look at Tony. He started like, Have-Gun-Will-Travel. Now he's my *Segundo."*

The first man, Tony Dee nodded at the gun in Leslie Wright's hand and said, "Okay, Lady, drop the pea-shooter."

Leslie started to drop the Beretta, but she looked down at the smoky silver-gray tile, as if concerned that the weight of the gun might damage it. Seeing her hesitate, the gunman Randall, said, "Now, lady, before we blast you in half!"

Even with his threat, she moved over two feet and dropped the gun carefully on a plush area carpet.

Tony Dee gave a dark little laugh. So did Randall.

"I can't believe you, lady," said Randall, stepping forward. "We're getting ready to shoot you in your head. You're worried about this *floor—?"* His words cut short; the front door swung wide open. A large hole appeared in the middle his forehead as the loud blast of a gunshot roared throughout the large dark house. The woman let out a short scream.

Delbert Moss had frozen in place, but he thawed out and stepped sidelong toward the dropped Beretta, seeing Eddie Vango take a step inside the open front door, a 9mm semi-auto extended arm's length at the other gunman. Tony Dee, the other gunman, stood with his hands raised chest high in surrender, but the .45 still grasped tight in his right fist.

"Don't shoot, Mr. Vango! Please don't shoot. I don't want to die!"

"Then lay your gun down, *Paladin,*" said Vango, "easy like. And I don't mean drop it."

"Gunman Tony Dee stooped and carefully laid the gun on the floor. When he stood up, Delbert Moss had stepped over and picked up the woman's small Beretta. He held it toward Gunman Tony who stood disarmed, wearing a worried look.

"Say the word, Eddie," said Delbert. "I'll burn down the *Segundo* here." He tightened his grip on the Beretta.

"So will I, Leslie Wright put in. "How dare you threaten to shoot me in the head!" She extended a hand toward her Beretta, but Delbert didn't give it up.

"That wasn't me, lady," said Tony. "That was Randall! I never said nothing! Look, I don't want to die. Please stop this." He eyes went to Vango, pleading.

"If you're his *Segundo,* his number two," she said, pointing to the body bleeding on her smoky tile floor, "I have no qualms about—"

"Hey, hey, everybody," Vango cut in. "What is this,

a spaghetti western?" He looked back at the frightened, trembling gunman. "We're not going to kill you, Tony, *so shut up* before I change my mind." He looked back at the woman and Delbert; both looked disappointed.

As Vango spoke, he reached over and closed the front door.

"As it stands," he said, "I just drove your dead pals here from up the street from where I ran into them—you know, the ones chasing Delbert and me? Now I've got this one dead on the floor here." He looked at Delbert and Leslie as he picked up the gun lying near the dead gunman. Then he walked over to the gun lying on the floor in front of the second gunman who still held his hands chest high. "If I kill this one, what am I going to do, send them all four back to Lambert in a taxi?"

"I should have thought of that," Delbert said in a humbled tone. "My bad, Eddie." He looked down at the floor.

"No problem, Delbert," said Vango. "You're doing good. Keep paying attention." He nodded at the second gunman's 9mm on the floor and said to Delbert, "Take *Paladin's* gun and keep him covered with it." He looked at Leslie Wright and said, "Mrs. Wright, please get us a mop and let's get the blood off this tile."

"You want me to mop the floor?" She almost gasped.

"Not you, Mrs. Wright," Vango said. "Get a mop, we'll ask *Mr. Have-Gun-Will-Travel* here to do the mopping." He gave Tony Dee, the second gunman a stare. "Make it look good and clean and I won't ask Delbert to put a bullet in your face. Sound good to you?" he asked the frightened gunman, who was now looking a little less tense than a moment earlier.

"You bet it does, Mr. Vango!" Tony Dee said. "I'll mop this whole place if you want me to—and I'll get all four of these stiffs loaded up and out of here most *rickety.*"

All four ...? Vango let it go.

"Then let's all get at it, people," he said. Leslie stepped over close to Vango on her way to a utility closet in the kitchen.

"You can call me, *Lee,* Eddie," she said in soft tone. "I would like that. I really would." She gave him an easy smile.

Vango nodded and said in an equally soft tone, "So would I, *Lee.*" He returned her easy smile. "Don't forget a bucket, and some soapy water." He looked at Tony. "Anything else you need, *Paladin?* We don't want any blood stain on the travertine."

"Some bleach, maybe, if you have any handy?" Tony said.

CHAPTER 6

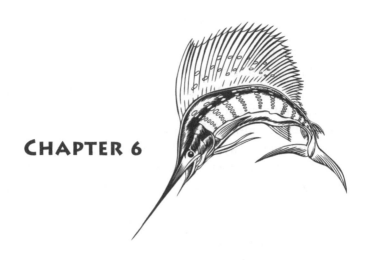

Vango, Delbert and Gunman Tony heard the woman rummage around in the kitchen utility closet searching for a mop and bucket. After a while Vango shook his head and walked over and locked the front door. "Looks like it might be awhile...." He dimmed the overhead lights both outside in the porch ceiling and in the foyer where they stood. Then he stopped for a moment beside Delbert Moss.

"You doing okay, Delbert?" he asked.

"Couldn't be better, Eddie," Moss replied, leveling his shoulders. He wasn't used to people inquiring about how he might be doing, or anything else that might imply they even knew he was alive.

"Good work," Vango said. He patted Moss on the shoulder and said. "It looks like Mrs. Wright has difficulty locating her house cleaning items."

"I saw that," said Delbert. He winced at the sound of a pan crashing to the floor from the kitchen closet.

"I want you to keep a close watch on *Paladin* here while I go upstairs and look around, Vango said. "If he gets squirrely, drop him." As he spoke, he gave Gunman

Tony Dee a hard stare.

"You got it, Eddie," Moss replied.

On the way up the stairs, Vango heard the slightest sound of movement along a row of potted palm plants lining the second-floor hallway. Without looking toward the sound right away, he walked on. At the landing, as he turned toward an open bedroom doorway, he heard the sound again. This time he looked just in time to see the big cat come loping to him. Instead of the big cat rubbing his ankle, it leaped up into his arms. Vango heard the deep rattling purr in its chest.

"Yeah, glad to see you too, *Bruiser,*" he said. He rubbed the cat's head for a moment, then lowered the animal back to the floor. It continued purring, walking alongside him into the master bedroom.

The overhead track lights were turned on but dimmed low. Vango felt the switch plate beside the door with the palm of his hand. *Warm* .... The way a dimmer gets when it's been too low, too long, he thought. He turned the dimmer up and looked all around, the cat sticking close beside him. A closet on the wall beside the bed stood open a few inches. Across the room, glass doors stood open out to a balcony. *Okay* ....

He stepped over and opened the closet door, expecting anything. But the closet was empty except for some various items stacked on the right wall. On the floor, amid the items, he saw the leather handle of a large canvas bank bag. He pulled it free and stepped back out of the closet and laid it on the bed. It felt empty. He unzipped the bag's top and started to open it. The cat leaped up onto the bed and sat watching him. At the same time the ceiling lights dimmed low again. He jerked his attention to the light switch.

"Eddie ... Eddie, it's *Lee,*" he heard Leslie Wright say in a soft tone. In the darkness he saw her standing as if posed in the shadowy darkness, her fingers holding open her unbuttoned blouse. "I thought you might like some company?"

Aw-man ... He looked around again, back and forth between the balcony doors and half-naked woman as she dropped the blouse to the floor and took a step toward him, a bottle of champagne in hand. *Times Square ...!* The cat bounced down from the bed and loped over and sat looking up at the open balcony doors.

Thinking quick, Vango said in a rush, "Lee, quick! Turn up the lights! I've found a bank bag full of cash!"

"What? Really?" the woman said. The lights came up full strength.

"There must be a *million bucks* in here!" Vango said.

Lee appeared like magic beside him. She looked down into the large *empty* bag. But before she could mention it being empty, Vango clenched her wrist strong enough to get her attention and shut her up. He gave the slightest nod toward the balcony door. The big cat sat looking up, growling low in its chest.

"Take it easy, Bruiser," he said to the cat in almost a whisper. "Here," Vango said to the woman, "I'll take it downstairs. We'll count it *there.*"

The woman gasped when a silhouetted figure filled the balcony doors and said in a gruff voice, "Not so fast. I'll take the money bag." As he spoke, he stepped closer and closer, saying to Vango, "Lift that cannon from behind your belt and drop it on the bed."

Vango did as he was told. Leslie Wright clutched the champagne bottle to her breasts. At two feet away the gunman tapped his gun barrel on Vango's chest. "You know, I almost wish you would have made a *hero* move. There's nothing I would have liked more than to—"

His words stopped short, seeing Vango reach sidelong and snatch the champagne bottle from the woman's hands. Before the gunman could make a move Vango swung the full bottle around, wide, full strength and crashed it on the side of the man's face. Under pressure, the unopened bottle popped with the sound of a muffled shotgun. Champagne and glass flew. The big cat squalled like a panther; *Lee* Wright cursed loudly. Vango heard Delbert Moss's footsteps hurrying up the stairs, Tony the gunman in front of him.

The big gunman struck with the bottle did not go down as he should have. He staggered around, crouched, his head bleeding, searching for his gun on the floor. Vango opened both arms wide and brought them together full swing, his palms cupped on both of the gunman's ears at once. But the man still did not go down. Instead he staggered around and managed to head out the balcony doors.

Okay then .... Vango helped him along, guided him out, gaining momentum every step to the balcony rail and helping him flip over it. The man landed with a hard, splattering thud on the concrete pavers below.

Vango walked back into the bedroom where Delbert Moss stood with his gun on Tony, who stood with a blood-pink sponge in hand. Leslie Wright stood topless beside the bed, holding the big cat against her breasts. Vango picked up her blouse from the floor, shook it out and handed it to her. She set the cat on the bed and inspected the blouse and put it on.

"Well …" she said, quietly, "that was certainly *real.*"

"I didn't know he was still alive," said Tony Dee, looking worried. "You said they were dead in the car, I just figured you meant—"

"Forget it, *Paladin,*" Vango said. "You're still the transportation guy." He looked at Delbert and nodded them both downstairs.

As the two walked down the stairs, the woman started to follow them. Vango stopped her, saying, "So, *Lee,* you and I are becoming much *closer* friends, it appears?"

She stood with her hand on her hip, her breasts only partially visible now, her blouse back on but not properly closed or buttoned.

"I hoped we were," she said, smiling coyly, the both of them knowing how good she looked. "Only my most intimate friends call me *Lee,* Eddie. I hope I haven't been presumptuous."

"Not at all, Lee," Vango said. "Nothing I would like better. But there's a couple of things I've been wondering about. Maybe you can tell me."

"Of course, I'd love too, if I can," she said.

Vango looked toward the stairs, then out through the balcony doors. "How long have you and Harold been married?" he asked.

"Three years, actually a little over," she replied.

"You've been together that whole time?" Vango asked.

"Yes, except for the past year I've traveled a lot."

"Maybe a lot more traveling lately?" Vango asked.

"Yes, that's true," she offered. "Harold with his new business …"

"And you traveling to the Keys a lot, lately." Vango pressed.

"Yes, I am. Sadly, Harold and I have had to go our own ways more than usual."

Vango smiled. "Okay, that explains why you didn't know where the coffee filters are in your own kitchen." He fixed an expectant look on her. She stood stalled for a moment, but then came around quickly.

"Well, aren't you the highly-attentive one, Eddie Vango," she said, smiling brightly—a little too *brightly,* Vango thought.

"No, no, Lee—if I can still call you *Lee,"* Vango replied quietly. "I'm just paying attention to whatever is moving around in front of me."

"I see," Lee said. "Of course, you can still call me Lee." But Vango noted her voice had gone a little cold. She continued. "If you think that my forgetting where we keep the coffee filters means anything, I suggest—"

Vango cut in, "You didn't know that the tan leather bag was Harold's, not mine or Delbert's."

She paused and let out a breath.

Busted! Vango thought.

"Okay, Eddie," she said with a certain element of relief in her voice. "I'll come clean. Harold and I have been married for three years, but it's always been in name-*only,* especially for over the past year." She waited for a moment, then added, "You see, I have a lover, that is, I *had* a lover, down in the Keys. Lately I've spent most of my time there, in Key West."

"I see," Vango said. On the big bed, the cat—now called Bruiser—lay comfortably watching the two of them talk.

"But that's all over now," the woman cut in quickly, causing the cat to jerk its head toward her. "We broke it off. There's no one in my life now, except … Harold, my *husband,* of course, if that counts for anything." She paused again. "Does it?"

"I don't know," Vango said. "You tell me."

"No, it doesn't count," Lee said. "I mean it *doesn't to me,* if it *doesn't to you."* She struck an intentionally seductive pose. "Does it, *Eddie?"*

Vango picked up her invitation. He couldn't keep from looking her up and down. *Who could? Lee, Lee … what a straight-up beauty you are …,* he said to himself.

"Well, *does* it, Eddie?" she asked.

Vango snapped back into the conversation.

"Not in the least," he said.

"So, are there any more questions I can answer for you, Eddie Vango?" she said.

He had more questions, plenty of them. But this wasn't the time or place.

"We're going to send *Gunman Tony* to deliver his Mobile Death Squad back to Lambert. Then Delbert and I are getting out of here. You're free to go with us. That is, I want you to go with us, but it's your free choice. *Yes, or no?* We're not kidnapping you."

He motioned his eyes around the room slightly, indicating the place could be bugged.

At first, the woman looked surprised. But then she seemed to understand.

"Yes, I want to go with you." She gestured slightly

around the room as if making sure she was being heard should anyone be listening.

"Thank you, Lee," Vango said with a slight smile. He lowered his voice to barely audible. "When we get somewhere *safe,* we'll talk more."

"Yes, I understand," the woman replied.

On the bed, the cat stood up and looked at them as if wondering what the next event on the day's calendar might be.

"What's up, Bruiser? All this action making you hungry? Let's go see if we can find you something to eat."

The cat stepped over to the edge of the bed, making a sound that was between a purr and a growl. He hopped from the bed to the floor and followed them out and down the stairs.

"Where do you think he came from?" Vango asked.

"Cats don't typically belong to anyone," Leslie Wright said. "The neighbors on either side are gone for the season. I hope one of them hasn't left him to fend for himself while they're globetrotting."

"Looks like he's doing all right for himself," Vango speculated. If you'd thaw him out some steak from the freezer, I bet he'd kill for you."

"We'll just have to thaw some out and see," she said.

CHAPTER 7

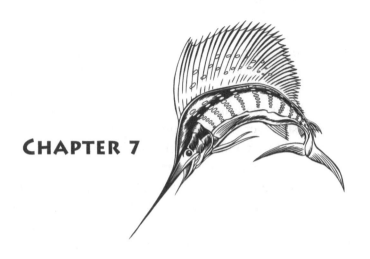

"Before you leave, tell me something, Paladin," Vango said to Gunman Tony, having helped him and Delbert drag the bodies of Randall and the upstairs gunman into the car they'd all arrived in, "where did Ian Lambert find all these gunmen on short notice?"

"If I knew, believe me, Mr. Vango, I'd tell you," Tony said, giving a worried look at the 9mm in Vango's hand. "But work's really bad right now. Everybody's looking for a way to get by. Everybody on the street knows a guy who *knows-a-guy,* you know?"

"Yeah, I know," Vango said. He caught an aroma of steak grilling in the kitchen. Leslie had thawed a New York strip in the microwave and cut it into hefty bite size chunks. Bruiser had devoured most of the chunks raw, or barely warm. He sat stretched out in a high kitchen chair, licking his paws.

"A guy like Lambert wants some temps," said Tony, "he makes a couple of calls here and there, feels out a couple of Miami parole officers—passes them a few bucks. All of a sudden it looks like you've got an army showing up. Right?"

"Yeah, I get that," Vango said, knowing that what Tony said was true, but only partly true. At least it told him the kind of men he was dealing with. This crew of Lambert's were newly formed and thrown together. If this issue over Stanley's money got too hot, most of them would fold and run. This told him that Victor and Lambert were only middlemen.

They might have a handful of reasonably good gunmen, but unless they were guarding a big drug move, the kind of men they needed weren't easily found, unless top dollar was being offered. Instead of *guns-for-hire,* Lambert might be surrounding himself with window dressing—*guns-for-show.* But why? Didn't big drug-dealers like them need *real security, full time?*

Maybe not .... Vango told himself. That was something else that needed to be talked about. Maybe Leslie Wright knew. *We'll see*, he thought.

He took note of the nervous look on Gunman Tony's face.

"When you get to Lambert, give him this message from me. He still owes Stanley the Pole *fifty-bucks.* Tell him his world has stopped turning until I get that money and get out of here with it." He gave Tony a grave look. "Can you remember that?"

"I can, Mr. Vango," said Tony. "He's going to be awfully pissed when I tell him, but I will tell him. You've got my word."

"Good man, Tony," Vango said.

Delbert Moss, Leslie Wright and Vango dimmed the foyer lights and stood watching through the windows until Gunman Tony drove out of the driveway with his grisly load of dead gunmen. As the car turned out of the private community onto the two-lane road, Delbert shoved his newly acquired .45 cal. into his waist and turned to Vango and Leslie Wright.

"I made Tony sponge the walls down, too, Mrs. Wright," he said. "I knew you wouldn't want to leave brains and goop and blood all over—"

"Good job, Delbert," Vango said, cutting his details short.

"Yes, thank you, Delbert," Lee Wright said, her shiny little Beretta shoved down in the waist of her skirt, Bonnie Parker style, her blouse hiked up behind it. She glanced around at the clean walls and floor. Then she turned to Vango and said in a much-lowered voice, "Okay, I know a nice quiet motel near here where we can talk."

"A motel?" Eddie asked, his voice equally lowered. "How safe are we talking about?"

"It's local, not a part of a chain. And it's *very* safe," she replied, a bit defensive. "I know the desk clerk— he's also the owner." Before Vango could comment, she added, "Motel owners here are good at keeping their mouths shut. And, the place I'm thinking of has some very *discreet* parking around back. It's the Blue Dolphin Inn. You can't see anybody's car from the street unless they want you to."

"That's our kind of place," Vango said. "Call ahead on your hand phone after we've left here. Set us up a couple of connecting rooms."

The woman nodded.

Vango also glanced around the foyer. "Only take what you need with you. Maybe you shouldn't be here by yourself for a while. Maybe a *long* while."

"Is there an offer in there?" she asked.

"That offer is always there," Vango smiled. "But for now I'm thinking about your safety."

"I understand," she replied. "I don't think Lambert's the kind of man who gives up easily."

"Neither do I. We'll have to see," said Vango. He glanced down at the big cat who'd showed up and started sidling against his ankle. "You got anything to leave out for this guy? He seems to like it here."

"I saw some cocktail crackers in the cupboard," the woman offered.

Vango just looked at her.

"Delbert, please put this guy out, and set a bowl of water out for him. See if there's any canned meat or tuna in the cupboard."

"You got it, Eddie," Delbert said. He turned and set about his task. "I sure hope he's gotten over his mad-on at me."

Vango stood waiting in the foyer, keeping watch through a part in the drapes. Delbert and the woman came walking back, hurrying along. Delbert carried a four-bottle wine-carrier bag; the woman carried a shopping bag with a thin loaf of Italian bread sticking up from it.

"What's all this?" Vango asked Delbert, seeing the wine bag.

"Mrs. Wright asked me to bring it along," he replied.

"It's getting late," the woman said. "I thought we might want a drink of wine …." She let her words trail. Vango just looked at her, then at the shopping bag in her arms.

"I thought I should bring these few things," she said. "Just something for us to nibble on if we get the munchies?"

"What are we, hippies, smoking pot?" Vango asked.

"Okay, we won't take any of this," the woman said with a pout. She and Delbert started to set the food and wine down.

"No," that's fine, bring it," Vango said. "You're right, we might want it later." He looked around at the house, the surroundings, and at Delbert Moss.

"Why don't you drive, Delbert?" Vango said. "I'll go through the leather bag Harold left behind."

"You got it, Eddie," Delbert said, sounding pleased to be called upon.

"Harold's bag?" said Leslie Wright, looking the tan leather bag sitting at Vango's feet.

"Yes, it is." Vango tapped his foot sideways against the bag and smiled at her. "That's something else you didn't know about your husband."

The woman gave him a flat stare but didn't offer an excuse.

"I don't suppose you'd have a key to it?" he asked as they walked to the car.

"No," she said frostily. "I'm not familiar with it."

"No matter, I can open it," Vango said. He opened the door for her on the passenger side and offered her the front seat.

"Thank you, Eddie," she said.

Vango closed the door and walked around and got in the back seat. Delbert slid into the driver's seat and adjusted himself behind the wheel.

"And we're off," he said, the tan leather bag on his

knees. "I want you to cruise around for a while, Delbert, then come back past here every few minutes."

"Sure thing, Eddie," Delbert said, sitting rigid, staring straight ahead.

Vango took note that Delbert was driving unusually slow, both hands tight on the wheel.

"You okay, Delbert?" he asked.

Delbert paused, then said, "The fact is, I ain't suppose to drive an automobile," Delbert Moss said, creeping along down a palm-lined sandy road a couple blocks from the Wright home. Beachfront mansions stood in a row on the left; Indian River widened and spilled into the ocean on the right. Vango leaned forward and looked at him from the back seat. Leslie Wright sat in the front passenger seat. She gave Delbert a curious look.

"You're not supposed to *drive?*" he said. "What's that about?" He glanced at Leslie Wright who sat listening intently without taking her eyes off the road ahead.

"Yeah, I should have told you," Moss added. "I had my privilege revoked back in seventy-two. Can't drive, can't vote. I have a fake Montana license, but if the police ever checked it out, it would only get me busted."

Vango tapped his fingers on Harold's tan leather bag lying open on his lap. The woman turned her eyes from the road and looked at Delbert in surprise.

Vango said, "I think you're okay in Florida, Delbert. As long as *somebody* in the car has a driver's license, you're good to go."

"Really? How you know that?" Delbert still straight up in the seat, still gripping the wheel.

"It's just something I heard somewhere," Vango

said. "One licensed driver per car, it doesn't really matter who." He smiled at Leslie Wright and said, "Makes sense, don't you think?"

The woman didn't answer; she looked uncomfortable.

"Well, that's good enough for me," Delbert said. He let out a tight breath, getting relaxed. Dropping one hand from the wheel he gunned the car forward.

"I would still drive very carefully, Delbert," she said. "In case the law Eddie is talking about has changed."

"Yeah? What do you think, Eddie?"

"She's right, Delbert. Slow it down some. Don't want you to get pulled over," Vango said. "And stop listening to everything people tell you."

As Delbert cruised them around the plush area, Vango took out a pocketknife and began jimmying the lock on the leather bag. The woman watched with interest when Vango pulled up a small leather-bound appointment book from the bag and flipped through it, at names, addresses, columns of figures that could only mean money. *Victor's street connections?* He wondered.

He handed the woman the notebook with the pages open to the list of names.

"See anybody you know?" he asked. He held the pages for her in the glow of the dash. They both studied the long list of names for a moment.

"No," she said finally. "They might be Miami dealers, not from around here." Her eyes continued down the list of names and the column of figures alongside them. "I left Harold's metal box at the Blue Dolphin earlier on my way home. I'll get it when we get there and see whose names are in it."

"Hold it!" Vango said. "You were at the Blue Dolphin Inn earlier? You left a metal box there—with names and numbers in it? Just how friendly are you with the *owner?*"

"It's nothing like that," the woman said. "We're good friends. A small community like this, we all look out for each other. It's nothing else."

Vango just stared at her.

"I've heard of some of these guys," Delbert put in, having cut a sidelong glance at the list of names. "They're dealers from all up and down the coast here." He reached over and pointed a finger at the name, *DD Spike.* "He was a bad Haitian gang leader out of Miami—dead now. The cons in Dade County lockup called him the *Haitian Wolf.*"

"Good work, Delbert," said Vango, looking impressed. "What about these other names? Anything ring a bell?"

"Not really," said Delbert. "Word is, Trio and Lambert slipped in while the market was so good, nobody was paying attention, at least not like they should have been. I would bet that everybody on that list is big enough to boot Victor and the Lamb out of business if they only had their suppliers. I guess they have a large enough market they don't want to start messing with the upper end of distribution? Bert says nobody's minding the store." He paused.

"Wow, good information, Delbert." Vango looked impressed by Delbert Moss's input.

Moss shrugged.

"I listened a lot while Bert and some others talked about things. Some of it made sense. The bigger the drug demand gets, the more these dealers make. The more they make the less they attend to business."

"Same as any other big business," Vango said. He closed the notebook and ran things through his mind.

Nobody minding the store ...? What an opportunity for a new player to come into the game—catch everybody off-guard. It sounded too good to be true, but he might just be that new player. It was worth a closer look.

He handed the notebook over to Leslie Wright. "See what you think?" he said to her. He sat back, relaxed for a second and asked Delbert, "Are there wolves in Haiti?"

"I don't know," said Moss, "I guess, maybe? Nobody ever said. Why?"

"No big thing, just wondering, Delbert," Vango said. "Turn up here and swing back past the Wright's house. We want to check something out."

"You got it, Eddie." Delbert grinned, liking the "We" part of *we want to check something out* .... He swung the car around the end of a palm-lined meridian, and headed back, gunning the Corsica, fishtailing a little in some loose sand. "I think I'm going to like working with you, Eddie Vango," he added, his wide grin growing wider.

"Same here." Vango smiled and nodded.

As they drove through the intersection, Vango looked down the darkened street and saw the shadowed outline of a white delivery van parked two doors down from the Wright's driveway.

"Yep," Vango said. "Even money says that's the same J W Home Cleaning van from this morning." He smiled to himself and looked at the clock in the dash. "Going on midnight they're still out here working?" *Yeah, right....*

Delbert just nodded, having no idea what Vango was talking about; but he pulled the car over when Vango motioned him toward the curb.

"If I'm not back in twenty minutes," Vango said, "take off without me."

"And go where?" Delbert looked confused. Leslie Wright perked up in her seat.

"Anywhere you like," Vango said, swinging the car door open. "Just be sure, you *give* me twenty minutes."

"I'm not wearing a watch."

Jesus ... Vango rubbed his forehead. "Delbert …." He tapped a finger on the dash indicating the clock. "Okay?"

"I got it," Delbert said. "It's been awhile since I've been behind a wheel."

"I understand," Vango said quietly. He looked at the two of them. "Forget the twenty minutes. *Just wait right here* for me. Don't move an inch until I get back. How's that?"

Delbert nodded, patting the steering wheel. "We'll be right here. You can count on it," Delbert said.

"Be careful, Eddie," the woman said.

Vango eased the car door shut, walked back to the intersection, turned, and staying close to the bordering walls and overhanging shrubbery. He slipped along the narrow sidewalk until he ducked into the pull-off next to the Wright property. Once again, he went up over the five-foot wall and dropped down into the cover of foliage. From there he crept back along the wall to the rear of the sprawling house, stopping at a spot where he could see across the tops of hedges and into the well-lit kitchen through double French doors.

The kitchen sat empty. But he waited, watched. In a moment a light snapped on in an upstairs window, and he caught a glimpse of a man moving in a hurry, room to room. Then the light snapped off. In a second a woman, a brunette in a business-cut pants suit, came into the kitchen, also in a hurry. Behind her came two men, both wearing dark blue wind breakers and matching caps.

DEA, maybe ...? Vango speculated. One thing for certain, they'd had this place bugged from the start. The minute Vango, Leslie Wright and Delbert left, they'd swooped in. He'd have to ask the woman just how much product Harold and his partners brought in at one time. This was looking bigger than he suspected.

The woman in the window of the Wright's home said something to the men, gesturing an arm around the kitchen. The men began rummaging through cabinets and drawers, straightening everything up behind them. She checked her watch while they worked.

Vango smiled. *They're good, whoever they are ....*

CHAPTER 8

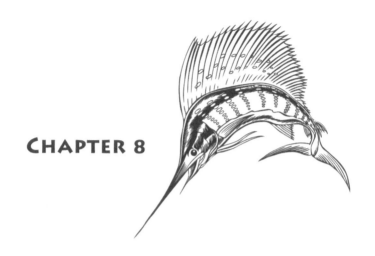

For a couple of minutes Vango watched the woman and the men from the J W Home Cleaning van toss the Wright's home. When they stepped away from a drawer or a closet they'd finished searching, you could hardly tell they'd been there. *Real pros ...? Maybe.* Vango cautioned himself to keep these people in mind with any move he made. They, in their semi-anonymous white van, would be circling like hawks. Either avoid them, he reminded himself, or find a way to work them into whatever plan he had to follow.

Keep them busy? he asked himself. *We'll see.* Let them make the first move. He smiled to himself. *You're only here to collect a gambling debt ....*

He watched. Whatever these people were looking for, they better find it quick. The Lamb was on his way. Vango was sure of it. If not the Lamb personally, certainly some of his hired help. Vango had seen all he needed to see. *Yep*— He raised up slightly and eased back along the wall. *—When Lambert or Trio or any of their gunmen came sliding into this driveway, they'd have their hands full.* Vango didn't want to be here when it happened.

He had slipped along in the shadows and just gotten back to the corner when he recognized the black Mercedes with darkened windows come shooting along the dark street. *Uh-oh. Too late. Here's Lambert now* ....

He dropped down into some foliage and watched the car blow past him on the way to the Wright's. He watched as the car's brake lights come on and the big vehicle nosed down, coming to a hard stop in the middle of the dark street. Glancing past the car he saw the tiny pin light come on from inside the cleaning van. The light blinked twice, then went out. *A signal from someone inside the van*, he decided.

As soon as the light blinked inside the van, the Mercedes gunned backward, swung around and shot away like a dart, leaving Vango crouched there in the shadows for a moment as the big car sped out of sight. He looked back at the dark van, then eased along through the cover of darkness to the Corsica sitting out of sight around the corner.

"I saw the Lamb's Mercedes zip by! What was all that about?" Delbert Moss asked as Vango slipped into the back seat. Delbert and the woman had been ducked down in the front seat, Delbert with the big .45 ready in hand.

"That's what I call our tax dollars at work, Delbert," Vango said. As he spoke the woman and Delbert both sat up in the front seat.

"What are you saying?" Leslie Wright asked. She stared into the darkness toward her home.

"I'm saying somebody back there is working both sides of the street."

"What does that mean?" Delbert looked around as

he put the Corsica into drive.

"It means somebody back there in the delivery van just tipped off the Lamb, or whoever that was in the Mercedes. Get us out of here, quick, Delbert. We've seen enough of this."

"Okay, I got you, *Boss.*" Delbert adjusted himself to the steering wheel, looking eager. "Where to now?" *Boss ...?*

Vango just stared at him. "I don't know about you two, but I'm ready to hang it up for tonight," Vango said. "Swing us over to the bus station, Delbert. I'll give you some money and get you out of town. Keep you out of all this. How does that sound to you?"

"No thanks, Eddie." Delbert shook his head, having dropped the *Boss*. "I don't want to go nowhere. I've got no place to go." He drove down the street with the headlights off for a full block, until he reached the two-lane Indian River Road running past the community. Good thinking, Vango thought.

"Delbert," said Leslie Wright as they stopped at the stop sign, "Eddie's trying to keep you from getting any deeper into this thing—"

"Yeah, I got that," said Moss, easing the Corsica forward, turning left. "But I'm not going to leave. I'll just stick around, you know, do some driving, take you where you need to go?" He looked at Vango in the rear mirror.

Vango let out a breath.

"Delbert, I got to be honest with you," he said. "You and me working together might not be good for you. Nothing personal, but it's going to get red-hot once the Lamb realizes I'm holding the names and dollar amounts of a lot of his clientele. Not to mention what could develop with these folks back there, *one of which,* just tipped off Lambert that there are pros back there tossing the place right now." He gestured in the direction of the house behind them in the darkness.

"I know all that," Delbert said. "But I ain't leaving."

Vango just stared at him. So did Leslie Wright.

"Who are they, DEA?" Delbert asked, getting uncomfortable with the silence. He drove on.

"Yeah, maybe DEA." Vango shrugged. "Who knows. The point is, they'll have to be dealt with if I'm going to collect the money. And I *am going to* collect the money, whether anybody believes it or not. Right now, you can still get out and disappear, Delbert. Later might be too late."

Collecting the gambling debt was getting to be the least issue on his mind. But it was his open seat at the table. Drug dealers always considered themselves the elites in the room.

Suits me, he told himself. Keep an eye on them for now, you'll know when to make a move.

"How you planning on doing it—get the money that is?" Delbert glanced at him, then back to the street ahead. Leslie Wright just shook her head.

"I gave him enough to know he's got to deal with me," Vango said. "Now I'll let him search for me until I decide to let him find me." He smiled. "By then he'll be begging me to take the money and split town. Tomorrow, the vig and penalty are going to up the thirty-eight thousand."

"Damn." Delbert grinned, bumping his palm against the steering wheel. "See, that's why I want to hang out with you. I could learn something. All my life, all I've done is pull time and listen to a bunch of cons talk about what went wrong. I've never had what you could call a *skill.*"

"Collecting gambling debts is not exactly a skill," Vango said, gazing ahead toward downtown Jensen Beach as neon and streetlights began flickering by.

"I've got a hunch you do more than collect gambling debts, Eddie. But you know what I mean," Delbert said. "I ain't getting no younger. I need to start knowing how to play the game, get streetwise as they say. Like throwing that cat in my face? I would never have thought of that."

"You ever shot anybody?" Vango stared at his face in the green glow of the dash light.

"No, but I would … I mean, as long as it ain't some innocent person."

A silence passed as they drove on. Then Delbert said: "I know all the places where the Lamb and his guys hang out. The past two weeks I've probably been to every place on that list, riding with my pal Bert, while he made deliveries. I can save you some time, taking you around."

"Yeah?" Vango considered it. "How much we talking about, pay wise?"

"I won't charge you nothing," Delbert said with a shrug.

Vango looked at him for a second, and chuckled. "Man, Delbert, you're right. You really *do* need to learn a couple of things." They rode on another block and Vango said: "Pull over at the next phone booth. I'll call my partner and let him know we're coming." He looked at the woman. "We're not making any calls from the Blue Dolphin once we get checked in there." He looked at Moss. "Okay, Delbert, you're the driver. Take us to a pay phone so I can call and check on my backup man."

"Alright!" Delbert grinned and swung across two lanes of traffic toward the corner while Vango and the woman held themselves in place.

At a corner pay phone, Vango called Lew Stucky's motel room, but when Stucky didn't answer, he got back in the car and Delbert drove on, only stopping long enough for Delbert to pick up three packs of Camel cigarettes for himself on their way. Inside Stucky's empty motel room, the strong smell of vinegar hung in the stale air. As soon as Vango clicked on the light switch, Delbert said in a strained voice, "Aw man!" He reeled a step to the side.

"What's he been doing in here?" Leslie held a hand cupped over her mouth.

Vango smiled, looking around the disheveled room, at the empty vinegar bottle on Stucky's un-made bed.

"Disgusting huh? It's my partner's room," he said. "He got sunburned to a crisp, then laid out in it again the next day. He called himself a *burnt pork chop.*"

A small white card leaned against the telephone. Vango walked over, picked it up and looked at it. On the front it read: Martin County Emergency Medical Service. On the backside he saw Stucky's scribbled handwriting.

"He's gone to the hospital. Can you believe that?"

"Must be pretty serious," the woman said, leaning closer, looking at the card. "Didn't he know any better than to get back out in the sun? This Florida sun is a killer."

"I tried to tell him. Some people don't listen." Vango put the card in his shirt pocket. "Okay, folks, let's ride. It's after midnight."

Delbert spun the cellophane from a pack of Camels, opened it, then pecked one out of the pack and lit it. Vango looked him up and down. Delbert blew smoke all around in front of him.

"Let housekeeping air the place out," Vango said. "Tomorrow morning we'll go by the hospital and check on Lew."

"You got it, Eddie. Think we can go somewhere and find me a change of clothes?" Delbert asked. "I left the rest of my clothes in the trunk of Bert's car. Don't know if I'll get any of them back."

"Sure," said Vango. "We'll do that on our way." He looked at Leslie Wright. "Want to point us to the Blue Dolphin Inn?"

CHAPTER 9

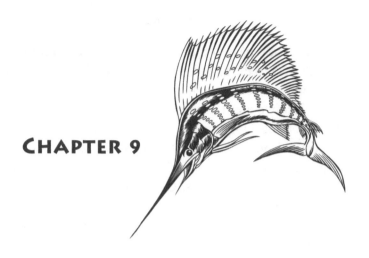

At 1:00 a.m., the small town of Jensen Beach lay shut down for the night. The only food and drink place still open was Crawley's, a blues and crab joint at the west end of a two-block stretch of businesses and tourist shops. The dimmed neon glow of a large crab hung above the doors. Electric Led Zeppelin redo style blues whined out from an alfresco garden where a half dozen stoned patrons gyrated like zombies on a small dance floor.

A waiter stood out front of Crawley's folding the menu board for the night. A shielded glowing joint moved from fingertips to fingertips among band members.

From the Corsica's passenger seat, Leslie Wright said, "When you get the opportunity, you both should check out this place."

Delbert and Vango gave her a bemused look, each of them carrying a loaded gun in their lap.

"Yeah, when we get a chance," Vango said dryly.

"I'm just saying," she added. She quickly nodded ahead of them as the small beach town melted into a purple hazy darkness behind them. The road they were on left town and merged onto a sandy two-lane state highway. They passed a draw bridge on their right that led back over to the island. Ahead of them the white glow of a single bulb shone in the near distant sky.

"Here we are, Delbert," she said. "Up there on the left—the Blue Dolphin Inn." Delbert slowed the little Corsica and pulled into a long gravelly path leading to the office of the small motel. Three cars sat out front of three motel room doors. One room had a light in its window. An outdoor light shined slantwise on the office sign. A doorbell button hung beside it. Bugs circled and swarmed.

"Don't stop out here," the woman said to Delbert. "Follow this path around back. I set us up two connecting rooms *as per request.*"

When Delbert had parked the car and the three stood at the door to the room on the right, Leslie Wright reached up and took two room keys from above the door frame. Eddie gave her a look; she smiled as Delbert pushed the door open for them and stepped aside. A full fresh container of ice sat on the kitchenette table beside a new corkscrew.

"Not bad," Vango said, quietly.

"I told you, I know the owner," she replied, the shopping bag of snacks and airline flight-sized vodka shot bottles clinking as she walked in, crossed the room and set the bag on the table. Delbert stepped in and set the wine carry bag beside it. Vango gave an extra searching look all around the dark parking lot, past a large, recently remodeled pool and Jacuzzi area. Then he closed the door and stepped over to the air conditioner embedded in the front wall and twisted its dial to the coldest setting.

"If you gentlemen will excuse me," Leslie Wright

said. "I'm going to take a shower and prepare for *beddy-bye?"* She shot Vango a coy look that carried the hint of an invitation and said, just between the two of them, "Are you?"

Delbert, either not hearing any of it or pretending not to, pulled a bottle of wine from the carrier bag, picked up the corkscrew from the table and stepped around and seated himself on a sofa. He picked up the TV channel changer.

"Guess I'll have some wine and see what's on the boob-tube this time of night." Before Vango could say a word, Delbert clicked on the power and looked away from Vango at the fizzling TV screen. "You two get some rest—don't mind me out here."

They didn't ….

Inside the attached room, when the woman closed the door and latched it behind them, she crossed the floor into the bathroom, walking out of her clothes a little more with each step. Vango followed, loosening his trousers, losing his shoes, pitching his gun over on the bed for now.

In the bathroom, Leslie reached into the shower and turned the water on. Before she turned around, she felt Vango's arms encircle her from behind. He stood fully against her, a hand spread wide on her breast, his other hand reaching down into the V of her thighs, pressing her more firmly to him. She gasped a little, feeling him there, feeling his mouth on the side of her throat.

"My goodness, Eddie, but aren't you one to get right in and get acquainted," she said in a teasing little laugh. "I wondered if we would ever get around to this—" Her words stopped short as he turned her around to him and put his mouth on hers. He felt her breath quicken, her wet breasts firm on his chest.

"Now you don't wonder …," he managed to say as their mouths gathered each other hungrily. He raised her higher up on him and helped her lower herself down, fitting herself easily into place. She moaned aloud as thy began their lovemaking.

She twisted her lips away from his long enough to say, "Oh, God, Eddie! Do me good and hard!"

It went without saying. He lowered them to the shower floor, on his lap, rising and falling with him. *Oh, Jesus …!* She needed this so bad.

"Do me, Eddie! *Do me!"*

He gripped her in both hands, rising and falling with her, going deep. As he took more of her, she gave it up completely. Warm water poured down on them from the shower head. When they slowed for a moment the sound of the theme song from *The Good, the Bad and the Ugly* seeped in from Delbert's TV.

When they had sated themselves of each other, Vango reached up around her and turned the shower off. When he leaned back, she stretched out atop him.

They lay gathering their breath on the tile floor in the draining shower for a moment, hearing the faint sound of the Good, the voice of Eli Wallach (Tuco The Rat) at the end of loud gunfire, "When you are going to shoot … *Shoot!* Don't talk!"

"Do you think Delbert heard us, Eddie?" she said against Vango's throat. Vango gave a slight shrug.

"I don't know," he replied. "Do you care if he did?" He adjusted himself up, bringing her up with him. They both stood up pressed together.

"I do now, a little," she said. "I didn't care at the time." She smiled. Vango noted a sniffle. He saw her eyes were filled and she wiped them with her fingertips.

"Are you crying?" he asked.

"No, not really." She shook her head. They stepped out of the shower. Before he could ask if anything was wrong, she ran a hand down between them and cupped him firmly but gently.

"Sometimes I *tear-up* when I cum," she said. She wiped her eyes again with her free fingertips. "Okay? So, I'm one of those women."

Without reply, Vango took a soft bath towel from a wire shelf, let it unfold and pressed it to her breasts. He dried her softly, liking the feel of her through the towel.

"Do you tear-up *sometimes,* or *every time?*" he asked. They still stood close, very close, indicating to him they were not finished with each other, not just yet.

"This time," she replied, looking in his eyes, as if putting an end to the subject. She reached a hand down between them. Held him. "Oh, *yes!*" she said, already feeling signs of life stir in her hand. She led him out of the bathroom to the waiting bed, feeling the excitement her touch caused in him, feeling excited herself.

They lowered onto the king-sized bed, already pressing together, writhing. The gun he'd pitched there earlier lay on the pillow beside them. Later, he would move it. *Later* ....

Near dawn as the two of them dozed against each other, her warm hands moved across him again, and again. She seemed to know all the places to stop and let the pleasure she created simmer for a moment, then her hand moved away lightly before that pleasure came to a boil.

"Are you asleep, Eddie?" she finally whispered against his face.

"You're kidding, right?" Vango whispered in reply. He guided her face back down to his throat. She gave a slight little giggle. She stopped exploring with her hand but held him firm in it, not giving it up.

"Maybe I should have told you," she replied in the same lowered voice, though there was no need to whisper, "I am a wanton, sex-crazed woman—I can never seem to get enough."

"I believe you, Leslie," Vango whispered.

"It's *Lee,* Eddie," she corrected him.

"I believe you, *Lee,"* Vango said, liking the warm feel of her against him, the AC in the wall keeping a coolness overall.

"Am I depraved, Eddie?" she whispered.

"Maybe," he said. "If you are, it must be catching."

She gave another giggle and squeezed him tight down there, holding on a little longer this time. He loved it, even as he moved her hand away. She took his right hand and clasped it between her warm thighs.

"So, my *new* lover," she said, "is this place safe enough we can talk?" She pressed her thighs together tight before letting his hand go.

Her new lover …?

"Sure, we can talk here, if we can keep our hands off each other," Vango said. "I just didn't want to talk at your place. Turns out I was right." They both adjusted themselves, lying naked only a foot apart.

She pulled a sheet over her from the waist down and lay gazing at him on an elbow. Her breasts were spectacular for a thirtyish woman, with money and gym time to keep her confidence peaking.

"Okay, ask me anything, Eddie Vango," she said.

Vango let out a breath.

"First of all, what is this about a *metal box* you brought here earlier? Your husband, Harold, had a metal box under his arm when he left with Lambert. I didn't mention it before," he added.

"You didn't need to, Leslie said. "I figured if he left with Lambert, he would be carrying that metal box if nothing else. Lambert would have insisted on it."

"Oh?" said Vango. "What's so important about that box?"

Leslie said, "It has keys to several bank deposit boxes all along the Treasure Coast." She paused, then said, "Or, at least that's what Victor Trio and Ian Lambert thinks are in it."

"What does that even mean?" Vango asked.

She paused, as if carefully deciding just how much she could, or, at this point, *would* tell him.

With a breath of resolve, she said, "Okay, Eddie, here we go. The truth, and nothing but the truth."

At last .... Vango listened intently.

"To answer your curiosity about my husband and me, Harold is gay." She spoke flatly and paused for his reaction; Vango gave none. Not a nod nor a flinch—a good collector's response.

"When I told you ours is a *marriage of convenience,* that's what I meant. When we married, we both knew that Harold is gay, and in an ongoing lifetime of trial and error we both knew that I am not."

An ongoing lifetime of trial and error ...?

Vango kept silent. Leslie Wright paused, then said, "Before you get the wrong idea and think you have just spent the night making love to a lesbian, let me assure you, that's not true."

"Again, proven by *ongoing trial and error?*" Vango asked.

"I hope that doesn't offset you, Eddie," she said. "But yes, by trial and error. Should I go on, or does that stop us in our tracks?"

Us ..., Vango noted. Once again, she linked them up.

"I didn't ask. You didn't have to tell," he said. "But I'm good with it if you are. Take us to any part of all this that might help me get the money I'm here to collect."

"It's all interrelated, so please indulge me," she said quietly. She reached a pack of Virginia Slims on the nightstand. Vango watched her light it and breathe in a deep draw. She let it out.

"I met Harold though his assistant—I won't mention her name. She had just swallowed a bottle of downers because she and I had quit being *close friends.*" She stared into his eyes for a moment. "Harold managed to put two and two together—sharp accountant that he is." She gave a slight smile. Vango noted to himself— her skin, creamy, sun-touched, her hair ashy silk, blonde, almost natural, her eyes blue but changing constantly with the light—*God, you are a beautiful woman ....* And now he knew the taste of her, the deep feel of her body, her scent— *Stop it,* he had to tell himself. *Pay attention!*

"Once Harold thought I might be the same as him, he admitted his homosexuality to me. We became friends, and from that came our marriage of convenience. Harold knew, or I should say, *feared* his clientele would leave him if they found out he was gay." She shrugged. "They would not have, of course, but that was how Harold thought."

"Okay, I get all that," Vango said, keeping his patience in check. "You said you hadn't lived with him this past year. That explains why you didn't know where anything was at in your own home."

"Yes, I have been living with my friend in Key West," she said. "But not anymore, that's over. All right, *fast forward,*" she added, "to when Harold started up with Lambert and Victor Trio. He soon realized the LL Partnership he set up, Wright Way Venture Capital Investment Company LLC., was only a scam to help big-time drug dealers launder money. He set up a system that brought other drug dealers in with Venture Capital and held large amounts of their cash until drug deals were made. Then, he made short-term investors of them. When he released their money back to them, he did it in form of bearer bonds made payable to them or whomever they wanted to make them payable to." She smiled. "It was the latest rage among the big dealers at the top of the drug chain. The government is getting ready to ban them, but for now they are legal as far as using bearer bonds go."

"I know a little about bearer bonds," Eddie said. "And I know a lot of legit businesspeople have dropped out of the stock market because the returns are so low in this bottomed-out economy. So, you're saying Harold setup a business that collected cash money from these same investors and invested it in major drug deals." He shook his head a little. "Why not? It's worked for

American corporations for over a hundred years."

"Exactly," she smiled. "Instead of Wall Street, investors are going to the drug world, where the money is," she said. "They can invest as little or as much as they want to risk, make more interest then they will ever make in the stock market, and never pay tax on it. Are those good selling points?"

"Dynamite," said Vango. "So, the term *venture capital,* in this case, means money gathered from investors large and small and used to buy and sell drugs across the globe without anybody having to dirty their hands with the details?"

"I'm impressed, Eddie," she said. "You catch on quick." She smoked and watched for his reaction. He gave none.

"Now back to the box," he said.

"All right, back to the box," she said. "Lambert and Trio both think the metal box has the keys to the deposit boxes in it. They are wrong. Harold saw this business was losing its sharp edge, like a lot of corporations. And we both knew these dick-heads, Trio and Lambert, couldn't be trusted. While funding of this present big deal has been coming together, we have been coming up with fake deposit box keys. The real keys are in another metal box, in the trunk of my car."

Bingo...! Vango told himself.

"Sounds *real* safe to me," he said critically.

"I know. Who would have *thunk* it?" She actually giggled a little. "So, today when Lambert starts going from bank to bank, he might gather some small amounts of cash. But the bearer bonds he's really after are gone. They are spread along the Treasure Coast. All the bonds need is Harold's signature. Which Lambert will never have, of course."

"And if Harold is dead, which I'm betting for sure he is," said Vango, "neither Ian Lambert nor anybody else will ever have it."

"That would be true," she said. "I don't have my husband's signature, but I have the next best thing. I have an affidavit on file with the source issuer of the bearer bonds. As head of Wright Way, he has given me the right to sign for my husband in any event that prevents him from being able to do so for any reason."

A marriage of convenience .... Vango just looked at her, imagining he could see wheels turning inside her head. If all of this was true, why was she even telling him? As if hearing his thoughts, she said, "I need someone I can count on, Eddie. Can I count on you?"

"Jesus, Lee," he said. "How much money are we talking about here?"

"I'm not sure, Eddie, but here's the best answer I can give you," she replied in a dead-serious tone. "We could be talking a few thousand dollars, or two or three million dollars." She studied his eyes letting it sink in, then said, "Or, we could be talking about some *really big money.*"

Two or three million! Or, some 'really big money?' *Slow down,* Vango warned himself.

"I have a couple of things I need to take care of first thing today," he said. "But for the kind of money we're talking about, you can count on me."

"Good," she said with resolve. "How much are you going to charge me?"

"Let's talk about that later, once we know what's

involved," Vango said. "This might all get *real* dangerous *real* quick. First thing, we've got to stop at a couple of banks, make sure the keys you have *in your trunk* are the ones it takes to open the deposit boxes."

"What if one of Lambert's men has gone there and already tried one of the bad keys?" Leslie asked.

"Don't forget there are two locks on the deposit box," Vango reminded her. "The bank clerk has to open one lock first, then leave the customer in privacy. When Lambert's man tries his bad key and can't get in, all he can do is leave—go tell Lambert what happened."

"So, it might be awhile before Lambert catches on," Leslie said.

"I don't think so," said Vango. "I think he'll know right away someone has put the screws to him. But he has to decide who's doing it." Vango smiled. "Then he has to figure what to do about it. Meanwhile we've moving from bank to bank, ahead of him. Not a bad idea Harold came up with," he added.

"This part was not Harold's, it was mine," Leslie said.

"Okay," Vango said. "Let's get out there and start putting some numbers on the board."

The woman giggled with excitement.

"We're here on the Treasure Coast. This will our *treasure hunt* on the *Treasure Coast!* And before we start, as far as I'm concerned, if you're in for a penny, you're in for a pound. Whatever we make … we're partners, *fifty-fifty!"*

"That could be a large amount of money," Vango said, in almost a cautioning tone.

"Large or small, that's my position, Eddie," she

said. She laughed. "Are you going to try to talk me down?"

"No, I'm not, Lee," he said. "Let's both remember what we said here and get to work."

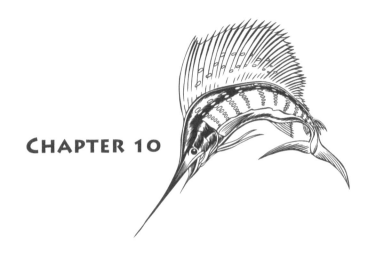

CHAPTER 10

Leone Morez arrived at Victor Trio's former apartment in Oceana Princess II early, with his personal bodyguards, Joe Paso and Cuban-Russian Hector Chebreski, walking close, in position, Paso six feet in front, Chebreski four feet behind him. The two men carried a combined solid-muscle weight of five-hundred pounds. When the door buzzer screamed through the apartment, Ian Lambert caught a tight breath. When he looked through the peep-hole and saw Morez and his men standing there, he hurried to open the door, knowing that if he didn't the next thing he would hear would be Leone's voice saying loud, "Open the door, we know you're in there."

And there it came, before the second ring. *"We know you are in there."*

Christ! Damn it! He didn't need this crap first thing this morning. He had just finished a quick once-over of Victor's apartment in case he had missed anything. Still he'd found nothing! He'd been ready to leave, and go check the Wright's home, see if the drug search he'd been tipped off about had left anything uncovered. *But now, here's this sonofabitch!*

"Yo, Mr. Morez, what a surprise!" Lambert said, swinging the door open, seeing both bodyguards, each standing with their right hand close to the holstered 9mms in their belts. The loose lapels of thin linen day-jackets partially hid the gun butts.

Lambert watched, hand extended, as each huge bodyguard stepped in and faded to either side, allowing Morez to step inside, look all around and remove his sunglasses before shaking Lambert's hand.

This sonofabitch! Lambert repeated to himself. He took a step back, giving Morez wider entrance. He tried not to flinch when the dapper-dressed Uruguayan turned suddenly to him.

"How do we know you are in here?" Morez said, standing close, face to face.

Here it comes! Lambert had heard all this before, many times. Still he played along.

"No, Mr. Morez," he said. "How did you know?"

"Because *'here'* you are," Morez replied. He turned a cheesy grin at the bodyguards. They returned it.

"Oh, yeah, okay, I get it." Lambert gave his own cheesy grin, walking along with Morez into the apartment with a guiding hand, unnecessarily. The Uruguayan had already moved past him and began making himself at home. He glanced at the empty space near the balcony door where Bones' chair always sat.

"Where is the old man?" he asked.

Lambert smiled. "He retired, Mr. Morez. I heard him tell Trio he was going back to Cuba."

"I expected the *fat* man, but I get you," Morez said. "I look for old Bones but he is also gone." He gave a quick glance around, then back to Lambert. "Where is

Trio? Somewhere eating a restaurant to the ground?" Again, the cheesy grin, but it had waned some. He stood close to a plush sofa; Lambert motioned him to have a seat.

"Actually, Mr. Morez," said Lambert. "Victor is no longer with us—"

Morez raised a hand, imitating a gun and pointed it at his head and said, "You mean …?"

"No, no, nothing like that," Lambert replied quickly, although that was exactly what had happened. "You're the first of our investors I'm telling this to, but I bought Victor out. He's gone two days, already I miss him." He shrugged and studied the man's dark eyes to see how that news would set with him. It seemed all right.

"He'll still have a hand in furnishing the product, but the new business is *all mine* from now on." He grinned and added, "As they say where I come from, I'm now the man with the *fuzzy nuts!*"

"Ah, that is great for you," said Morez. His smile melted away. I'm glad to hear you are a *fuzzy nut,* because now I know who to ask about what I came here to ask about."

"No, wait," Lambert said quickly. "I didn't say I'm a *fuzzy nut!* You misunderstood—"

"You are the boss, eh? The *big-shot man*, no?" said Morez, cutting him off. "You are who I come to now that the fat man is gone."

"I am the man," said Lambert getting irritated, "but just so we both understand, you always dealt with Victor as your go-to guy."

"And now my *go-to* guy is gone," said Morez, "so now I *go-to* you, the *fuzzy nut."* He pointed a rigid finger at Lambert, coming within an inch of poking him in his chest. "So, I ask you, where is the two million in *funny money* I signed over to the fat man last week?"

What the ...? Lambert stood stunned for a moment. Finally, he said, "You signed an additional two million dollars in bearer bonds over to Victor Trio, last week?"

"Did I stutter?" said Morez. "No, I did not stutter."

"I think you mean that you signed them over to Harold Wright?" Lambert said, feeling sourness stir in his belly. Trio hadn't said a word about it, neither had Harold Wright. *Of course they didn't mention it, they were skimming!*

"*Sí,* I signed them to Harold Wright to be recorded, but I sent them to Trio *personally,* the way Mr. Burge told me to—the way Trio himself instructed us to do."

Oh shit ...! Victor you underhanded son of a bitch!

Lambert took a breath, feeling very much screwed, trying to take in what Trio had done to him. But there was more coming.

Morez said, "Three days ago when none of my people heard of any product arriving like we were expecting, Mr. Bruge tells me, take Joe Paso and Chebreski and go to Florida, see the fat man. He says to me, 'Leone, either come back with the two million or the product we wait on. But don't come back empty-handed.'" He paused, then said, "Without him telling me, I know he wants us to shoot some bullets into Victor Trio's head—or whoever the new *Fuzzy Nut* is—if we don't get the dope *or* the money." He gave Lambert a flat stare and a cruel little grin.

"Whoa now, let's not get out-of-hand." Lambert glanced around, wishing Bones was here, rising from his chair, the shotgun cocked and ready in his weathered hands. "Whatever is going on, I'll get it straightened out! Could be with all that was going on with Trio, he got Burge's two million in bonds and forgot he even had them, the way everybody has gotten loose lately, throwing their money around." He shrugged, with a weak grin. "And that's one thing I want to stop right away now that I'm in charge."

"Sure," said Morez. "Mr. Bruge and I can both understand all that. Many times, I, myself, forget a couple of million here, a few million there. What is a few *million* among *amigos* like us, eh?"

Lambert heard the bodyguards stifle a little laugh under their breath.

Leone Morez drew a patient breath.

"Look at me and listen carefully," he said to Lambert. "We are going to be here in Florida a few days, three, maybe four. We'll experience the topless beach here, which I understand is right up the island road toward Fort Pierce?"

"Sure it is," said Lambert. It's called Blind Pass Beach." He pointed north. "It's real close."

Morez went on. "Then we will cruise down to Miami, check out some clubs. But we'll stay in touch, make sure we are keeping everybody's interest. Especially *yours.*"

Both bodyguards nodded in agreement.

"Good, good," said Lambert. "Believe me, if I can't get it straight, I'll take care of it myself. Meanwhile you fellows go enjoy the nude beach." He cupped both hands up against his chest. "Those naked babes will knock your eyes out! You can tell Mr. Burge I've got it covered here.

I need to check on the product. It should have already arrived. Either way, you'll either get the money or the dope. No sweat." He looked back and forth between the three sinister faces fixed on him. "Where are you guys staying?"

"You are right, *Fuzzy Nuts,*" said Morez, "it should have already gotten here. I'm here to find why it hasn't." He gave Lambert a sharp stare.

Lambert fidgeted and said, "Hey come on, fellas! It'll get here any day. It always has! Give it a chance." He changed the subject. "Where you staying while you're here? I've got some discounts you can have for the—"

Morez cut him off with a raised hand. He and his two men looked at each other again.

"How far is it to Disney?" Morez asked. The bodyguards stood listening with interest.

Hunh ..?

Lambert waited a second to see if he was joking about Disney. When he realized Morez's question was serious he considered it for a second.

"From here, Disney is two and a half hours, three at the most, depending on the traffic. From Lauderdale it takes a lot longer. They're in opposite directions."

"Okay, first we go to the nude beach and let them knock out our eyes," said Morez.

As daylight crept up on the eastern horizon, Delbert pulled the Corsica into the Wright's driveway and kept the engine running. Vango looked all around for any sign of Lambert or his men.

So far so good ....

From inside the Corsica, Leslie Wright opened

the garage door with a keychain clicker from her purse and watched it rise. In no more than a minute Vango had backed the Mercedes out. Top down, he turned the Mercedes around in the wide driveway and waited for Delbert to turn the Corsica around and ease up alongside him.

"You want me to lead or follow?" Delbert asked.

"You two go to the motel until the mall opens," said Vango. "I've got a couple of stops to make." He didn't like sitting there in an open-topped convertible.

"Shouldn't I take the box of keys from the trunk before we pull off?" Leslie Wright asked.

"Don't get nervous, Lee, the metal box is safer where it's at until we sit down and go through the keys," Vango said. "Run by the mall when it opens, get Delbert some new threads. Then meet me in the hospital parking lot. Park in the shade. I've got to see Stucky and tell him the news."

"What news?" said Delbert.

"That he's going home," said Vango. "You're going be doing the driving."

Delbert just gave him a proud nod. Vango smiled as he pulled the Mercedes away along the palm-lined street, Delbert followed in the little Corsica. At Indian River Road, Delbert and Leslie Wright split off toward the motel and Vango checked the level of the gas tank and drove away south, down Indian Lagoon Drive, in the direction of the airport.

Three miles down the lagoon-side road, he pulled off into a small ancient development of old crabber shack houses and vintage Airstream silver bullet trailers that had sat so long the wheels had rusted away to nothing.

They sat, some on concrete blocks, others with their rusting frames sunken down into the sandy dark soil.

Vango pulled into a rutted sand and gravel path winding around through a jungle of wild palm and Bougainvillea to the last trailer on the lagoon shoreline.

On a rickety porch Vango stepped up and knocked on a pitted aluminum storm screen door and heard a parrot squawk and curse angrily and bounce around inside his cage in the small darkened living room. Through the parrot's madness a thin oriental woman in a gauzelike kimono ventured in from the next room and called back over her shoulder to where Bones sat on the back porch.

"Hello, Teensie," Vango said.

"Hello, Eddie." The woman offered a faint nod and smile. The bird settled a little and emitted a shrill piercing whistle.

"It is your friend from Chicago," the woman spoke quietly, but her words found their way through the darkened empty house as she motioned for Vango to come inside. *"... Awwk! Friend from Chicago,"* the bird mimicked in a crackling voice. Vango walked in and followed her through two rooms of smaller-scale antique wicker and ornately carved seaside furniture. She held the rear storm door open for him with a tiny outreached arm and moved away silently when he stepped out and stood looking at Bones seated in a faded pale green metal glider.

"I didn't think I would see you this soon," he said to Vango, barely looking up. His blackout shades were off, lying on a flat cushion in the glider beside him. "What do you think of our *paradise?"*

"Nice," said Vango, "but you were right. I don't

109

like the heat here."

Bones gave a slow nod. Vango saw a slight smile move on his lips.

"But you're staying longer anyway?" he said. He waited a second and when Vango didn't answer, he asked, "What'll it be, Uzi or Mac?"

"I want more than one," Vango said, taking a nice thick fold of cash from his pants pocket. "Make it two of each, with plenty of ammo. Are they close by?"

"Be here in ten minutes," said Bones. He noted the size of Vango's folded cash. "What else can I get you?"

"I could use a bazooka," Vango said, half joking.

"Done," Bones said flatly.

"Seriously? You've got a *bazooka?*"

"I've got an M79 grenade launcher" Bones said. "It'll do lots more for you than some outdated *bazooka.*"

"Okay, I'll take it," said Vango.

Bones stood up to walk inside and call his contact.

"While we wait, maybe you can tell me more about our friends Lambert and Trio," Vango said.

"I'll tell you about Lambert," Bones said, reaching for the pitted storm door handle. "Trio is gone. We don't want to talk about him."

"Gone?" said Vango.

"Yeah, gone *far away,*" said Bones. He stared at Vango.

Vango got it.

When Bones returned from inside the house, the parrot raised a screaming, whistling ruckus and shouted loudly as Bones passed its cage. *"Get the door! Awwk, get the freaking door!"*

"Freaking door?" said Vango.

"He watches his language when people are here," Bones said, sitting down. "Sometimes I want to cut his throat, but he's good at watching things." The parrot cackled with creepy laughter from the front room as if he knew what was being said. "Anyway, he's Teensie's bird. If it was me, I'd have a toucan. Parrots never shut up. Toucans don't talk, *period*—but they're smart as hell."

Parrots? Toucans? Okay, Vango nodded.

They let the bird settle down. Bones leaned closer to where Vango sat and said in a lowered voice, "Your goods are on their way."

"Thank you, Bones," Vango said.

Teensie stepped out the door carrying two tall frosted glasses of rum mojito-style drinks on a battered wooden tray and sat it on a wrought iron table beside the glider. Bones saw Vango glance around as if wondering about the hour of morning.

"Rum starts early this time of year," Bones said. The two raised the cold glasses in salute. With their glasses still raised, Bones said quietly, "This business is changing hands right now, Eddie. Whatever you're doing, get in, get it done, and get out of here. You hear me?"

"I hear you. Thanks," Vango said. He jiggled his glass of mojito in hand. "Here's to breakfast."

Bones had just laid out everything he was wondering about in one short sentence. *This business is changing hands right now ....*

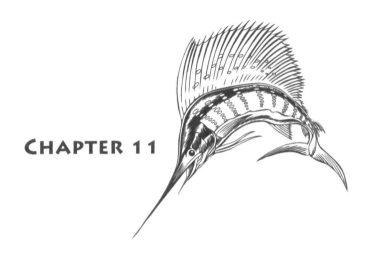

CHAPTER 11

It took longer to stop and see Bones than Vango had intended. But it was worth his time, he decided. He'd picked up some serious weaponry, and spent a few extra minutes gathering information on the drug operation Harold Wright, Lambert, and the late Victor Trio were a part of.

Just as Vango has suspected, Trio and Lambert had never been a part of the Santo Trafficante Family now headed by Santo, Jr., who, like his father, stayed low profile at all times. Santo Trafficante, Jr. was known to give independents a lot of room in Florida, so long as they kept their beaks out of his well—as Bones put it. He wondered for a moment how it would go over when an independent operator like Lambert and Wright Way LLC. screwed over an entire network of top-end drug dealers. He was ready to find out. He had a hunch the high-end dealers already had themselves and their money covered. The smaller investors, *not so much.*

Wright Way LLC. He described the business in his mind: *A drug dealing, money laundering, venture capital corporation, under the guise of a legitimate lending company. Un-frigging-believable!*

Okay. Leslie Wright had already told him much the same as Bones had just ran past him, except for the part about Trio being indescribably gone. But it was different hearing the full lowdown from Bones who had sat listened and watched who came and went through Wright Way Inc. ever since day one.

As he thought about it, Wright Way LLC. did exactly what their mission statement would purport to do, if they, indeed, actually ever detailed a "Mission Statement." They raised venture capital from their list of investors to support their list of entrepreneurs whose business ventures needed cash—short-term cash—from time to time. It didn't matter that their investors and entrepreneurs were illicit drug smugglers, and more often than not, one and the same.

Pulling into the parking lot at Martin County Hospital, he saw a line of cars parked in the slim shade along the lot's perimeter and spotted the Corsica sitting under a large blanketing live oak. As he slowed and cruised closer, he saw Delbert and Leslie in the front seat, windows up with the AC and engine running. He pulled the Mercedes in beside them, its top down and the 10:30 morning sun already blazing down.

"The top won't raise," he said, seeing Delbert and the woman staring at him curiously as he raised the windows all the way around and stopped the engine. He felt his shirt sticking to his back as he stepped out and closed the door.

"It's practically brand new," Leslie said. She stepped out of the Corsica long enough to look the Mercedes over. "The top always works fine for me.

Anyway, it's under warranty. I'll call the dealer, right now." She looked at Delbert for the keys to the Corsica. "I'll need to leave the engine running, for the AC."

Delbert gave her the keys and she slid into the driver's seat and started the engine. Vango and Delbert walked away to the hospital entrance doors.

"Is she all right?" Delbert asked. "She won't cut out on us with all the deposit box keys?"

"I don't think she will," Vango said. "It's time we decide if we can trust her or not."

It was 10:50 a.m. when they walked into Lew Stucky's room and found him in his hospital bed, looking out at Vango and Delbert from beneath strips of wet gauze across his red face.

"I was wondering when you would show up," Stucky said to Vango, ignoring the stranger, Delbert Moss. Stucky's breath smelled of vinegar from five feet away.

"I had some things to do on the way here," Vango said. He walked across the floor to the second floor window and looked down on the parking lot, seeing the Corsica and Mercedes both through the broken shade in the live oak perimeter.

"Yeah?" said Stucky, his breath smelling sour of vinegar from five feet away. "I've got some things to do, too. First thing when I get out of here, I'm killing that two-bit Irish punk," he said, talking about the Lamb. "This wasn't right, him doing this to me." He gestured a red arm down his naked stomach covered with wet gauze. Over near the door stood Delbert Moss, watching from beneath the brim of his new white Panama straw hat, his hands down in the pockets of his triple-pleated lightweight summer khakis. Tattoos on his arms stood out against his loose shirt—a flashy, red, light-weight silk job covered with green and gold sailboats and coconuts.

"Lew," Vango said, "I tried to warn you. The sun's not something to mess around with down here. What does the Lamb care that you burn yourself to death? Probably a big joke to him."

"I got his joke for him!" Stucky's hands clenched tight, then came loose as he hissed in pain. He took a breath and settled himself. "You made things worse," Stucky added, looking away from Vango, "you and your vinegar treatment. Now I've got the diarrhea from drinking it."

"I didn't mean you should *drink it,* Lew. I said get *soaked* in it. I even left you some towels to soak with."

"Yeah, but to me, *get soaked ...? You know?"* He paused, then said, "Forget it. I'm burning inside and out." He looked away, then nodded his red face toward Delbert over near the door. "Who's the coconut?"

Delbert stiffened slightly, staring at Stucky. Vango stifled a little chuckle, motioning a hand at Delbert. "This is Delbert Moss. Delbert, meet Lew Stucky from the *Chi."* He turned back to Stucky. "Delbert's going to do some driving for me. I figured with you out of commission, I better get some help."

"Yeah?" Stucky looked back and forth between them. "You clear this with Stanley? You know he don't like bringing in outsiders."

"Sure, I cleared it with him, this morning. It's cool. I told him maybe you better *fly* back up, the shape you're in."

"Maybe ... we'll see. But I'm not going no-damn-

115

where until we get things done here. You've let this Victor Trio and the Lamb dick you around. I get out of here. I'm killing Lambert, maybe both of them."

Vango sighed. "I might be meeting with the Lamb today. Things got a little screwed up, but now it's all about to turn around," he lied.

"I don't believe ya," Stucky said, raising a little then easing down, wincing. "I think you're going to fool around with this deal and make us both look bad. We're getting stiffed. And I ain't leaving town without I first give the Lamb the beating of his life. You got that?"

"No," Vango said firmly, "that's not the game plan. Here's what Stanley wants done." As he spoke, he pulled an airlines envelope from his shirt pocket and pitched it onto Stucky's bed. "He wants you back in Chicago as soon as you can travel. Something important, it sounds like."

"Yeah, what?" Stucky asked in a suspicious tone.

Vango said, "He didn't say what it is, so I didn't ask. It's between you and him." He nodded at the flight ticket envelope. "Must be something big, pulling you away from me down here."

"Yeah, maybe so," said Stucky. Listening, watching, Delbert liking the way Vango handled this guy, getting rid of his backup, making it sound like the guy was needed elsewhere.

"Anyway, there's an open ticket for you. It's good for any regular Chicago flight, straight through. A flight jumps out about every four hours here. Meanwhile, Stanley says for you to get well quick. That's the main thing for now. I figure he expects you tomorrow, maybe the next—"

Stucky cut him off, jerking a nod at Delbert Moss, then back to Vango.

"Whatever you pay this guy comes out of your end, I hope you know," he said.

"We'll talk about it when we're both back home," Vango said.

"Bull shit. I'm telling ya now. You brought him in, you pay him. I'm not making nothing as it is, time you figure this hospital bill. I've got none of the freaking, what-you-call, Blue-Cross."

Vango shrugged. "We'll get square on it. Don't worry about it. Can we bring you anything? You got everything you need?"

Stucky stared at him for a second. "Yeah. Bring me some booze. Make it a bottle of vodka, so's they can't smell it."

"Okay, I'll have a tall vodka brought up to you this afternoon," Vango said. "By then I'll have Stanley's money and we'll be able to laugh about all this." He turned to Delbert and nodded toward the door. "Come on, Delbert, let's go get this thing settled ... make everybody feel better."

"Don't forget my vodka," Lew Stucky said as Vango and Delbert left his room, "or I'll be pissed. I'll start burning like fire when my pain meds wear off."

"I won't forget you, Lew, how could I," Vango said back over his shoulder. He shot Delbert a look, the two of them starting down the hall. "Bring him some vodka, Delbert. Pour it into a ginger ale bottle so's nobody sees it."

"For two cents I'd pistol whip that jackass," Delbert said in a lowered tone.

Vango smiled to himself—*Delbert getting his legs under him, talking bold and ballsy for a change.* Vango liked that.

"I know what you mean," he said. "Stucky has a way of bringing that out of everybody. But get him some vodka, okay?"

"I'm on it," Delbert said.

The two took the stairs down one flight to the first floor and headed through the parking lot where they found Leslie Wright with the top raised on the Mercedes.

"Can you believe this?" Vango opened the driver's door and felt the AC purring, a stream of chilled air engulfing him. He heard the stereo playing cool rhythm on a commercial-free Latino jazz station. Leslie Wright sat smiling, sprawled leisurely in the passenger seat.

"It worked fine for me," she said. "I didn't have to call the dealer."

"That's good, Lee." Vango smiled. He said to Delbert, "Hop in back. We'll leave the Corsica here for now and pick it up after a while, when you get the vodka."

"Sure thing," said Delbert.

"What vodka?" Leslie asked.

When Vango explained the vodka for Stucky, Leslie said, "I've got a bottle in the trunk. You can take it up to him." She clicked open the trunk for Delbert. They watched him shove a bottle down into his belt and go back inside the hospital. As Vango slipped into the driver's seat, she put her hand in his lap, gripped him firmly and put her face on his neck.

"Want to make-out some until he gets back? Pass the time?" she asked. Her voice went to a warm whisper.

"I'd love for you to put your hands on me right here, right now." She took his free hand and closed it on her and clamped it in between her hot thighs. Jesus! Vango moved his hand around firm, easily.

"Oh yes, *do me! Do me good, Eddie, just like that,*" she purred, breathless.

When Delbert came back, he opened and closed the Cosica's trunk lid, then slipped into the Mercedes rear seat pulling the cellophane from a fresh pack of Camels with his teeth. In the front seat, Vango and Leslie Wright had straightened themselves up.

"Get us to the motel, *quick,* Eddie," Leslie whispered in Vango's ear. Vango nodded, then looked back at Delbert in the rearview mirror.

"Did he give you a hard time, Delbert?" he asked.

"He started to," said Delbert, but then a nurse came by and gave him something she had hidden in her hand. He shut up all of a sudden. He was already drunk." Delbert shrugged.

"Already drunk?" said Vango. "We just left there! I could tell he'd been drinking some. But he didn't seem *drunk.*"

"He grabbed the bottle from my hand and drank a third of it *straight up!* He washed down whatever the nurse gave him!" said Delbert. "He took a breath, made some shitty remark about my hat, then took another swig, with me telling him to slow down! I was afraid it would stop his heart, the way you hear of it. I'm thinking, what if he dies while I'm standing here—?"

"Good thinking." Vango gave a little chuckle. "So, ole Lew had managed to score something in a hospital! That's fine by me. I told him we'd bring him some vodka, and we *did*. Now we're done with him." He raised Leslie's hand from his lap where she had placed it and continued with short little squeezes. He gave her a look that promised he would hurry; then he started the car and pulled out of the hospital lot and shot down the street like a getaway driver.

When they reached the Blue Dolphin Inn, he led the woman urgently through the adjoining suite to his room and closed the bedroom door behind them. They fell across the bed, leaving a trail of clothes and shoes.

In the kitchenette, Delbert walked to the refrigerator, poured red wine over a glass of cracked ice and walked out to the pool area and settled back into a lounger. He sipped his wine, looked at his new clothes, new shoes, and the straw panama resting on his crossed knee. *This is nice ...,* he told himself. He smiled and relaxed, without a memory of anything ever being this good in his entire life.

An hour later in the darkened room, Vango rubbed his hand up and down Leslie's naked back.

"That *really* is a great way to pass time, Lee," he whispered.

She turned onto her side facing him, and sighed, "That's what I call some great pastime," she said. "I hope you don't think I'm terrible, Eddie. I just love sex. Sometimes something just comes over me, it's all I want to do. Do you think I'm a wanton woman? A slut? You can call me *Slut,* I mean, I won't mind. I might even like it." She smiled and started to reach for him. He slipped away and sat up.

"Lee, you have been the surprise of my life," he

said. "Right now, we have to keep our minds in the game, don't you think?"

"Oh, okay …." She feigned a pout.

The three seated themselves around the small kitchenette table and sorted through the metal box full of the authentic deposit box keys. All of the keys had the words, *Do Not Reproduce,* stamped on them, with readable bank or institution number stamped beneath it. A little white tag hung from each key with the bank initials hand printed in it.

"Bless his heart. Harold made these tags to tell him and me which *real* key went to which box," Leslie Wright said.

"That helps," Vango said. "It'll keep us from carrying all of these with us from bank to bank." He looked at a clock on the kitchenette wall. "We still have time to hit a couple of boxes before the banks close soon. The sooner we're gathering all the bearer bonds, the better," Vango said. "It won't be long before Lambert starts to do the same thing. When he gets stopped cold by a couple of the fake deposit keys, he'll see we're out there dipping in his cashbox." Vango picked up the keys to the Mercedes from the tabletop.

"You mean *right* now?" said Leslie Wright, surprised.

"Yes, right now," Vango replied. "We need to open an account so we can cash the bonds and put them somewhere. We don't want to gather lots of cash and have Lambert rob us." He looked at Delbert and said, "Don't worry, I'll see to it you're taken care of."

"I'm not worried," Delbert said. He stood up and

adjusted the chair back under the table. "I'm ready when you two are."

Vango turned to the woman as the three of them readied themselves to leave the motel.

"Make sure I understand, Lee," he said. "We pick up bonds that are signed, all we need to do is deposit them into our *account?* If a bond is not signed, you have the legal written authority to sign it? Right?"

"Right, both ways," the woman replied. As she spoke, she slid two brand new looking keys away from the rest. "Wait a minute," she said in surprise. "Look at these!" She handed the keys to Vango. "These have no tags on them!"

Vango said, "What's that about?"

"Right here, look," the woman said, pointing out tiny letters imprinted on each key. The imprint on one read: CPWM. The other one read: CPI.

"Okay, "What do these two keys go to?" Vango read the stamped imprint on both keys.

"These are brand new," said Leslie. She looked stumped for a moment. "Harold said he was opening accounts off-shore. I'm guessing one stands for Cayman Pearl Investment. The other one stands for: Cayman Investment and Wealth Management. Both owned by the same corporation, Cayman Pearl International."

The three fell silent, studying the keys.

Leslie Wright said quietly, "The letters are almost too small to read."

"Where in the Cayman Islands?" Vango asked, taking the keys and looking at them up close.

Getting more excited, the woman said. "These are the new boxes he rented in George Town, on Grand

Cayman! He said he was going to do it real soon. Wow, he didn't wait around, he did it!"

Vango asked, "Are you saying these are new enough that Lambert might not even know about them yet?"

"I'm certain he doesn't know about them yet!" said Leslie Wright. "Harold would have told me first, in case something like this happened. Lately, he was always expected the worse from those two. He would have told me before telling them."

"Jesus, these guys," Vango said, posing a question. "They make so much they lose any regard for it?"

"Handling so much cash for so long makes them avoid handing it at all," Leslie Wright said. "And then the wolves move in," she added.

Delbert grinned and gave a quiet mocking howl at the ceiling.

"I agree," said Vango. "When we get back, we'll all howl together." He wasn't going to mention that Trio was dead. Not just yet. Lambert would know that Bones was the only one who knew. Vango wasn't going to risk Lambert finding out the old Cuban had told anybody.

"Get back?" said Leslie. "Aren't we going to the bank today?"

"Yes, but with a change of plans," Vango said. "Today we get to a bank before closing time and open an account. Tomorrow morning instead of checking every deposit box in town, we fly out of Miami to Grand Cayman and see what the Islands hold for us." He looked at Delbert. "Any problem, you leaving the country?"

Delbert hung his head. "Yes, there is, Eddie. I've never had a passport and I'm pretty sure I can't get one."

Leslie Wright cut in. "Maybe they issue a three days *in-and-out* travel visa, or something?"

"Even if they do," Delbert said, "they'd have to run a quick check on me. If they did, my record would burn down the terminal." He offered an apologetic smile.

"That's too bad, Delbert," said Vango, "but I get it." He sensed there was something more to it than Delbert's criminal record, but he'd let it go, for now.

"I really wish you could go with us. You're part of this venture same as we are."

"Thanks, Eddie," said Delbert, but I'll be right here watching over everything while you two jump over there and back. Leave me some money if you don't mind, for cigarettes and walk-around?"

"You've got it, Delbert," said Vango, "however much you want. Only don't be walking around too much. Lambert and his crew will be circling the streets for any of us."

"I know," said Delbert, "but don't worry, I'll stash up some Camels and wine, I can lay low like you wouldn't believe."

Vango looked at Leslie Wright and said, "Okay, Lee, pack a bag for a couple days' stay. We head out tomorrow."

"I can get us a flight on my phone," she said, already rummaging in her purse. Pulling her hand-held phone out, she paused for a second. "Oh, wow, I'm just thinking," she said. "I don't believe I have a new bikini for the trip! I have one I've never worn ...? Okay?" She looked at them as if for approval. "And it's yellow? Okay?"

Vango and Delbert gave each other a look, each

picturing her in a yellow bikini.

"We're not going there to swim, Lee," Vango reminded her.

"I know that, Eddie," Leslie said, still considering it.

"All right, I suppose the yellow one will have to do. Like I said, I've never worn it."

"Just a hunch," Vango said, picturing how good she would look in any bikini of any color. "I bet they sell bikinis all over Grand Cayman."

Leslie smiled. "Of course, they do. I was only—"

The phone buzzed in her hand, startling her. The three of them stared at it.

"Who has your number?" Vango asked.

"Harold had it," she whispered as if the phone would hear her. "My friend in Key West … and my hair salon." She looked at the buzzing phone as is searching for a clue, "Should I answer it?" she whispered.

"Go ahead," said Vango, "leave the speaker on. If that's Lambert, stall him a little, give him a hard time."

"A hard time?" she said. "I would, but I know it won't be Lambert," she added. "He *definitely* doesn't have this mobile number! No way in the world."

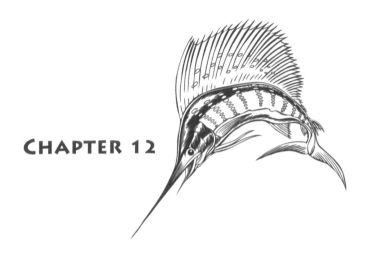

CHAPTER 12

"So, you finally answer the damn phone!" Ian Lambert said to Leslie Wright in a slurred, raspy voice. "Where's your frigging boyfriend?"

Around the table, Leslie, Vango and Delbert looked at each other. Vango winced and smiled a little. He gave Leslie a wave to let her know he wasn't going to talk to Lambert just yet. She got it. "He's drunk," Vango whispered, "play him off a little."

She gave an approving smile.

"Don't be vulgar Mr. Lambert," she said, her voice turning icy. "I'm afraid I don't know who you're talking about." She checked Vango for his approval. He nodded and stood and walked to a window looking out toward the gravel trail around the side of the motel. "I think you're drunk, Mr. Lambert!" she said. "I'm warning you I won't forget this!"

"Warning me? You won't *forget* this?" Lambert gave a crazy little unbelieving laugh. "What? You're going to report me to the operator?"

"I just may," the woman said, "so watch your step!" On the other end, Lambert's red watery eyes stared at the receiver in his hand in disbelief.

Unprepared for her response, he said, "Did you say, 'Watch my frigging step?'"

"Yes, you heard me," Leslie said. Vango and Delbert both stared at her, stunned.

"Watch my frigging step—?" Lambert repeated.

Leslie cut him off. "And by the way, where is my husband, Harold? Did you kill him? I heard you did!"

"Easy, lady," Lambert said, suddenly tensing a little. "I don't know anything about Little Harold—"

"Oh! Then how did you get my private number? Only Harold knows it!"

"What about your boyfriend in the Keys?" Lambert said. "The one you've been screwing every time—" He stopped short and got back on track. "Okay, forget that. Look, beautiful, I don't care about your boyfriend, and I don't know anything about your husband. I want to talk to Van-go. Put him on!"

"He's not here!" Leslie insisted. "Anyway, how do you know I'm not screwing him too?"

"Lady, *please!* I'm sure you are." Lambert said, starting to grow weary and badly browbeaten by her. "I'm done with who you screw, have screwed, or will ever screw again."

"Then why did you bring it up?" she said. "It's none of your business!"

"Look, I know Van-go is there. Put him on," Lambert insisted.

Vango chuckled a little. He stood peeping around an edge of window blind, watching what he decoded was a black silhouette of a car sitting off to the side in bushy palmetto palms. He looked at Delbert and made a gun of his hand and nodded. Delbert stood and walked to his bed in the other room and came back with his .45. Vango reached behind his back and took out his 9mm.

Leslie Wright still railed at Lambert over the phone. "I think you're some kind of sick-o who gets off on knowing who's doing what, with whom. Do you go through dumpsters the next morning and see if you can find—?"

"Okay, Lee, that's enough," said Vango cutting her off. He took the phone from her and said to Lambert, "It's me. Where's the fifty-nine thousand?" He stepped back over to the window and peeped out, phone in hand. A dash light turned on and off as a car door opened and closed.

"Fifty-nine? *Jesus!* Hold on, Van-go," said Lambert. Vango liked how bumping up the vig always got everybody's attention. Truth of it, Stanley had told him for a reckless gambler like Trio, leave the vig alone this time. Right away Lambert began sounding a little more sober—not much, but a little.

"I went by the Wright's place to pay Victor's bill for him," Lambert said. "Instead of finding you, I got a tip there's a whole squad of DEA or ATF, or FSP or somebody shagging the place down and waiting for anybody who showed up." He paused again, then said, "That's the freaking truth, Van-go! Now, do you want this fifty-nine bucks or not?"

Vango stalled just long enough to make it sound believable.

"Okay, Lambert, you can tell Victor this is his last chance to pay the Pole. I'm headed north tomorrow, with or without the money. Show up or forget about it. You know where I am?"

"Yeah," said Lambert, "you and *Sweety Pie* are in the Blue Dolphin shithole, where she takes all her tricks. I know the place, I know her rooms, and I know her car."

"My *tricks?* My *tricks!* You son of a bitch!" Leslie Wright dived at the phone, clawing at it. Vango stopped her and held the phone out of her reach.

"Okay, good," Vango said. "When will you be here with the money?"

"I'm an hour from there," said Lambert. "I'll hang up and I'm on my way—money in hand. You be there! Let's get this settled! Victor wants it over with."

Yeah, right, Vango thought, knowing Victor was dead and disassembled.

The line clicked off. Vango handed the phone back to Leslie.

"You did good, Lee," he said, seeing the embarrassed look on her face, from hearing what Lambert said about her. "Don't let this guy get to you."

"Thank you, Eddie," Leslie said. "He's just a gross, vulgar pig. I don't turn *tricks.*"

"I know you don't," Vango said. He looked at Delbert who had turned toward them, the .45 hanging in his hand.

"He said he'd be here in an hour?" he asked Vango.

"Yeah, but he's not coming, Delbert. But his men will be at the door here in less than five minutes," Vango said.

"Five minutes?" said Leslie. "Then they must be here already…." She glanced toward the outside.

"Yes, they're out there right now, locking and loading over by the palmetto," Vango said. "Lambert didn't want to talk to me about anything. He just wanted to make sure I'm here, before his boys bust in. Makes me think he doesn't yet know that his keys are fake."

"Then what does he want?" Leslie asked.

"Probably just wants to kill me," Vango said. "I made a bad first impression. He thinks I have a video of him snatching Harold. Figures I'm the last witness who saw Harold alive." He smiled and looked at them both. "Don't answer the door for nothing. I want you to stay inside and let me handle this quietly. Lee, get your overnight bag ready." Turning to Delbert Moss, he said, "When this is over, Delbert, I want to you to drive us to Miami, tonight. Are you down for it?"

"I'm down for it, Boss, whatever you want," Delbert affirmed.

"We're leaving *tonight?*" Leslie Wright asked.

"Yes, we are," said Vango. "He might not know about the keys right now, but he'll find out any time. When he does finds out, he's going to blow up." He looked at the two again. "Be careful around the windows," he added. He turned away and walked into the attached suite, shoving his 9mm down in his belt.

"If we're going to Miami tonight," Leslie said, "I should get busy and make us a pitcher of mojitos." She looked at the two of them. "You know, for the drive down?"

The three men wore thin black sun masks rolled up on their foreheads. They unrolled and stretched the masks down over their faces and adjusted the eyeholes around their eyes. Each had a gun shoved down in their belt; one carried a gruesome-looking set of brass knuckles hanging loosely on his thick fingers. When they had silently closed the door of the big sky-blue Oldsmobile, they walked toward the adjoining motel rooms where Lambert said they would find the Wright woman and the two men. He'd said there would be a silver-gray Mercedes parked out front of the rooms, and *there it sat.*

"I want to get my hands on this woman," one of the gunmen whispered. The three of them stopped beside four tall palms standing in a cluster thirty feet from the row of motel rooms.

"Hey, Samuel! That's not what we here to do," the one with the brass knuckles replied in the same lowered whisper. "You leave the woman alone. We're here to give this Chicago boy a beating and take him and the woman to the *Lamb*. You copy that?"

"Aw-man. You seen this woman?" said the one named Samuel.

"I have," said the third men, a Florida stock car cowboy known as Racey. "She's a damn straight *smoking* filly."

"Copy that?" the one with the brass knuckles asked Samuel again in a stronger tone. "Don't make me foul you up, boy."

"Yeah, I *copy that,"* said Samuel. "Let's go play this thing out."

The three men stepped slowly forward, toward the room with a dim light glowing from its window. Samuel, the one walking closet past the four-palm-tree cluster let out a deep grunt, sounding as if he might have tripped over an exposed tree root. The other two didn't look around to see him disappear into the cluster of palms.

Vango had snagged him, dragged him into the four

palms and slammed his face four times, hard, against one of the thick rugged tree trunks. When Vango turned him loose, Samuel fell to the ground making only a slight rustle in the brush.

"What the hell? *Samuel?*" the man with the brass knuckles whispered, finally looking around, seeing no sign of the man who'd been walking alongside him in the gray darkness.

"Samuel?" the other man called out. The two shrugged at each other in the darkness.

Behind the palm cluster, Vango spoke into his cupped hand.

"Back here," he said in a muffled tone.

"Damn it! What the hell?" the man with the brass knuckles barked aloud. He walked back to the palm cluster and arrived just in time to feel Samuel's gun butt swing in out of nowhere and smash the bridge of his nose all over his face. He hit the ground with a painful yelp and tried to raise up on his hands. But again, Samuel's own gun butt, in Vango's hand, swung in, this time on the back of the downed man's head. The force of the second blow drove his face into the soft loamy ground.

Vango stood over the downed man long enough to unload Samuel's gun and stick the clip down in his pocket. He tossed the empty gun into the palms where he'd left Samuel laying sprawled, his face mask shredded by the palm trunk. Catching a glimpse of the third man vanishing into the darkness, Vango turned to follow him when he heard the loud *THWANG!!!* of a long-handled shovel Delbert had found behind the building when he slipped out to lend a hand. Delbert had swung the shovel and smacked Racey squarely in his face at a full run.

Seeing Delbert walk out of the gray darkness, shovel in hand, Vango watched him stop long enough to light a Camel cigarette then proceed forward until he stopped only a few feet away.

"I hope I didn't piss you off, Boss, coming out here after you said stay inside," Delbert said. "He was running so fast I thought you wouldn't mind if I slowed him down a little."

Vango said, "You slowed him down, for sure. Did you check and see if he's dead?"

"No, but I don't think he's dead," Delbert said. "He's bleeding too much for a dead man." He nodded at the brass knuckles Vango had slipped on to his fingers. "Are those yours, or a souvenir?"

"Souvenir," Vango said, slipping them off, offering them to him. "You want them?"

"Sure, I'll take them if you don't want them," Delbert said. He grinned taking the knuckles. "I expect he'll be too embarrassed to ask for them back."

"That would be my guess," Vango said. They both turned to the sound of the front door opening. From the open doorway Leslie Wright called out, *"Yoo-hoo,* Eddie? Delbert? Is it okay for me to come out?"

"Sure, come on," Vango said, liking the way they had all three become more comfortable around each other. Three people all on the make, about to collect *God Knows* how much money for themselves. Money nobody would ever know about if he played this thing right. "Watch these mosquitoes though," he added. "They're lethal tonight."

"Ha ...," she said, stepping out onto the first in a line of concrete walk pads, "Don't forget, I'm a Florida

gal, Eddie. Mosquitoes don't mess with me—" As soon as she spoke, she started slapping herself frantically all over and let out a little scream. "My God, they're eating me alive!"

"Get back inside," Vango called out. "We're coming in."

"Yes, please!" she said, hurrying back to the door. "I can't go to Grand Cayman beach covered with mosquito bites! My goodness!" She slammed the door behind her.

"A real trooper, this one," Vango said.

Delbert gave a little chuckle.

"If you don't mind me saying, Boss, she's about the best-looking woman I've ever seen."

"No, Delbert," Vango said, "I don't mind you saying so." He thought about it for a second and said, "I think so too."

"And I believe she really likes you," Delbert ventured. When Vango didn't reply right away, he added, "You know, the way she looks at you sometimes? And I think maybe you feel the same way about her. If I was you …." He left his words unfinished.

"You'd do what, Delbert?" Vango said.

"If I was you, Boss," Delbert said, "I'd hang onto her and not let go."

They both heard thrashing inside the palm cluster where Samuel lay bleeding, coming around from his face bashing. A long painful-sounding moan arose from the cluster. Knowing where it came from, Delbert and Vango kept talking.

"It's something to think about," Vango said, regarding Leslie Wright. He had to admit, given the short dangerous circumstances under which they had met, this gorgeous, classy, *screwball* of a woman had, with the slightest move here and there, gotten to him. She was a real-life flesh and blood sensual dream come true. *Oh yes,* he realized it. But if there was ever such a thing as something being *too-good-to-be-true,* she was it. He was certain. Knowing it, he tried keeping his thoughts of her safely to a minimum—*There's no time for this, so stop it ...!* he told himself.

"What do you want me to do with these two?" Delbert asked, looking around, at the other knocked out gunmen lying strewn in the darkness.

"I unloaded that one's gun," said Vango, nodding at the palm cluster. "Shake them all down for any more weapons." He nodded at the Oldsmobile sitting in the darkness in the palmetto. "Get the car key and toss it away. They'll never know for sure what happened to them here or who did it to them." He looked all around. "They might figure it was a mugging."

Delbert gave a little chuckle. "There's never any muggings in these parts," he said. "But they can be thankful I don't finish them off with this shovel blade." He jiggled the long shovel in his hands. "They would have it coming."

"I like leaving them lay here without a clue—give the mosquitoes a buffet dinner," Vango said. "If we get a move on, we'll be headed for Miami Airport before these jerk-offs find their way home."

"Yeah, that's works for me too, Boss," Delbert said. "I didn't want to finish nobody off with a shovel."

"I know that, Delbert," said Vango.

"From here the airport is about a two—maybe a two-and-a-half-hour drive," Delbert said. He paused, then said, "What do you think about me staying the night in the Wright's garage?"

"It would be good having you there, seeing if anybody comes snooping around. But what about the extra driving you'd have to do, coming back to pick us up?"

"What, three or four hours more? In a big Mercedes convertible?" He grinned. "How bad is that?"

"I hear you, Delbert," said Vango. "But if you want to stay there you don't have to sleep in the garage. The place is full of guest bedrooms."

"I've never slept in a Mercedes," Delbert said, as if settling the matter. Again, the grin. "I'm ready to go when you two are. Think she's ready yet?" He looked at the closed door, the light glowing in the window behind a circling swarm of insects.

"I don't know," said Vango. "How long does it take to mix a pitcher of mojitos?"

No sooner then he asked they saw Leslie hurrying from the house carrying a tall pitcher of mojitos and three plastic travel glasses.

Vango opened the rear door; She slipped inside and said in a bubbly voice, un-phased by the day's events, "All set here. Let's get rolling." She folded down a service tray between the seats and sat the pitcher and glasses on it. Vango shook his head, handed Delbert the keys and stepped into the rear seat with her.

"What do you think of Delbert spending the night in your garage, Lee? Keep an eye on things?" he asked as Delbert started the car.

"That would be great, Delbert," she replied into rearview mirror. *"Mi automobile, su automobile."*

CHAPTER 13

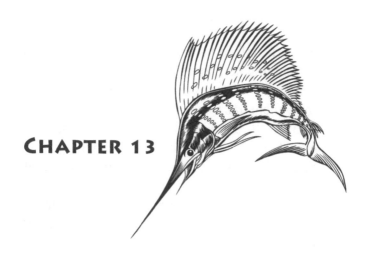

As soon as Lambert hung up the phone in Trio's condo, Morez's bodyguards, Joe Paso and Cuban-Russian Hector Chebreski, both stuck their guns back in his red sweaty face and shoved him back down into a chair.

"Fellows, please! Take it easy!" Lambert pleaded. "They're going to bring him here. I swear! First, they'll soften him up some, get his mind right for us—"

Leone Morez walked over to the railing, looking down at the moonlit ocean. He had listened to the conversation between Lambert and Eddie Vango, finding it had nothing to do with their money or their drugs.

"Okay, *Fuzzy Nut,*" he said to Lambert. "Your phone call tells me nothing."

Fuzzy Nut .... How would he ever get rid of that that name ...? "Look, things are happening quick here," he said. "With a big deal hanging in the winds, people are getting a little edgy. But trust me, my men are right now bringing this Van-go punk and Harold Wright's wife here! We'll find out what's going on with them and Trio and Mr. Bruge's two million!"

"They are not coming," Morez said flatly. "I could

137

tell the way he talked to you. He thinks you're an idiot! He is not coming here tonight."

An *idiot!* Wait until he gets this all turned around. He'd show them *idiot!*

"Oh, he'll be here. I promise you that," said Lambert. "And whatever he knows, he'll tell us."

Morez looked doubtful. His bodyguards looked restless as if they badly needed to beat someone senseless.

"Tell me about this fifty-nine thousand dollars you are supposed to pay this man. And don't try to bullshit me. I could kill you right now for lying about the nude beach."

"I told you where the nude beach is," Lambert said, "couldn't you find it?" He touched a soft tissue to a trickle of blood on his swollen lip where Joe Paso had given him a sharp rap with his gun barrel.

"Yes, we found it," said Morez. "You neglected to tell us this nude beach is made up almost entirely of very old men!"

"No," said Lambert, "There must be a mistake!"

"The mistake is that we should have already shot you full of holes! Which we do straightaway if this Vango man and Harold's wife do not show up very soon. While we wait, I think you better tell us about the fifty-nine thousand you are trying to stiff this Vango man on."

"Okay, here's the deal on Victor Trio and this Vango guy! Everybody knows Victor's a degenerate gambler. He lost a bundle of money last year on the games to a bookie in Chicago named Stanley the Pole."

"The *Pole.*" Morez nodded. "Okay, I know of this Stanley the Pole. I understand him to be a reasonable man. But he always wants his money. Why does Trio not pay him? You and Trio have plenty of money, don't you?"

There was the question Lambert needed to avoid, at least until he got his hands of the bearer bonds and cashed in a few of them.

"Yes, of course we have money. Millions! But every time I talk to this Van-go the price has ticked up. It started out at thirty-thousand. Now it's *fifty-nine.*"

"Ah, yes, the penalty and the vig," Morez said. He laughed a little.

"I understand," he said. "But still you have the money, so pay him."

"Okay, right, I get that," said Lambert. "But Trio is being a real hard-on about it. On the other hand, even though we're no longer partners I'm trying to do the *right thing.*"

"The right thing?" said Morez. "In that case cut off Victor's head, take it to this Vango in a plastic bag with the knife still in it. Tell Stanley that Victor won't pay so you cut off his head out of respect. Believe me, if he takes the head and the bloody knife to Chicago, the Pole will understand. Eh?" He laughed and looked at the two ape-size bodyguards. They laughed with him. Lambert sat staring.

Joe Paso stopped laughing. He stepped in close to Morez with a dark gleam in his eyes and said something just between the two of them. Then he turned and stared back at Lambert.

"Good idea, Joe," Morez said. He turned to Lambert, "Joe says there is nothing to do here while we wait. He wants to know if I mind the two of them hold you over the handrail out back and joggle you up and down by your feet—it helps pump their triceps. I told them they can but be careful not to drop you or they have to clean up the mess below." He grinned. Joe Paso and the Cuban-Russian stepped closer to Lambert.

"Hey, wait, hold on Mr. Morez!" Lambert pleaded, "This shit ain't funny!"

"Neither was it funny, us going to the nude beach to maybe score some nice *tush*. Instead, we see old men's wrinkled penises flopping all around us. It is a hurtful thing you did to us."

"Look, I had no idea about the beach!" said Lambert. "I swear to God, I've never been there! Everybody told me it's a super hot spot ...." His words melted away, "No no," as the two bodyguards picked him up and carried him out onto the fifteenth-floor balcony. Morez gave him toss-off, *saludos*.

Joe Paso and Hector Chebreski, each with one of Lambert's legs in hand hoisted him and swung him out over the railing. Lambert screamed, loud.

"Shhh! Don't scream! You make us nervous and we *will* drop you!" said Joe Paso. Lambert sobbed and pleaded but managed to keep his voice to a minimum. Morez slid the doors shut, muffling the sound, and walked to a bar and poured a Johnny Walker Black over a couple of ice cubes and looked all around the place, sizing it up.

These people at Wright Way, Trio, Lambert and Harold Wright, had never impressed him much. Given the opportunity he knew he could do better. He wasn't sure just how. But he was confident he could. When the big US banks got stopped in their tracks by the federal government, from laundering large sums of cash, Wright

Way Venture Capital became, overnight, the place to store big dollars weeks, or even months, ahead of a large shipment of cocaine coming in. Okay, he had to give them that. But that was Harold Wright's savvy, never these clowns Lambert and Trio.

Instead of showing up at a drop dock with dangerous amounts of cash drawing in killer thieves and the law alike, everybody had switched from cash to bearer bonds—deposited right into their accounts, anywhere in the world. *No muss, no fuss ....*

How sweet was that? Morez asked himself, smiling, sipping his scotch. He realized he was long overdue to branch out into his own distribution network. If jerk-offs like this Wright Way crew could do it, so could he. He was just waiting for the right opportunity, and a few million in cash, he reminded himself.

As the weightlifting bodyguards joggled Lambert up and down, Lambert watching the ground sway back and forth from some one hundred-odd feet below, Morez heard someone at the front door and looked over in time to see the lock turn and the door open as a utility cart carrying clothes and cleaning supplies rolled inside.

Seeing the cart, and seeing the woman pushing it look up in surprise, Morez eased his hand from behind his lapel away from his gun.

"Yoo-hoo, cleaning," the woman said. She eyed Morez up and down but stood perfectly still while he checked her out. She looked good! Maximum blonde, average height, a little fleshy, he surmised, but with a sexy almost cherub face, and breasts that tagged his attention and refused to let go.

"Cleaning?" At this time of night?" he said with suspicion. Yet, as he spoke, he let his gun hand ease down his stomach and hooked his thumb behind his belt. This one was too well-kept, too good-looking to be cleaning condos in the middle of the night. "Who are you, lady? Who do you work for?"

"I'm Jill Wray, with J W Cleaning," she said, calmly. "Get it? Jill Wray—J W Cleaning? But call me Jilly. It's less formal, don't you think?"

Sexy little thing .... Morez felt like saying. But he kept himself in check.

"Why are you here at this hour, Jilly?" he asked.

"Mr. Trio likes it when I come in the middle of the night," she said. She offered only a slight smile.

"I bet he does," said Morez with a wide sharp grin.

"No," she said. "What I mean is he knows he'll either be out, partying late, or he'll already be asleep. So, this is a good time for me to be here, when no one coming in or out the office." She looked in the direction of the muffled laughing voices on the balcony, then back at Morez. "Excuse me for just a moment while I fumigate the bedroom." She picked up a can of air freshener. "I'm afraid Mr. Trio's cigars leave their presence known."

"By all means, J W Cleaning." Morez gestured a guiding hand toward the bedroom. "Tell me, how do I get you to come clean my place?"

"Sorry," she said, "I stay booked up. I don't even give out my number." She walked away from her cart and smiled, shaking the can a little to mix it up. As she closed the bedroom door behind her. Morez walked to the balcony doors and knocked loud enough to get the bodyguards' attention. Lambert sat collapsed in a chair, trembling, his face soaking wet with sweat.

"Keep it down some," he said to the two men.

"Yes, sir," said Joe Paso. "He wants to talk to you. Says he wants to come clean about everything. There is nothing he will not tell you."

Morez saw Lambert looking up at him with watery, pleading eyes.

"After a while, maybe," Morez said coolly. "I'm busy right now."

Inside the bedroom, Jill Wray heard the muffled voices as she hurried and stuck the second listening device up under the foot of the bed. The first one she had stuck under the top of nightstand beside the bed. She stood up and quickly adjusted her tank top.

"Hello, hello," Morez said, opening the door and stepping inside.

"I've been waiting," she said in a soft, slightly sing-song voice. She stood in the middle of the floor and gave a cool seductive smile, her hand on her hip as Morez walked in and closed the door behind him. He loosened his flowery tropical tie as he walked forward and stopped again. He started to say something he thought would sound really cool. But his words came out broken and strange as the woman's shoe toe came up hard and fast and jammed his testicles up into the bone-work just below his belly.

Morez jackknifed at the waist as her hand went down, caught his loosened tie, wrapped it around her hand and flipped him over her shoulder onto the bed. A handcuff ratcheted tight around his wrist. She yanked his wrist out and closed the other cuff around a bedpost.

Then she squatted atop his chest. His gun—*his own gun, for God sakes!*—stuck an inch deep inside his mouth with its hammer cocked.

"Now that I have your attention, *Leone Morez,* who comes from Colonia Del Sacramento, Uruguay!" she said, letting him know she knew his full name and where he was from. "I've been listening to you and watching you. It's time you and I talk. I'm taking this gun from your mouth so you can tell your apes you're in here bagging the *cleaning lady.* But say anything else and I will kill you before they kill me. Get it?" She eased the gun out of his mouth.

Morez spit and rasped, "Got it." Before he could speak again, she stuffed his rolled up tropical-flowered necktie in his mouth, replacing his gun which she held close enough for him to see it at all times. *His own gun ...!*

A soft knock resounded on the bedroom door. "You good in there, *Jefe?*" Joe Paso asked. "We're getting hungry here."

Perched firmly on his chest, Jill Wray pressed Morez's gun harder against his cheek and pulled his tie from his mouth. She tapped the gun on his chin.

"Yes, I'm good, Paso. I have bagged myself a *cleaning lady.*" He looked up at the woman's eyes as he said, "See what Trio has to eat in his fridge. The lady and I are busy right now."

Outside the bedroom door, Paso and Chebreski both looked at the utility cart and grinned at each other. Paso made a fist and pumped it back and forth in short strokes. "You got it, *Jefe.*"

"Okay, Mr. *Leone Morez,*" said the woman. "I'm going to talk fast, so don't interrupt me."

She shifted her weight a little but remained firmly on his chest. "I am not a cleaning lady," she said.

"No, you're not," said Morez, "you are some Bruce Lee kind of devil woman sent here to—!"

"Shut up and listen. I don't have time for this crap." she said, giving him a slight thumb with his gun barrel. "I'm the leader of the community watch group, Reconnaissance And Tactical Services. We've been gathering and documenting information on Wright Way Venture Capital for the past year. My group works closely with DEA and other government sources to break the grip cocaine has on our cities and neighborhoods."

Morez stared at her almost in disbelief. She sounded like a person reading from a sales script.

"You're the leader of *Rats?*" he said. "You and your people are *Rats.*"

She bristled.

"Watch your mouth!" she said. "We're concerned citizens, out here doing our part. How dare you!" she started to smack him with his pistol.

"No wait, listen!" he said. "Reconnaissance And Technical Services. Spells *Rats!* Jesus, lady, do the math. R A T S."

She stared, blank for a moment, as if having never realized it. She ran it through her mind. "Wow …." She let the gun slump a little. "I never …, I mean, we never." She stopped cold and said, "Okay, it's a new name we only changed to recently. Although, in this case I think it's perfectly appropriate. What's wrong with *Rats?*"

"Lady, don't even ask," Morez said, "change the name." He raised an index fingertip and politely moved the gun barrel away from his face. "You can change it at your next meeting or whatever, right?"

"Well, yes," Jill Wray said. She still looked thrown off her game.

"Okay, enough about *Rats,*" said Morez. "Now that you have kicked my nuts halfway up my chest, tell me what you want to tell me. And tell me before those two go through all of Trio's groceries and start bobbing Lambert over the railing again."

When Jill Wray finished telling Lambert everything her listening devises had revealed about Wright Way Venture Capital, including Trio's death, she stretched out alongside Morez on the large bed and took a draw off a cigarette he offered her. She blew out a stream of smoke toward the ceiling. Morez lay on his side facing her, his hand still cuffed to the bed headboard post.

"Here's the part I think you'll like Leone—may I call you Leone?"

"We are in bed together, of course you can, *Jilly* Wray."

She smiled and took a deep breath.

"Keep—must keep—this hush-hush," she said. "My group gets up to twenty-five percent value of all the drugs we're connected to after it's seized, whether it's cocaine, heroin or whatever! It's a fluctuating *bounty* reward."

"All drugs *confiscated?*" He couldn't believe it.

"Every bit of it," she said.

"Holy *Madre!*" said Morez.

She nodded. "Yes, it is a very generous and highly innovative program. The bounty on drugs varies, of course, from case to case," she said. "But the U.S. is so serious in winning this war on drugs they've pulled out all stops. They have been paying our citizens' group ten percent and more, regularly. The percent goes up as the value of the drug deal goes up. I can't pinpoint how much value this Wright Way deal will come to, but the intel I've gathered has it to be safely over ten million dollars. That's large enough to draw over twenty-five percent bounty when and if my group brings it down."

"Holy *Madre—!*" Morez stated to murmur again. This woman was so wrong. Ten million dollars was nothing compared to the money invested in this next big shipment. But it was definitely a good start for him to step out and make a move on his own.

"How much would I make if I bring this deal to you?" he asked.

"The opportunity is limitless." She smiled and took another draw. "Now you know why I wanted to talk to you," she said. "I propose that with you on the inside and me on the outside we can start by taking this deal down and both making a fortune."

Morez said, "And all of it legal as hell?"

"Yes," she said. "Everything my group does is *legal as hell.*"

Morez looked her up and down, lying there close beside him. Yes, she was what some men would call a *chunky blonde,* but he saw her as sexy, with nice thighs, large but perky *gondabos*—his own barroom name for breasts. He was amazed at how she had happened along at just the time when he was considering his future in the illicit drug trade. *Twenty-five percent of the value of all large drug shipments ...? Oh yes,* he could do this. He could do this and set up his own distribution at the same time. He smiled and laid his free hand on her shoulder.

"Why don't you take this cuff off me, *Jilly* Wray?" he said. "Let's get better acquainted."

"I'm not here to screw around, Leone," she said in a semi-seductive tone. "I'm only here to do business—"

A muffled scream from the rear balcony, caused her and Morez to stare at each other.

"Un-cuff me, quick!" Morez said. She did.

They both reached the bedroom door; the woman reached to open it, but the door opened quickly from the other side.

"Mr. Morez! Something bad has happened!" said the huge Cuban-Russian. "Joe was bobbing Lambert by his ankles, and … he *dropped* him!" He tried handing Morez one of Lambert's shoes. Morez slapped it away.

"Damn it," said Morez. "Now we'll have police coming!" He looked at Jill Wray as they followed Paso to the open balcony doors. "Can you help us with this some way?"

"I'll make a couple of calls, get some of my crew here," she said calmly, walking out and looking down at Lambert's body lying on the plush green stretch of lawn. "After all, I own a Cleaning Service."

Morez smiled. "I like that about you." He turned to the bodyguards who stood watching, listening intently.

"Listen up, both of you. This lovely lady is a new friend of ours. She's going to show us how to make millions on our own without some big-shot like Burge looking down our backs. Are you guys good with that?"

Hector Chebreski raised his hand slightly.

Morez gave him an angry glaring look.

"You got to go to the bathroom, Hector? What do

you want?"

Hector asked, "This is not a deal where Joe and I bring in some guys under us, and they bring in guys under them, and we get a percent of everything they make—?"

"Jesus, no!" said Morez.

"You mean like a pyramid scam," said Jill Wray, picking right up on it. "No, it's nothing like that."

"Okay, that's good," Hector said. "In that case to hell with Paulson Phillipe Burge! I call him Little *PP.*" He gave a big stupid grin.

"Hey, Hector!" Morez said. "We never use Mr. Burge's full name!"

"Sorry, Boss," Hector replied, his head lowered. He looked up and said with a brighter expression, "In that case, I like you, Joe and me working for *Mr.* Burge—"

Morez shot him once, squarely between the eyes. The balcony fell dead silent. Morez turned the gun at Joe Paso. "Any more stupid-ass questions, or knucklehead remarks?" he asked.

"Not from me, Boss, I'm good," Joe said quietly.

"All right then," said Morez. "Throw Hector's dead ass over the rail and let's get on with it." He turned to Jill Wray. "Can your people handle this mess while they're here."

"Sure, no problem," the woman replied coolly, taking out a hand-held phone, punching in a number.

PART II

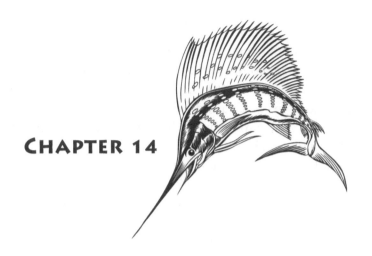

CHAPTER 14

Eddie Vango had checked his small travel bag into luggage with a 9mm stuck down under a folded pair of clean underwear for the flight back. Leslie Wright had carried her overnight bag on-board. Instead of placing it in the overhead luggage compartment she sat it over in the widow seat and seated herself beside it.

When the plane lifted off, she reached inside the travel bag, took out a smaller folded zipper bag.

"Excuse me, Eddie," she said. "Once I'm in the air I always have to *tinkle.*"

He thought he noted a slight edginess as she moved past his aisle seat, but he let it go. Tomorrow was a big day for them both, he told himself. She was doing fine just fine. *Doing fine, and is fine ... fine indeed.* He leaned back and rested his eyes. He felt good about everything. His only question was how much money would be waiting in the deposit boxes at Cayman Investment and Wealth Management, and Cayman Pearl Investment. He felt himself dozing off.

"Eddie? Eddie?" he heard her whisper into his ear, her breath warm and soothing, a part of whatever dream he was about to conjure up. "Can we make-out some?"

Please, no, he said to himself. He was so tired, so knocked out exhausted …. He felt her hand go onto his lap and to his belt buckle. His zipper. *Well, maybe …,* he thought. He heard her move her travel bag from between them and drop it by their feet. She tugged him over in the middle seat and helped him turn facing her.

"Do me good, Eddie, just like before," she whispered, breathless, surging against him in hot anticipation. She cupped him firmly in both hands, kneading, stroking. He swelled, hard.

Oh, all right …! He could sleep later.

A few minutes later he did manage to doze off for a while, Leslie with her head resting on his shoulder, not asleep, yet not quite awake. A gray, faded gold dawn crept into the cabin from the east. When the cabin bell rang, announcing a welcome to Grand Cayman message from the captain, she said blearily to Vango, "Don't answer it …."

Nudging her slightly, Vango whispered, "Rise and shine, Lee. Our adventure begins."

Instead of replying, the woman slumped over against the window. In doing so, Vango felt her bag fall over onto his foot. As he reached down to right the bag, he felt a few items fall from it onto the floor. Quietly, in the shadowy floor lights he picked up the bag and a few of contents that spilled from it. He'd began putting the items back into the bag when he stopped at the sight of a thin plastic syringe with a small plastic bag holding a slim portion of white powder. A rubber band held the dope bag in place.

Picking up the syringe and the accompanying dope, he looked back and forth between the syringe and the dozing woman.

Easy, he cautioned himself.

He wanted to confront her right then, on the spot. But one thing he didn't want to do was cause any kind of a stir sitting here aboard a commercial jet, especially not with a 9mm pistol checked into luggage, ready to lock and load. Jesus! There was too much at stake here. He took a calming breath, wiped the syringe free of his fingerprints, and dropped it back into the travel bag. He started to remind himself of the saying, *when something is too good to be true ....*

Shut up! he told himself.

Vango's first thought was to confront the woman with the syringe as soon as they arrived at the Trade Winds Beach Front Hotel Leslie had booked for them. The fact is, syringe or no syringe he was here with her to collect as much money as this bearer bond deal could offer up, maybe a healthy few thousand dollars, or maybe a few *hundred thousand.* With drug dealer cash, you never know.

Either way he wasn't going to kill a once in a lifetime deal over Leslie Wright shooting a little junk. *Who knows,* he thought, *it might not even be her needle. Stop it!* For all he knew the needle could even belong to her former *lover* in Key West. *Yeah, right ....*

Nice try, he told himself. He knew that a drug bust on a commercial flight would be a kiss of death on what they were trying to do here. What the hell was she thinking doing something like this? He sat thinking about it as the plane touched down and taxied a short way to the terminal. When the plane stopped and the interior lights came on, the sound of passengers preparing to leave caused the woman to straighten in her seat.

"Here we are," she said with a smile, reaching inside her bag for the paperwork and phone number of the Trade Winds Beach Front Hotel. "I hope we like this place. You know they have a minimum three day stay here. So, if we'd like to finish our *business* and stay a while longer, we can do so."

"Let's see how it goes, Vango said, standing, hoping nothing in his voice revealed his downturn in attitude. Leslie gave him a surprised look, standing with him, raising the carry strap of her bag up over her shoulder.

"You know if we get checked in early enough and have time to kill before the banks open, well ...." She gave him a seductive look, letting her words trail. "Maybe we'll think of something to do."

"I'm sure we will," Vango said, returning her smile, not wanting to reveal anything here, at this moment. He would wait. Why wouldn't he? Now that he had resolved himself and calmly considered it, hurt feelings aside, if everything went well here, he might never mention it to her at all.

Sure, that's the way to play it, he decided. He slipped an arm around her waist and pulled her to his side. "Let's grab a taxi and check out our new digs." He lowered his voice. "If we get enough bonds cashed and deposited, we might stay here the rest of the year."

After checking in at the Trade Winds and requesting a wake-up call in two hours, Vango and Leslie Wright took the elevator up to their room and dropped their bags respectively into a stuffed chair. They stood for a moment looking around at their drop-dead gorgeous surroundings.

"It looks like the place has been overtaken by a band of fashion-conscience pirates," Leslie said in weary but still attentive voice.

"I'm, dead," Vango said bluntly. With no energy for small talk, he fell across one of the two double beds in the tropical-accented suite.

"I'm tired too, but I'm not sleepy yet," Leslie replied. "I might just lie down beside you and close my eyes for a while." She undressed down to her panties and fell across the bed beside him. Vango had taken a close look at her travel bag lying in the chair, housing her drugs and needle. He made a mental image of where and how the bag sat in order to see if she might have moved it while he slept.

Enough of that .... He dozed off thinking of her and the syringe and the small bag of dope, telling himself not to *obsess* on the matter, yet feeling himself do so all the same. When he did drift away, he only slept for what he guessed might be a few seconds, when the phone between the beds rang in a flat distant sound, somewhere far away.

"Thank you," he heard Leslie say quietly into the receiver. He began to awaken slowly, her hands warm on his neck. He felt her shake him slightly.

"Time to go to work, Eddie, *darling,*" she said jokingly, in a feigned chirpy voice. He turned over onto his back and started to sit up. She pressed him back down, raised up and adjusted herself atop him. He felt her start to move around slowly, teasing him.

Okay, get real, he told himself, looking up at her, her perfect breasts, perfect face, skin. Maybe he needed to take more time thinking about this drug situation. She owed him no further explanation of her personal life. She had already revealed more than most women would, about her husband, their play-like marriage, their outside affairs. She used a little dope like most everybody else in his crowd. So what?

She hadn't lied about it; she just hadn't mentioned it. Why should she? The two of them were out here trying to rake in a small fortune that her husband and she would have otherwise lost. Chipping a little smack, or skin-popping some recreational blow was none of his business.

He knew she had offered herself as a part of a package deal. And she was right. He couldn't blame her. A lot of people, men and women alike offered themselves up for a lot less than this had the potential to be. They had both had a feeling they were on the trail of what could be millions. Maybe they were wrong. But meanwhile, for good measure she had made herself up as the icing on a very sweet cake. He had to admit, looking up at her, feeling her warm against him, affecting him this way first thing in the morning. Drugs or no drugs, he liked the taste of this cake. The taste, the texture. Everything about it.

Damn ...! He liked it a lot. "Come down here, Lee," he said, quietly resolved. "Let me get these arms around you."

"Here I come," she said in a soft voice, leaning down atop him. She gave him a warm smile. "I thought you'd never ask."

CPI, Cayman Pearl Investments and CIWM, Cayman Investment and Wealth Management, occupied an entire shaded glass and gunmetal gray building taking up half a city block in the emerging restored George Town area. Leslie had called ahead and spoken with the Manager of Customer Services, Mister Trange, who appeared to be watching for them as their taxi swung to the front curbing.

Mr. Trange met them inside the door with his hands at his side, waiting to see if offering a handshake would be acceptable. It was.

"Mr. Adams and Mrs. Wright," he said, reaching out a hand to Vango. "Welcome to our island. It's a pleasure to meet you both. I'm Lawrence Trange, Customer Services." He smiled at Leslie Wright. "We spoke over the phone? Please come in." He ushered them across the lobby, seated them in his office and offered them coffee, which Leslie accepted and Vango declined respectfully. On the flight over, she had given him a driver's license with the name James Adams on it, in case anyone at Cayman Pearl asked for identification.

Vango relaxed while Leslie took the lead on a brief round of cordial small talk. When her coffee arrived, she thanked the young woman who brought in on a small ornate silver tray. She took a sip as if tasting a vintage wine.

"Lovely," she said. She smiled at Mr. Trange, sat the cup down and said, "Now then, to business."

An hour later, after taking notes on a plain unlined desk pad, and making three interoffice calls, Lawrence Trange hung up the phone on his desk and smiled, first at Vango

(AKA Mr. Adams) then at Mrs. Wright. Vango noticed the manager could not keep his eyes off her for over a few seconds at a time. Vango understood completely.

"Very good then," Trange said. He slid a folder across the desk to Leslie's fingertips. "If there's nothing more I can do for you today, please allow me to escort you both to our brand-new deposit vault," he added proudly. "I want to thank you both for opening your new account with Cayman Pearl." He picked up a key that a young man had brought to him. "Thank you, *Sheppard,*" he'd said, letting the young man know that he, as Customer Services Manager, would be escorting these two lovely people to the deposit boxes *personally.*

Key in hand, the manager stood as Vango and Leslie Wright stood up with him.

"If you will follow me, please," his free hand guided them from his office and down a long hallway.

When the manager unlocked his side of the deposit box, he gave a slight bow and turned and left. Alone in the big deposit vault, Vango and Leslie Wright looked all around. Seeing no sign of a camera anywhere, Vango followed Leslie to the box and watched her unlock the box and slide it out. He helped her by taking it and laying it on a long marble-topped table.

Stepping back, he took a deep breath and said, "I feel like we've just robbed a bank or something!" He looked around again as if making sure no one was watching.

Leslie held up the folder of paperwork they'd received for their new joint account. She wagged it and smiled.

"Eddie, we are *so* legal I can hardly *stand it.*" She

stepped in closer. "If we have time, right here, right now—"

"Lee, let's get busy," Vango said, knowing where this was headed. "We'll have the rest of the day to ourselves." As he spoke, he folded back the lid of the long deposit box. They both looked down, stunned at banded stacks of large denomination US bills.

"My God, Eddie!" Leslie said just above a whisper. "Maybe we have robbed a bank. Some international drug cartel bank." Her words cast a sinister pall.

"Watch your language," Vango said quietly with a slight smile. "I don't hear any alarms going off, or machine guns yakking."

"So far so good?" she offered.

"So far, so good," Vango repeated.

Taking in the stacks of cash spread along the sides and filling in an eight-inch space on one end of the metal deposit box, he lifted the top bearer bond from a stack of bonds in the middle of the bands of cash. He looked it over letting out a deep breath.

"Here's twenty-thousand, Lee," Vango said, handing her the bond certificate from atop the stack of brand-new bonds. "Buy yourself that new bikini."

"I will, Eddie," she whispered, sounding almost dazed by the stack of cash, and now the deep stack of brand-new unissued bearer bonds just waiting for her official signature.

"Wow, Eddie," said, looking at her travel bag she'd sat atop the marble-top table, "I hope I brought along a nice ink pen."

Vango turned up another twenty-thousand-dollar bond, looked at it and handed it to her.

"If you don't," he said, "I'm betting the manager will be happy to lend you one."

"Yes, he would, I'm sure," she said. She looked at him and gave a little giggle. "Eddie, I'm so happy I'm getting teary-eyed."

"Uh-oh," Vango said. He slipped an arm around her waist. "Let's get you a seat and let you start signing these into our new account." He nodded at the cash and bonds.

"How much do you think all this comes to?" she asked.

"It's hard to guess," Vango said. "Much more than we expected. More than enough to pay for this whole picnic. Don't forget this is only our first stop. We've got all day here, and more waiting for us on the Treasure Coast." He saw her eyes, teary and glistening.

"Eddie, I love you," she said in a hushed tone.

Whoa .... He hadn't expected that. He drew her close and touched his lips to her face.

"I love you too, Lee," he whispered. He surprised himself saying it. "Now *you* start signing, *I'll* start counting."

CHAPTER 15

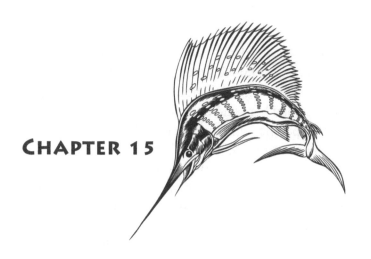

For the rest of the morning, Vango passed along signed bearer bonds to the young Customer Service Manager, Sheppard McCoo, who carried Leslie's freshly signed bonds from the vault lobby to Manager Trange's office. Having approved and made a copy of Leslie's signature of authority, the manager looked at the large amounts of bearer bonds being deposited into *his bank on his watch* and made an executive decision. He quickly ordered a desk, a computer and a telephone set up for himself just outside the vault door. An unopened bottle of spring water stood in a silver bucket of ice.

"I want you to *handle me, personally,* Lawrence," Leslie had told the stricken manager in a comely tone. She'd passed her smile from him to Sheppard McCoo. "And you too, Sheppard, the two of you together. I'd love both of you *handling me."* Vango looked away and smiled to himself. *Nothing could move the earth like big money and a gorgeous woman on the make ...,* he told himself.

At Leslie's feet sat a large canvas bank bag reinforced with stiff leather binding. Inside the bag lay two million, seven hundred thousand dollars and change—the stacks of cash from the deposit box. He had to admit, all of this felt too good to be legal.

But it is legal ...! he reminded himself. Whatever laws applied here had been long broken, beaten to death by the people who had made all this money—them and their attorneys. So much big powerful money that they had created an entire industry out of just hiding it, stashing it out of sight, cleaning it up enough to deny it ever existed. 'Legal as hell ...,' just like Leslie Wright had told him.

That's okay .... If Leslie Wright, himself, and Delbert Moss managed to pull this off, take all of this huge, crazy, absurd, vulgar amount of money and give it a good home, he was okay with that. He looked at Leslie Wright and gave her a wink as she looked up, rubbing her writing hand. She returned his wink, wiggled her fingers to loosen them, then picked up the pen and went back to signing.

Perfect ...!

"Mr. Adams, sir," said Manager Trange, interrupting Vango's train of thought as he stood up from his desk and walked over beside him. "I believe you and Mrs. Wright are both staying at the Trade Winds?"

Vango gave him a curious look, not only for knowing their accommodations, but also for calling him Mr. Adams, the name on his fake driver's license. It would take getting used to, being called Adams. Leslie had given Trange his name when she'd called ahead.

"Please excuse me for prying, Mr. Adams," said Trange. "I had to perform a brief and very *routine* check for our records. Everything is wonderful, though, I assure you."

Vango only nodded as Trange continued, "I simply want to let you know—" his voice lowered "—Pearl International owns the Trade Winds Beach Front Hotel, and I would like to upgrade your accommodations there and make everything *complimentary* for your entire stay in Grand Cayman. With your permission, of course," he added discreetly.

Vango kept himself from looking taken aback. "Of course. Thank you, Mr. Trange," he said. "Mrs. Wright made the reservations for us with the three-day minimum, I believe?" He posed it as a question.

"Ah—" Trange waved it away. "Yes, but I've corrected your reservations. Please feel free to stay with us as long as you like." He glanced around and said even lower, "And Mr. Adams, if I may be so bold, many of our clients like to travel *incognito.* Should you prefer an anonymous name, for security sake …." He let his words trail but gave him a look that masked any unspoken secrets with utmost discretion.

Vango replied, "For security sake, my name, 'Adams,' will be just fine for me." He said it with no confirmation or denial.

Trange understood. He dismissed the matter of names, but not of amenities.

"I hope I'm not being presumptuous, Mr. Adams, but I noted the two of you arrived here in a taxi? I've taken the liberty of arranging for one of our cars and a driver, to be at your service when we're finished here. Please feel free to use our service for as long as you need us."

Aw-man …! Cayman Pearl appeared to be turning into Las Vegas for The Rich and Famous. How much money were they depositing here in Cayman Pearl, to bring about this quality of service? Vango almost asked, but he caught himself and relaxed, realizing that at any time he chose to see the latest amount, he could step over to Trange's desk and look at the figure on Trange's computer. *But no hurry,* he told himself, this money wasn't going anywhere until he and Leslie said so.

Every time the screen flickered on the manager's desk, a substantially larger total came up, making a cute little beep each time it reset the total. *So, this is how it's done* .... He looked all around. Leslie Wright at a desk, signing her name to bearer bonds and having the manager accept them and add the higher amount to their new account. Watching, he breathed in deep, savoring a full and engulfing sense of satisfaction. His only leveling affect for the moment was that he might awaken and suddenly realize that this was all some sort of Dom Pérignon dream.

Stop it ..., he told himself. This was for real. He smiled to himself.

"One more thing, Mr. Adams," said Trange walking up with a separate folder in hand. "Your other account is right here in the building. With your permission I can have it brought to you, under lock, of course."

"That would be wonderful," said Vango. He and Leslie looked at each other and smiled.

Instead of calling the hospital from a pay phone, the way Vango had advised him, to see if Lew Stucky had been released, Delbert noted for the first time a coiled phone cord hanging just beneath the dash. He couldn't resist using it. He waited until he arrived at the Wright home and pulled the car in next to Harold Wright's Buick Park Avenue and closed the garage door with a touch of a remote clicker. With another touch of two buttons side-by-side on the driver's door, he lowered both front windows and relaxed in the plush leather driver's seat.

Pushing a green lit button on the dash, he saw a lid raise and reveal not only the car phone, but also a step by step list of how to use it.

Okay, Delbert, buddy, you can do this, easy as pie, he told himself, his inner voice sounding like Vango's. He took the piece of paper from his shirt pocket and looked at the numbers Leslie Wright had written down for him. As a practice run, before calling Stucky's hospital room he called one of the two suites where Stucky and Vango stayed at the Surfside Motel. On the fifth ring a mechanical voice took over.

"Your party does not answer," the recorded voice said. "If you wish to leave a message please dial *1* for the front desk."

Okay, Delbert did.

"Surfside Motel," said the male all-night clerk in a sleepy voice.

"I'd like to leave a message for Lewis Stucky—"

"Mister Stucky is no longer a guest here," the young male said, before Delbert could finish.

"All right," said Delbert. "Can you tell me what time he checked out?"

"I'm sorry," said the voice, "I don't have that information in front of me."

"Okay. This is Eddie Vango, in the room adjoining my friend Lew Stucky?" Delbert said. "Do I have any new messages?"

"Yes, Mr. Vango, you do have three! All three from the same person." The clerk's voice suddenly sounded tense. "Let me get those for you." A moment passed.

"Here we are, Mr. Vango. The first came at ten p.m. A call from Intermediate Care, Nurse Jennifer Collins," The clerk read, "As the contact person for Mr. Stucky, I'm sorry to inform you that Mr. Stucky has signed himself out of our facility against the doctor's orders."

Delbert held the receiver away from his ear and looked at it and said, "What the hell …?"

The clerk said, "The other two messages are from the same Nurse Collins and say very much the same thing. Shall I read them?"

"Uh … no," said Delbert. "But if anyone else calls for me, please give them this open message—that I'll be home the rest of the night. They'll have my number."

The clerk repeated with a hint of uncertainty, "You'll be home all night, should anyone wish to reach you. And anyone calling will already have your number? Is that all, sir?"

"Yes, thanks," Delbert said.

What the hell was going on …?

But before he had time to gather his thoughts, he jerked his head sidelong, toward a loud squall from the cat and a metallic thump as the big animal landed on the hood of Harold Wright's Buick.

"Whoa, Bruiser!" Delbert shouted, startled by the cat coming out of nowhere, the painful details of his and the cat's previous chance meeting coming to mind.

The cat hunched its back up and hissed at Delbert. Delbert watched as the big fierce-looking animal paced back and forth, looking at the back door leading into the empty house as if someone had just pitched him out and shut the door. *What is all this ...?* Before Delbert could step out of the Mercedes and investigate, the big cat half-spun atop the Buick and shot though the Mercedes' open passenger window.

Like one of its ancient ancestors out of the wilds the cat zeroed in and pounced, went for a strangle hold on Delbert Moss, and pinned him down behind the steering wheel. Delbert screamed! He cursed! He fought hard to loosen the big cat from his chest. But the cat wasn't giving an inch. It tightened its sharp hold on him. Delbert fought hard.

The cat squalled and hissed and bit and dug. Blood flew as its dangerous front claws sunk into Delbert's forearms and held on. Rear claws dug into Delbert's chest. The cat ran in place, a ball of mad fur and wild determination that quickly turned Delbert's new silk shirt into a shredded tangle of ripped printed palms and coconuts.

"Man! Look at this!" Tony Dee shouted as he stepped into the garage from the house. He held a .45 caliber with a long silencer attached to its barrel. Three other gunmen spilled out of the house around him, each armed with a semi-automatic pistol, all of them pointed at Delbert Moss sitting inside the Mercedes.

Tony Dee wagged his silenced .45 at Delbert, motioning him out of the car.

"Lay your gun over on the hood, Moss," he said. "We've been waiting here all day and all night for you! Where's Vango? I've got a score to settle with him!"

A score to settle ...?

Delbert stepped out and left the driver's door

loosely open. He stepped over coolly, laid his pistol on the hood of the Buick and turned facing the guns aimed at him.

"You should have mentioned settling your score before. You could have saved yourself a trip," Delbert said.

One gunman muffled a laugh; Tony shot him a hard look. To Delbert he said, "Shut up, Moss!" To the other gunmen he gave a harsh order, "If he runs his mouth again, shoot him in his big *stupid head!*"

Another muffled laugh came from the gunmen. Looking close, Delbert could tell they were all four drunk and high on reefer. He could smell whisky and reefer. He shut up.

"Check yourself out, Moss," said Tony, gesturing his gun up and down Delbert's shredded clothing. "That cat has *messed you up,* big time." This time laughter exploded, un-muffled. Delbert kept quiet.

Tony pointed at the Mercedes and said to one of the three gunmen, "Check out the back seat for cash, Charlie … and the trunk. I'm going to hang onto any cash we find until we hear something from the Lamb."

"What if we don't ever hear from him?" the one named Charlie Betz asked as he stepped away toward the rear of the Mercedes.

"Then we'll just have to keep it safe until get word what to do," said Tony Dee.

"Word from *who?"* Charlie Betz asked, reaching inside the Mercedes and pushing the button raising the trunk lid.

"For a dumbass off-loader you talk too much, Charlie! That worries me!" said Tony. He started to raise his silenced .45 towards Betz, but the slow rising trunk lid caught his attention.

Delbert raised a hand for permission to speak, like some well-mannered schoolboy.

"Yeah what?" said Tony, sounding impatient.

"I need to warn you, there's a shoulder held rocket launcher back there, and those things are tricky," Delbert said, his hand still raised, least the reefer infused Tony Dee forget he'd given permission.

"Yeah, right," Tony said. "We've been here all night. I don't want to hear any silly shit from you." The two gunmen still standing near him gave a little chuckle. Liking their attention, Tony grinned and added to Delbert, "Any *ray-guns?* Something we can use here?" As he spoke, he could hear his gunman, Charlie Betz rummaging around in the Mercedes' trunk.

Delbert kept a serious tone.

"No ray-guns, Tony," he said. "But there's couple of machine guns, locked and loaded. Everything back there is ready to fire. So, be careful."

"Hear that, bros?" Tony said to his gunmen with a short reefer buzzed laugh. "Delbert Moss, *concerned citizen,* giving us a little *safety with firearms* spiel.

Forget it then .... Delbert let out a breath and shut up, knowing what they would find back there. The big cat had leapt back atop the Buick. He watched the gunmen intently.

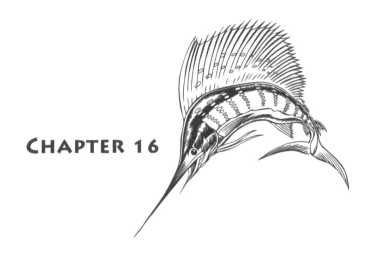

CHAPTER 16

From the trunk, Charlie Betz called out to Tony Dee.

"No cash back here, Tony. But he's right, there's some heavy fire-power in here, for sure!"

Tony had started to walk back to the trunk but stopped cold when he heard the words *No Cash.*

"Damn it …," Tony said under his breath. He let the silenced .45 hang down his side and gave Delbert a cold look.

Delbert raised his hand again.

"Take your hand down, *jerk-off,"* Tony said. "You can talk for now!" Then he went on, saying, "I keep hearing about *big money* every time I turn around." He spread his hands. "So far, I haven't found nothing—well, except for a couple of thousand, and the Lamb took it from me before I could hide it from him."

"Wow." Delbert nodded and listened and tried to sound interested. This was good, he decided, let Tony Dee talk. Delbert had learned from watching how Eddie Vango operates: When somebody like Tony Dee is talking, and especially if he's holding a silenced gun aimed at you, let him talk. At some point Tony would let his guard down. At that time Delbert would grab something strong and heavy and hang it over Tony's head.

End of story ..., he told himself.

He listened to Tony as he looked around the garage, for something—*anything.* On a wall shelf only four feet away he saw a metal-framed aquarium, twelve by eighteen inches overall, half-filled with loose golf balls and aquarium stones. *This will do,* he decided. He wondered how heavy would this thing be, snatching it up and over above his head. *Forty—fifty pounds?*

"You know, you could have come back with me when I drove those stiffs back to the Lamb," Tony Dee said.

"He would have killed me, Tony," Delbert said.

"Naw, Lamb ain't real smart. I would have lied for you, convinced him how much help you were when I escaped Vango and the Wright woman," Tony added, with a grin. "By the way, where are they?"

"Mexico," said Delbert. "Vango picked up a big bag of money from Harold Wright's stash, and they split with it."

"That explains why we found no money here," Tony said.

"I took them to the airport yesterday. I'm starting to wonder if they might have cut out on me."

"Might have ...? Duh!" said Tony. "Did you see them get on their flight?"

"No," Delbert said. "But I dropped them off out front of the terminal."

"So okay, Moss, break it down," Tony said. "They leave you standing there like a *dip-shit,* they get inside, buy tickets to anywhere in the world but Mexico. And they are gone like two gone-dogs! Laughing their asses off."

Delbert tried picturing *two gone-dogs laughing* but couldn't get a clear image.

"You think?" he asked looking disappointed at the prospect.

"Yeah, I think. And you got nothing!" Tony said.

"I wouldn't say *'nothing,'*" said Delbert. "Vango gave me three hundred dollars *walk-around money* until they get back—"

"Hey, Tony," Charlie Betz called out from behind the car. "What do you want us to do with all this?"

"Bring everything around here, let me see all of it." Tony replied.

"This bazooka—*whatever,* has to be set up, or something," Betz said.

"Is that your weapons expert?" Delbert asked flatly.

The remark went over Tony Dee's head.

"No," he said to Delbert. Then he called out in a louder tone, "Damn it! Set it up, Charlie! Let me see it!"

Delbert looked at the aquarium, ready to grab it up and make his move, bring it crashing down on Tony's head and leave it there. But before he could get started on it, Tony looked at him and wagged his silencer at the open trunk lid.

"You go first, Moss," he said. "Don't forget, I've never fired this big forty-five through a silencer. I'm itching to hear how it sounds."

Moss said, "If you think it's going to be really quiet, you're in for a disappointment." Before they stopped behind the Mercedes, Delbert asked over his shoulder, "How long since you've seen or even *talked* to the Lamb?"

"It's been awhile," Tony said. "But that's cool with me. He knows I'm a *can-do* guy. He can tell me what to do and I'll get it done, big time. He sent me to get Vango, and that's what I'll do."

"It's a long drive to Mexico," Delbert said. "By 'get' Vango, you mean kill him, right?"

Tony chuckled. "You don't catch on real quick, do you Moss? Sure, he means kill him."

"Hey, Tony," Charlie Betz called out. "I dropped one of these curly looking do-dads down the barrel of this bazooka—whatever. I think it's stuck! Should I shake it?"

"No!" Tony bellowed. "Don't do nothing!" Delbert stopped at the truck where the high gunmen stood staring at him and Tony. Charlie Betz stood holding the launcher backward, staring down, the wide barrel. Another gunman held one of the machine guns with its magazine inserted in the chamber, his finger on the trigger.

"Jesus, Charlie!" shouted Tony. "Give me that before you kill us all!"

"Here you go, Tony." The big man turned the launcher around to hand it over. But he dropped it.

The butt end of the launcher struck the concrete floor and made a hissing sound.

Good God!

Delbert dived to the floor scrambling to get under the Mercedes. The cat streaked from atop the Buick to the floor, slid under the Mercedes and tumbled to a halt against Delbert's side. A deafening explosion rocked the house on its foundation. Pieces of drywall, wooden and metal framing, chunks of furniture, rained down. A huge belch of fire and smoke engulfed the Wright's plush walled and gated home.

Pieces of broken barrel tile that had flown high from the roof crashed down through the screen enclosure surrounding the swimming pool. Delbert tried to slide away from the cat, but the cat held onto him as if the two of them were old friends.

"All right, *Bruiser,* come with me," Delbert said, coughing, talking loud above his ringing ears. He scooped the big cat up on his arm and pulled him from under the Mercedes with him. He stood up fanning smoke, dust and debris with his free hand. The cat clung.

Even in the thick swirling air Delbert Moss squinted at a long, wide, ragged hole reaching upward through the entire house, exposing the sky. Making his way to the blown-out garage door he saw the body of Charlie Betz lying face down, broken and smoldering on the littered floor.

The big cat turned nervous, growled, and burrowed its head into Delbert's side.

"I've got you, Bruiser. Take it easy." He stroked the cat's fur back, trying to calm him.

The driver's door on the Mercedes, loosely closed had swung wide open. The garage roof above him creaked and sagged. He had to get out of the garage before it all fell in on him. But seeing the ceiling breaking up, long pieces of it starting to break free and fall, he leaped into the Mercedes front seat just as a half sheet of drywall board fell and broke up on the hood. The big cat stuck to him like a terrified child.

Through the sound of the ceiling popping and creaking, he heard Charlie Betz calling out in a weak voice across the littered floor, "Help, me …."

"I can't! The place is falling!" Delbert replied above the sound of the ceiling. He saw the keys hanging from the ignition.

"Help ... me," Betz repeated.

"I *can't—*" Delbert started to shout again but stopped himself. "Damn it!" he said, looking around at the wobbling ceiling. "Hold on, Charlie!" He tried prying Bruiser from his side, but Bruiser would have none of it. "Hang on! You're coming with me!" Delbert shouted at the shaken cat.

With the cat shivering in the crook of his arm, Delbert came out of the car in a crouch and made his way to Charlie Betz and dragged him back to the Mercedes with his free hand. Betz didn't make a sound.

"Charlie, you got to help me get you into the car." He turned Betz loose long enough to open the back door, then grabbed the bloody, smoldering gunman again and raised him enough to stuff him up into the backseat. Betz smelled of burnt hair and skin.

"Bruiser, will you *please* get up there!" Delbert said, pulling the clinging cat loose. He held him up and over the front seat, the cat growling at him until he dropped him onto the passenger side.

"Thank *you!*" he shouted above the sound of the cracking ceiling framework. He pulled Betz's limp feet inside and slammed the rear door. "Okay, let's get the out of here while we can!"

The ceiling popped so loud it caused the cat to fling himself over against Delbert's leg and hang on again, trembling while Delbert started the car, jammed the gear shift into reverse and started burning rubber in place as the rest of the ceiling gave way and fell, looking like one large shattered overhead dance floor with a large black hole blown through it.

At the break of dawn, the J W Home Cleaning van had pulled into the Wright's driveway silently and stopped under an outstretched live oak. Jill Wray shoved the van gear shift into park and cut the engine off. She gave Morez a sidelong glance and picked up her cup of coffee from atop the console and paused before taking a sip.

"If your men are inside, we better let them see you first. I don't want to get shot dropping off Lambert's body."

"Don't worry, *Jilly* Wray," said Morez. "These will mostly be Lambert and Trio's men. They are all drifters and dick-heads. This will go like clockwork—"

"You told me you have men here?" she asked.

"Yes, I slipped a few men into Wright Way's operation when I noticed shipments slowing down." He gave a thin sly grin. "I don't like surprises. My inside guys help me keep my hand on top of things—"

At that second the launcher shot erupted, blowing a wide hole almost straight up through the garage ceiling, the second floor, the attic, and out the roof. It left a hazy wake of smoke and debris streaming, zigzagging up into the morning sky. Behind it a long sinister whistling sound followed it out of sight.

Jill Wray sloshed coffee in her lap. She and Morez stared up, dumbstruck, watching until the missile disappeared from sight.

"Holy Mother—!" she whispered as if speaking any louder would bring the next blast whistling her way. She sat the coffee down quickly, grabbed the ignition

key and twisted it hard. The engine only gave a low mechanical grunt.

"Damn it, *woman!*" Morez shouted. "Get us out of here! We've got a *dead man* rolled up in a throw rug!" His concern was not for his men who might be inside the wreckage, but from knowing that at any second there would be police, firefighters, maybe even news people with cameras rolling up.

"It'll start, it'll *start!*" the woman said. She twisted the key again. Still only a grunt.

"What? *We've got to walk?*" Morez shouted. "Get us the hell out of here!" They looked at the falling garage roof as the loud sound of screeching tires cut through the bellowing smoke and the crash of lumber. They stared, stunned, wide-eyed, watching the charred and battered Mercedes streak from under the downed roof.

Like a scene from some hellish nightmare, the big car with its top half-raised, flapping and waving, raced across the long front yard. It mowed down small palms and ornamental shrubs, ramped upwards, leaping islands of stone-lined flower beds and leaving a swirl of broken, flying landscape in its wake. Through the cleaning van's windshield, Morez and Jill Wray saw the car fishtail onto the road, and speed out of sight, still spewing foliage, gravel and mulch along the way.

"What the hell was that ...?" Morez said as if in awe.

Jill Wray didn't answer. Instead, she made the sign of the cross and took a deep breath, sirens wailing in the near distance from three directions.

She turned the key again. It grunted again. Once! Twice! On the third grunt it came to life with a powerful roar. Morez rolled his eyes and loosened his collar. Jill put the van in reverse and started to back around from under the tree. She stopped. "Uh-oh. We can't leave now! Look!"

Behind them a police car swung around on the sand street slipped in and stopped within three feet of the van's rear door, with no siren, but with its light flashing.

"To hell with this!" shouted Morez. He reached inside his silk jacket and wrapped his hand around the butt of a 9mm.

"No, wait, hold it!" said Jill Wray, "I know these guys! I've got this."

"You've *got this?*" said Morez. He didn't like not being in charge, of anything, any time. *Now this bitch ....*

"Trust me, *I've got this,"* she repeated. She reached over nudged his hand away from his gun. "Be cool, Leone."

Be cool ...? Be cool! Morez boiled. He'd straight-up choke her to death! *So help me!*

They heard the police car doors shut behind them. Sirens still wailed, getting closer.

Jill Wray hoped out of the door and closed it as the two officers approached her. Morez sat slumped, as if abandoned.

"Thank God somebody called it in, Sergeant *Dan,"* she said to the officer. "My squawk box and scanner are both in the shop."

Squawk box? Police Scanner? Morez mused to himself. His gun hand relaxed, a little. *What have we here? Ah, yes, the leader of RATS,* he reminded himself. He shouldn't be surprised. *Once a rat ....*

"I tried my phone ...." Jill Wray said, letting her

words trail. She yanked her phone from her hip pocket as if it were proof she'd tried it. "We were just riding by and *Boom!* This is what we found!"

"Don't worry about it, *Jilly,*" said Police Sergeant Dan Hicky, who'd been in the passenger seat. "We had calls come in from everywhere." He looked over at the blown-out garage door, the scorched barrel tiles at the uppermost edge of the roof. Others scattered in the front yard. "What have we got here, a blown water heater?"

"You got me," said Jill Wray, the van idling beside her.

I've never seen a water heater blow up. I didn't even know they blew up."

Morez sat staring straight ahead. The other officer who'd been driving walked forward past the van and didn't stop until he stood ten feet in front, looking at the house, his hand atop his holstered gun. Morez lightened up. But then the officer turned around, gave Morez a cordial nod and returned to the patrol cruiser. A large fire engine came rolling in through the Wright's open entrance gates, its siren screaming.

"All right, we'll get out of your way here," Jill Wray said the sergeant. She turned to open her door.

Officer Hicky came forward and said, "I'll talk to the tech at our radio shop—tell him get busy with your radio and scanner."

"Thank you, Sergeant Dan, you're an angel," Jill said in her *Jilly* voice.

Morez sat staring at her with a blank expression. She closed the door and gave him a little smile. "See, that wasn't so bad, now was it?"

Thank you, Dan, you're an angel .... Morez mocked

her in silence. He was still seething with some strange sort of anger at her, he wasn't sure why.

Jill turned toward her window as Sergeant Dan Hicky tapped his large police academy ring on the glass.

Jesus! Now what ...? She smiled as she lowered the glass. Morez was all set to go for his gun, again.

"Tom just reminded me" —his voice lowered— "you might have been on some sort of stakeout here, for your citizen's group?"

"We're always watching things," Jilly Wray said, still smiling, as if admitting nothing. She lay her forearm on the open window frame, trucker style. Thirty yards closer to the house, the blown-out garage doors, the fire trucks had taken position, ladders out. An inch and half fire hose unrolled from a large spool atop the engine.

"I understand, *Jilly,*" Sergeant Dan said, "and we all appreciate what you and Recon Tech Services do for us." He patted the back of her hand, leaving his hand lay there. Morez watched intently. *This cop prick ....*

"This is not according to *procedure,*" Sergeant Dan continued, "but I have a hunch you were here on surveillance. Would you like me to take you up there closer, let you have a better look around?"

"Aren't you the sweetest thing!" *Jilly* said. "Hear that?" she said, turning to Morez. "These officers are going to drive me closer, let me look around. Why don't you take the van back to Oceana Princess and maybe these wonderful officers will drop me there when we're through here?" She looked back around at Sergeant Dan with the question pending.

"Of course, we will," he said, barely giving Morez a glance. He opened the van door and Jill Wray stepped out. She looked through the glass at Morez and gave him a subtle wink. He stared back, seething with anger.

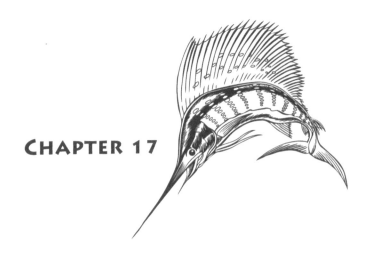

CHAPTER 17

Jill Wray and Sergeant Dan Hicky walked all around the perimeter of the Wright's home compound while the fire department went about its work hosing down the partially blown-away house and its attached four-car garage. A few feet back from a missing garage door, Jill pointed down at the maimed and blackened body of Tony Dee lying twisted in the path of black tire treads coming out of the wreckage.

"Yep, that's Tony Dee," she said. "I've watched him so much lately, I'd recognize him anywhere, dead or alive."

"Good work, Jilly," Sergeant Hicky said in a serious tone. He said Tony Dee's name into a small Dictaphone 210 he carried in the palm of his hand. As the two watched, a firefighter threw a heavy blue plastic cover over Tony Dee and hurried away. Farther into the garage, four feet stuck up under another plastic cover.

"Want me to show you their faces?" Sergeant Hicky asked.

Jill looked at the fire-hose water slouching around on the concrete floor, a heavy shower coming out the house from the hose.

"No," she replied. "None of these punks are worth us getting our feet wet. I'll wait to hear from the coroner." She tilted her head up and stared through the large ragged hole, running tunnel-like through the entire house and said, "What do you suppose did this?"

"A rocket launcher, no doubt about it," said Hicky.

"Someone got tired of fooling around with a handgun and said to hell with it?" Jill speculated.

"If I had to guess, I'd say it was an accident," said Sergeant Hicky. "Nobody is stupid enough to do this intentionally. Besides, look at this hole. It wasn't aimed at anything; it was just fired." He looked around again. "But it was here to be used. Maybe things are heating up, with the drug shipments being stalled the way they are."

"How late is the big shipment?" she inquired.

"A full week or more. But it'll all come back around," Dan Hicky said with confidence. "Once the money gets *right*. It's all about the money."

"Yep, it slows down, it speeds up," said Jill.

"Yes, it does," said Sergeant Dan.

She shot him a smile as they stepped away. "Thank you for sharing that with me, Dan. As soon as I hear anything, I'll get right back to you."

"*Quid pro quo.* Tit-for-tat," he said in a lowered tone, "Was that one of the cartel *higher-ups* sitting in your van?"

"Yes, higher-up, but not too much higher," she said. "I thought he would piss himself when you two rolled in behind us."

"I knew you were up to something, that's why I straight-up avoided him," said Hicky. He paused, then asked, "Does the big deal appear to be getting any closer from your end?"

"Any day," said Jill. "That's what I've got him around for. He's going to let me know well ahead."

"Any idea on the amount?"

"Not yet," said Jill, "but I'm told we're looking at twenty-five percent of close to thirty million."

"Holy *Mouther Toledo!*" said Hicky before he could stop himself. "When this goes through, I'm buying a *brand new* fifty-foot Bertram fishing yacht! That's all there is to it."

"Is a fifty-foot fishing boat a *yacht?*" Jill chuckled.

"It is to me!" Sergeant Dan grinned. "I live in the sailfish capital of the world, and I don't even own a boat! What the hell is that?"

Jill chuckled again. "You deserve a big boat, *yacht,* whatever. Stick with me, Dan. Be the king of the Treasure Coast."

"Oh, yes! I'm sticking!" Sergeant Hicky said. "Just keep reminding me we're doing some good here."

"We're wiping out an entire drug cartel," she said, "So, yes, we're doing good. After this, an everyday investor will think twice before putting any money in these shady bond investment deals. But we've got to hit it hard before the government puts a stop to it."

"I hear you," said Hicky. "They say bearer bonds are under-going some tight regulations next year." He grinned. "I better get my brand-new boat and get out."

Jill moved in closer beside him, let her fingertips brush his hand. "Will you take me onboard your big new *fishing yacht,* Sergeant Dan? We won't have to even leave the dock."

"That's *my favorite* kind of boating," he said, glancing all around at the busy firefighters. "Let's get you over to Oceana Princess before that coke merchant with you thinks you're playing footsy with the police."

Before leaving the Cayman Pearl offices Vango managed to get Trange alone while Leslie went to the ladies' facility. "When we leave this afternoon," he said, "I'd like you to take half of the balance from the new joint account and set up another account in my name only. Any problem?"

"No, sir," Trange replied quickly. "And I take it you'd like me to be discreet?"

"Yes, please, by all means," Vango said. "And on the other account, please do the same, half in my new account and half in the other one."

"Very well, Mr. Adams," said Trange. "And I have ordered three ten-thousand-dollar bearer bonds like you both requested, and an additional two million dollars in new bearer bonds the way you both requested." He smiled. "Is there anything else I can do for you?"

"Thank you, Mr. Trange," said Vango. "I believe that will be all."

Leslie Wright and Eddie Vango lay together looking out at the rise and fall of a foam-streaked blue and turquoise ocean. From a double-wide lounger under a wide scalloped umbrella, they watched large pelicans and gulls appear to rise up out of the distance and fly landward, early-birds looking for early-bird delights.

Beachgoers had thinned out for the afternoon, drifting away to seek what delicacies the eatery chiefs would conjure up with their magic whisks and knowing fingertips. The aroma of Jamaican Coco bread wafted on a sea breeze.

"I still can't believe it," Leslie whispered sidelong to Vango who sipped an icy bottle of Red Stripe Lager. "This whole trip has been like some beautiful impossible dream."

Vango let out a breath.

"Believe it, Lee," he said, trying to let himself accept what they had done and not get too excited about. He didn't know what they would have to face back on the Treasure Coast. But here, right now, he needed to relax. A metal bucket stood beside the lounger with three more bottles of beer peeping up from a bed of chopped ice.

The two of them had swooped in here and over a two-day period, having caught everybody with their pants around their ankles, taken possession of over *forty-four million dollars!*

Was that right ...? he asked himself. *Yep! Damn right*, he grinned. *Forty-four mil –and change.*

He still felt a little guilty of *something*, but he was getting better with it every hour.

"Eddy? Did you hear me?" Leslie said. "You got so quiet all of a sudden." She made a gesture toward his beer.

"Yes, Lee, I heard you," he said, handing her the short-necked beer bottle. "I'm just enjoying the day."

She took a sip and handed him the bottle.

"How do you do that?" she said.

"What, enjoy the day?" he asked.

"No, I mean, just let things go that way. I'm still so psyched, I'm tingling all over! Aren't you still excited?"

Needing a fix ...? Maybe. But this wasn't the time to mention it. He reached over and took her hand in his.

"I'm *still* excited," he said calmly. "But we've still got things going on."

She gave him a questioning look.

"For instance?"

"For instance, I haven't heard from Delbert. I don't know if Lew Stucky checked out and flew to Chicago." He added, "In fact I haven't heard what's going on with Delbert, *period.* Still no calls on your car phone? Your home phone?"

"Nothing," Leslie said. "Okay, I've wondered about that too. But we're heading home tomorrow. So ...."

"You're right," Vango said. "Everything is okay." He handed her another sip of beer; he looked her up and down as she touched the bottle to her lips. "By the way," he added, "Have I told you how *knock-down gorgeous* you look in the new bikini?"

"Yes," she whispered, drawing closer to him. "You *told* me you like it, but you didn't *show* me how much."

Vango glanced around at the near empty beach.

"Easy, Lee," Vango cautioned her. "We don't want to make all this money, then get ourselves busted for indecent exposure."

"Oh? What's *indecent* about us?" she whispered.

"Nothing I can think of," he said. He settled and relaxed against her. She wasn't making a move on him. She was simply asking for conversation. He was learning to read her. He liked that. He knew he'd read her right when she stood up from the lounger and slipped a breezy cover up over her bikini.

"Feed me, Eddie," she said. "Thinking about

money makes me hungry."

"Me too," said Vango, standing up, picking up the towel he'd spread over the lounger.

After dinner when they returned to their *upgraded* suite, a bottle of Louis Roederer Cristal Champagne stood in a silver ice bucket on serving table in the dining area. Leslie stepped over and placed a fingertip daintily atop the foil-wrapped cork and gave Vango a smile.

"I love this place, Eddie," she said. "Can we see about living here forever?"

"I'll ask around," Vango replied. He picked up an opener and reached for the bottle.

Leslie's brow clouded slightly.

"Can we talk, Eddie?" she said.

Vango looked down at the champagne, then back up at her.

"Sure," he said, laying the opener down. "It sounds serious."

She took a seat at the long dining room table. Vango sat down across from her.

"I hope it's not our first argument," she said.

"So do I," Vango said. He reached across the table and cupped his hand over hers. "Go with it."

"I should have told you this before. I was just afraid of what you might think of me."

"We'll find out, won't we," he said quietly. He added a slight shrug. He felt relief for having had Manager Trange set up a separate account in his name only. "Give it up before our ice melts."

"Here goes," she said. "I'm an *intravenous* drug user." She paused for a reaction from him.

"You're a junkie?" Vango asked, trying to keep his words soft.

"I won't go so far as to say I'm a *junkie.* I do inject minimal amounts of cocaine, heroin." She looked off, then back at him. "Sometimes I only snort, but more often I inject."

"You shoot–that is you *inject*–eight balls?"

"Some people call what I use *eight balls,*" she said.

"Oh? What do you call them?"

She paused, considered it, then said, "Okay, I call them eight balls. And *yes,* I shoot them." Vango noted a slight defensiveness come into her voice. "I'm not asking for your approval."

"Good," Vango said, "Because I don't like giving approval. I don't judge, so, I don't like justifying what people do to keep them ticking. It's not my business."

She gave him a curious look.

"To be honest," he said. "I thought you might be chipping a little. I saw a needle fall out of your travel bag on the plane while you were sleeping."

"I see," she said. "So, you just figured–"

"Hold it right there, Lee," he said. "I didn't figure anything. I kept in mind what we came here to do. And we did it."

"Okay, I appreciate that," she said. She relaxed a little. "Were you ever going to mention it to me?"

"I don't know," Vango said. "I suppose I don't consider it a big thing. I used some junk growing up. Most everybody I knew did. Almost none of them became hard-core addicts. They liked getting high. So did I. But I drifted away from it."

"Are you going to say maybe I'll quit someday?"

she asked, a slight smile coming on her face.

"No," he replied. "I'm going to say, watch out getting on the plane with it."

"I'll run out by then," she said. "I've spaced it out about right."

"Good, Vango said. "In that case I'll say, 'It's *your thing,* do what you want to do.'" He returned the slight smile she offered.

She laughed under her breath, shook her head, and said, "You know if you ever get the urge–"

"Thanks, I'll keep it in mind," he said, reaching for the bottle in the bucket of ice. "I like being with you. I like what we do to each other. I like it very much. Now that I'm rich, I'll probably like it even better. And if I ever need an eight ball you'll be the first person I come to. Although I've got to say, you know eight balls are deadly."

"I know," she said, and she gave him a *no-lecture-please* look. He stopped with his hand on the bottle. "I'm sorry … are we through talking?" he asked cordially.

She let out a relaxed breath.

"Yes, I think we are." She watched him strip the foil from the bottle, twist the opener and pull the cork with a moderate *'pop.'*

"I wish we weren't leaving tomorrow, Eddie," she said. Vango poured two glasses and handed her one.

"I know," he said. "But I'm glad we can come back anytime we feel like it. They touched glasses and sipped *Cristal.* When they finished their silent toast, Vango said, "While we're being honest, I need to tell you something."

"Oh …," she said.

"When we started out, you said I would be in

this for half of whatever we found. This would be *our treasure from the Treasure Coast?"*

"Yes, I remember," she said. "Back when we thought we might divide a few grand, maybe a couple hundred thousand." She paused, looked at him, seeing him wonder if she was going to back out, now they'd tipped the scales for such a staggering amount. She held out her glass for another toast. "Don't worry, Eddie, we're still partners, Fifty-fifty."

Vango touched his glass to hers.

"I'm glad to hear that," he said. "Now I need to confess. I talked to Trange before we left his office, I had him take half of our account and set up an account in my name only."

She fell silent for a moment, then said quietly, *"So,* the honeymoon is over." He saw her eyes mist a little. "I already knew you did that, Eddie. I was just waiting, wondering when you were going to tell me."

Vango looked surprised. He managed to reply, "Okay. You knew. I'm glad you said when I was going to tell you, not *if.* So, you knew I wasn't out to get one over on you, stiff you out of your half."

"I never doubted you," she said. "I am a little sorry you did it."

"I thought it best," he said. "We don't know what we might be walking into when we get back to the coast. I wanted this money thing out of the way."

"I understand, and I feel better," she said. "I was worried that you might intend leave me at the airport."

He sat the glass down and took her hand. He wanted to ask how a knockout like her could underestimate herself, but he was certain she'd heard some version of that same line so much it meant nothing to her.

"I can't leave you at the airport," he quipped. "We came here in your car, remember?"

"That's right," she said. "But we haven't heard a word from Delbert. We may not have a ride home——I may not even have a *car!"*

They laughed and raised their glasses.

"Here's to Delbert Moss and your Mercedes," Vango said, "Wherever they may be."

CHAPTER 18

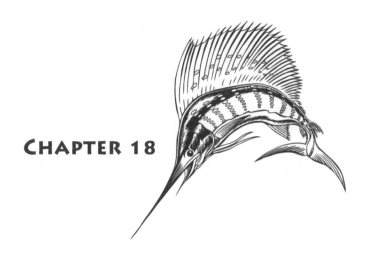

In the afternoon, Delbert drove the scarred and blackened Mercedes, its flattened convertible hardtop mashed down a full three inches from the garage roof falling in on it. He felt lucky just to be alive! The front windshield was spider-cracked top and bottom along the edges of the smoky glass, from the pressure of the weight and the blast. The slamming down of the garage roof had broken a shock, a spring, or something—he wasn't sure what— causing the car to dip forward and sag onto the left front wheel.

What an awful mess ....

But Vango had asked him to keep tabs on Lew Stucky, make sure he got aboard a Chicago flight, and that's what he intended to do, whether he found Stucky drunk or sober. Along the way to the hospital parking lot to drop the Mercedes and pick up the Corsica rental, he'd stopped at a local pharmacy and picked up first aid supplies he needed to patch up Charlie Betz who lay knocked out in the back seat, and a can of aerosol spray he needed to in order to deodorize Bruiser the cat.

Charlie Betz remained as limp and quiet as a corpse

while Delbert sat in the rear seat beside him and attended to him as best he could, using alcohol wipes to clean his face and scrub dried blood out of his eyes and hair. As an ambulance sped by them with its siren screaming and pulled into the Emergency Room entrance, Betz's eyes sprang open; he gave Delbert a terrified look.

"Don't let them take me …," he said in a faint but labored breath.

"They're not here for you, Betz. They're bringing in an emergency patient. Hold still," said Delbert, putting gauze and tape on the battered man's forehead.

"I— I'm lots better now," Betz whispered. His eyes moved all around, taking in his surroundings. "I never … fired a bazooka before. Do they all … do like that?"

"Not really," Delbert said. "I think it went off by accident."

"Wow, man," Betz said. "I hope they never ask me to fire another one …."

"I don't think you'll need to worry about that," Delbert said.

"How about … Tony Dee? Is he all right?" Betz asked.

"No, he didn't make it," Delbert said. "He was laying in the garage doorway. I think I backed over him."

"You backed over Tony?" Betz asked.

"I'm not sure. It sounded like it," Delbert said.

Betz let out a breath and relaxed.

"That's too bad," he said. He closed his eyes.

Delbert looked at Bruiser who sat perched atop the front seat, staring down at them. The aerosol had minimized the odor of burnt fur, but left Bruiser's coat bushed out and stiff. He looked twice his ordinary size, appearing as if his tail had been stuck into an electric socket. Delbert tried to pat the dried fur down but found it had become as spiky as nails.

"At least you don't stink now," he said to Bruiser. The cat offered a sound that was between a purr and a growl.

"Okay! Easy, big guy!" Delbert backed away, lit a Camel and slipped out of the rear seat and walked over to the Corsica. The doors were not locked on the rented Corsica but reaching under the floor mat he found no key—not in the ashtray, not up in the visor.

Okay, he reasoned. *If Lew Stucky had the Corsica's keys on him, where would he have gone with them?* He decided this was the kind of question Eddie Vango would be asking himself if he were here. One thing he didn't want to do was get caught hot-wiring the little rental car and go to jail. The thought gave him a sour feeling inside.

All right, break it all down, he told himself, his inner voice sounding a lot like Vango's. He slipped back inside the Mercedes, up front, in the driver's seat

Who does Lew Stucky know here?

Delbert thought about it while he lit a Camel and blew out a stream of smoke. *Well, no one ...?* he decided, feeling a little let down by his findings.

All right, go deeper! He pressed his mental capacity. *What else ...?* He smoked the Camel and thought more intently on the matter. Bruiser hopped down in the seat beside him.

The gambling debt ...?

He considered the money Victor Trio still owed Stanley the Pole. Eddie had said he was concerned Stucky would start poking his nose in where it didn't belong. Delbert finished the Camel and lit a fresh one from its burning tip. He crushed the butt in the ashtray. Beside him, Bruiser had plopped down and began licking his paws and rubbing his bushy head.

"You look like a hedgehog …." Delbert shook his head, took a few draws on the cigarette and straightened behind the wheel.

Okay ….

Without trying to move Bruiser from his spot beside him, Delbert scooted out and shut the driver's door, which made a loud banging noise in its out-of-line hinges. Pushing Charlie Betz over onto the rear seat, he stuffed the medical supplies into a storage pocket on a seat back, got out and closed the rear door, with an even *louder 'bang.'* The sound startled the cat. He sprang up but took a stance in the middle of the passenger's seat.

Back in the driver's seat, Delbert checked the time on the dash clock.

Here we go ….

He started the Mercedes, pulled it out of the parking space and rolled away, the big car wobbly and maimed, rattling like a large bag of scrap iron. He didn't recognize Leone Morez streaking past him in the J W Home Cleaning van. Morez drove like a man on a mission, making his way to the pay phones set up in the lobby of a Heritage Suites Motel over on US Hwy 1.

Reaching the motel, Morez walked to a wide long hallway that had been constructed to accommodate over a dozen pay phones along one wall. For the benefit of traveling sales reps each phone station provided a fold-down seat and a long counter to support their client's needs.

At six p.m., Leone Morez found every phone seat full, every line in use. But he was undeterred. He walked up close and stood almost against the back of one of the users and stared down. He bumped slightly against the man's shoulder. The man turned enough to look up at Morez looming over him, a strange unreadable expression on his severe face.

"Uh … I'll have to get back to you on that, Ms. Sullivan," the man said into the receiver. He quickly hung up the phone, snatched up his notes and small calculator and got up out of there–no eye contact. Taking his time, Morez stared hard back and forth at the person on either side of him, until they each swiveled on their seats and turned away.

When the woman on his right stood and left the phone, he took off his slippers and laid them there. With an international call card in hand, he dialed the operator, casting a malevolent sidelong stare at a person venturing close to his shoes.

In the Netherlands—Bloemendaal in West Amsterdam, Paulson Phillipe Burge sat in his office inside his country estate, smoking a mild aromatic Cuban cigar. When his private phone rang, he stared at it for a moment as to say *are-you-kidding?* Then he laid his cigar in a marble ashtray and sighed and picked up the intruding receiver.

"Yes," he said quietly.

"It's me, sir," said Morez. "is it safe to talk?"

"One second." The line clicked as Burge reached over and flipped on a shutout switch. Music filled the room, not too loud, just loud enough to break up any unwelcome listeners on either end of the line.

"It's after midnight here," Burge said flatly, not using Morez's name.

"I'm sorry," said Morez, "I couldn't call you earlier."

"I understand," said Burge. "I take it you called to find out where your office supplies are?" Before Morez could answer, Burge said, "I'm happy to say you supplies are in the usual place, awaiting your approval."

"Aw. Great!" Morez breathed relief. The shipment had arrived. He knew the *usual place* meant an old scrap and salvage yard where Indian River flowed into the ocean. *This is good!* He thought about Jill Wary and her RATS–he smiled, thinking about telling her.

Who's your daddy now, 'Jilly ...?'

"Then everything is the same as always?" Morez said.

"Except for one thing," Burge said coolly. "The bond certificates you take with you will have a release date on them. The release date will be three days after delivery."

"Whoa! Sir! I don't think our friends will go along with this. It's never gone this way."

"Don't mention it unless they bring it up. If they bring it up, explain that this is the new regulations on how bearer bonds must be handled from now on. They'll understand. I have six *professional* friends headed there to lend you a hand, in case anybody doesn't understand."

Six professional friends .... Morez thought about it.

"All right, that will help," he replied. "Once the supplies are unloaded and laying on the dock with nowhere else to go, *yes!* They *might* go along with it," he added. "But if I'm the one who took possession, I will be the one they hold responsible if they don't get their money. I don't have to tell you what will happen to me."

"They *will* get their money, all of it!" said Burge, He caught himself short of revealing exactly how much money they were talking about. His voice turned a little strained, louder. He realized their conversation was not being as discreet as they had started out.

"Of course, if you think you cannot handle this, tell me now, so I can make other arrangements!" he said.

Morez paused, took a breath and calmed himself.

"I'll handle it," he said. "Just let me know when I can pick up the supplies."

"My friends are headed your way even now," Burge said. "Call tomorrow, I will give you the time." He paused, then added under his breath in a friendlier tone, "When we complete this, there will be an extra *twenty* coming to you."

Twenty-thousand .... That helped, a little. Unless this greedy prick meant a twenty-dollar bill would arrive in the mail. He wouldn't put it past him.

Before Morez could reply, Burge hung up.

Morez became a mad man. He spit on the receiver, once, twice, three times.

"Fuck you!" he shouted. Then he caught himself and checked to make sure Burge was no longer there.

"Hello, hello …," he repeated in a meek voice.

Okay, good. The line was dead. He jammed the receiver roughly back on its cradle and looked around at other users who sat, and stood, staring at him, aghast. *And fuck you too!* He shouted silently. He picked up the wet receiver, scrubbed it noticeably back and forth on the crotch of his trousers and hung it up. He put his slippers on and left.

Lew Stucky made a few passes through the parking lot of Oceana Princess II. When he'd settled on a loosely thought-out plan, he parked his green Pontiac, which he'd had his new friend, Nurse Jennifer, drive him to, and which he'd started with a spare key from his wallet. He parked the Pontiac as close to the lobby as he could get in case he needed to get to it quick and make a slick getaway.

He'd left the Corsica at the hospital parking lot. He could have hot-wired it, but the truth is, he thought, he missed his big comfortable Pontiac. Nobody he ever knew would drive a punk-looking little Corsica on their way to beat the living hell out of somebody. He patted the big Pontiac's steering wheel and smiled to himself.

Already drunk, and high on painkillers Nurse Jennifer had sold him he raised the half-empty bottle of Smirnoff vodka lying beside him. He took a long drink, capped the bottle and stared at it for a moment.

He loved vodka, he reminded himself, recalling times he'd sat and drank it for hours–he went blank for a minute, reminiscing. Then he shook his head. *Forget that ...!*

He cut himself short, reached over into the back seat and picked up a K-Mart bag with a baseball bat sticking up from it. Getting out of the car, he walked unsteadily to the lobby of the building complex. This wasn't the time or place for thinking about anything except for what he came here for–one thing and one thing only. He was going to collect the thirty-thousand dollars Victor Trio owed Stanley the Pole, and beat the living hell out of Ian Lambert for causing his sunburn, which wasn't burning so bad right now with his vodka and painkillers raging inside him. All right, that was two things. But *so what?* He knew why he was here.

He crossed an empty lobby and rode an elevator to the fifteenth floor, remembering where Vango told him he'd found Wright Way Venture Capital when they were here before. Standing outside the door to the address Vango had mentioned, he reached down and clasped a hand around the thick end of the bat, crushing the paper bag around it.

Using the knob end of the bat, he knocked on the door soundly, a good seven raps, not terribly loud. But it was loud enough to get the attention of the four men inside who sat stoned on cocaine and hash. They stared at the door wide-eyed.

"What the hell, Joe!" said one of the three men Morez had brought in to fill the gaps that killing Cuban-Russian Hector Chebreski and Bones leaving had created. "You said this place is cool!" He instinctively jerked a .45 Charter Bulldog revolver from his belt.

"It is cool, Dennis," Joe Paso said, waving Dennis Inman back to the sofa. "Who's there?" he called out. As he spoke, he walked quietly across the floor and stood to one side of the door and looked out through the peephole. Stucky stood wobbly and round in the magnified glass circle.

"State police," Lew Stucky called out. His voice had a drunken slurred sound to it.

Joe Paso laughed. The others started grabbing up the hash and a bag of cocaine and looked all around for a hiding place. Joe Paso laughed harder, bending at the waist.

"Check yourselves out," he said, holding his sides.

"It's not a cop." He looked back at the door. "Who's there?" he asked again.

"State police," Stucky repeated.

"What *state?*" Joe Paso cracked himself up. The others laughed too.

Stucky didn't answer. Instead he rapped on the door harder with the knob of the bat. "Open up or we'll knock it down!" he shouted.

We'll knock it down? Hunh-uh.

Laughing hard, Joe Paso held up one finger and said to the others, "It's one guy. He looks wasted. He's carrying a ball bat in a paper bag."

"A ball bat?" A new man, Ozzie Decker, from over on the gulf side suddenly took interest. "Hey, let him in. Let's check him out."

The third new man, Bobby Tomes, a black man from Louisville, tossed the bag of coke back onto the coffee table and walked over and stood beside the door, a gun in hand, hanging down his side. He carried a blue magic marker behind his ear.

"You're covered, Joe," he said. "Let this fool in."

As the door swung open wide, Stucky straightened up and walked in, convincing himself that he wasn't as drunk or as high as the alcohol and pills were making him feel. He knew that didn't make much sense, but his sunburn wasn't hurting–that was a plus. He stopped inside the door and looked all around as someone shut the door behind him. The men were standing, forming a wide circle around him. Two of them held guns, one with a silencer on it.

Be cool ....

Stucky let the K-Mart bag fall to the floor, the

ball bat still in hand. He pointed the knob end of the bat around the room, taking in everyone except Bobby Tomes, the man behind him.

"Hey, you're not a state cop," said Joe Paso.

"No, I'm not. I'm looking for Victor Trio, Ian the Lamb—or Sheep—or whatever you call him. And I want thirty-thousand bucks!"

"Why you want Lambert?" Joe Paso.

"I just want to"—*he belched vodka*—"get my hands on the Sheep, really bad!" Stucky said. "The rest of you"—*he belched again*—"clear out of here." He took a step to the side, to allow them an open exit route. The four men broke up laughing.

"He wants to get his hands on the *Sheep!*" one of the gun holders, Dennis Inman, said. He wagged a silenced .32mm.

"Can I shoot him, Joe? Won't nobody hear it," he said.

"Are you going to clean up the mess?" Paso asked. "And get rid of his dead ass?"

At the mention of clean up, Inman let the gun sag down his side.

"Oh," he said.

"Yeah, that's what I thought," said Paso. He turned to Stucky. "The men you're looking for are gone. I saw one of them leave here myself." Joe Paso held back a smile, picturing Lambert drop down the side of the building, leaving a shoe in Paso's hand. "I heard about the thirty-thousand Trio owed, but we don't have it." He gestured around the room. "Right, *hombres?*"

Everybody shook their heads. They didn't have it.

"There, see?" Paso said. "Those two guys are gone,

and there's no money here. Victor owed a bookie some money. Who did the Lamb owe anything to?"

"He owes me," said Stucky, "for causing me this sunburn. I'm going to beat him senseless."

The men tried hard to keep themselves from falling out laughing. Paso raised a hand silencing them.

Stucky felt a hand on his back and swung his head around. Bobby Tomes stepped back, his hands chest high in a show of peace.

Stucky was feeling half sober, more in charge of himself. He had this. "So, I want thirty bucks from Trio, and I want Lambert the Sheep, right here, right now, or I start busting everybody's head!"

That sounded good, he thought. He turned the ball bat and bounced the knob end on the palm of his hand. The men in front of him fell silent, starting to take him serious. But he turned his back long enough to wave Bobby Tomes over to stand with the others. The three men saw a sign Tomes had taped to his back, which read: I FUCK SHEEP.

Seeing the sign, the three men broke up again. This time even more so. Ozzie Decker fell out backward on the sofa, holding both his sides. *"Stop it!"* he laughed, clearly out of control. Even Joe Paso couldn't keep it in.

Quietly, Bobby Tomes stepped around from behind Stucky, who didn't understand what was so funny.

"Hey," said Tomes, "you're holding that bat all wrong." He handed Stucky a gun to hold on him. "Give it here, let me show you."

"You'll *show* me?" Stucky gave him a hard-skeptical stare.

"Yeah," said Tomes, "I'm from Louisville." He

reached a hand out for the bat, "I've seen where these bats are made. I played *Little League* growing up."

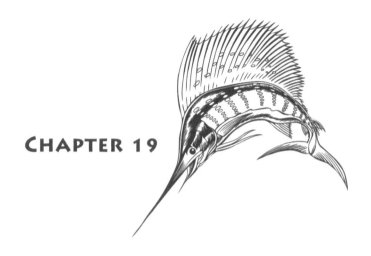

CHAPTER 19

Delbert Moss had swung by the Surfside and saw the empty spot where the big green Pontiac had sat. It was gone. *Bingo ...!* Delbert knew he was on the right track.

Twenty minutes later, cruising through the Oceana Princess II parking lot, he found the green Pontiac with Illinois license plates and pulled into a spot four spaces down from it. He had been to Wright Way Venture Capital twice before with a couple of Lambert's gunmen. He pulled up the big .45 from beside him, racked the slide a fraction of an inch, just enough to see the brass bullet casing in its chamber. He was good to go.

He got out of the ragged rattling Mercedes and stood half-hidden by the open car door. He slipped the gun behind his belt, smoothed his new tropical print silk shirt down over it, and closed the door. The sun had blazed in the sky all day like a cutting torch. Now it had started melting down into Indian River out front of the complex.

"I'll be right back," he said to Charlie Betz who sat slumped over in the rear seat, barely conscious. The big cat crawled deep up under the front seat, out of the sun.

Delbert felt only the faintest whisper of a cooling breeze on his way to the lobby. But he was grateful for the chilled blast of air-conditioning that welcomed him when he opened one of the double glass doors. The cool air continued following him, into an elevator and up to the fifteenth floor.

Yes, this is the place .... He absently touched his shirt where beneath it stood the big .45, locked, loaded and cocked. In his hip pocket he carried the brass knuckles Eddie Vango had given him.

The heat had returned harsh and unapologetic as he stepped off the elevator and walked along an outside tile walkway overlooking the river. At the door he stood for a few seconds listening to muffled laughter. On a hunch he reached down, turned the doorknob and found it unlocked.

Good enough ...!

Delbert shoved the door open and stepped inside, stalking forward, the big gun held out arm's length.

"Oh shit," said a voice.

Across the room, close to the doors leading onto the balcony, two men stood partially bowed over Lew Stucky who sat in a wrought iron balcony chair. His face was swollen and bloody; his wrists were duct taped to the chair arms. Two other men sat on the edge of a sofa leaning over a bag of dope. Lines of white powder had been formed up and lay ready for use. All four men looked at Delbert Moss, Joe Paso and Dennis Inman straightening from over Stucky.

The other two stood up from the sofa. Two guns lay of the glass-topped coffee table. "Get away from the guns," Delbert said, leaving no room for discussion. The two looked at Joe Paso, then stepped away from the guns, the coffee table, the bag of dope. Paso studied Delbert's face.

"Hey, I know you! You worked for the Lamb!"

"Not anymore," said Delbert. He saw Paso try to work his way in closer step at a time. "Don't any of you come any closer," he warned.

Joe Paso stopped. Bobby Tomes took a step away from Stucky's chair. "So, what is it you want here, man? You with this guy?" He nodded down at Stucky. "And he left you waiting down in the car?" He took another step closer. "As *hot* as it is?"

"I'm not going to tell you again to stop." He ran his left hand into his pocket and came up with the brass knuckles in place. He held his left hand half-cocked, ready, and gestured toward Stucky. He told Tomes, "Cut him loose."

"How am I going to cut him loose? Tomes said, starting to step closer again. "Oh, I get it. I'm a *black man* so I must be carrying a knife, a shank? I'm the *shank man?* Is that right?"

Paso and the other two moved forward along behind Tomes. Delbert didn't answer. Not until Tomes got much closer. Keeping close watch on Delbert's left hand, the big brass knuckles, he said, "That's some racist shit! I think you need to—"

Without moving his cocked left hand, Delbert swiped the big .45 across his face, full swing. Tomes stumbled sidelong, diagonally, and fell backwards over a lamp table. The lamp crashed on the floor. The other three men stopped cold. Delbert slipped the unused brass knuckles back into his pocket.

To Joe Paso, he said, "You, bring me that gun with the silencer on it—" He pointed at the coffee table. "—by the barrel." Paso stepped over, picked the gun up by its long barrel and brought it to him.

"Now cut him loose." He nodded again at Stucky. As Paso walked over taking a knife from his pocket, Delbert called over to Stucky. "Are you able to get out of here?"

"I— I think so," Stucky said, his lips swollen, his eyes, his nose. He tried to push up from the chair but couldn't.

"You," Delbert said to Paso, "Help him up."

"Hunh-uh, no way," said Paso. "He's all bloody!"

"All-righty then," Delbert said. He aimed the silenced .32 and shot Paso in the leg, right above the knee. Paso fell, letting out a loud yelp. Delbert swung the .32 at Ozzie Decker standing beside Inman, both with their hands raised. "Go help him up. I'm not telling you again."

"Whoa, I've got it," said Ozzie, already hurrying over to Stucky, pulling him to his feet. "There now," he said to the battered drunken Lew Stucky. "You want some ice or something?"

"Help him over here," Delbert said. "We're taking him down to the car."

Delbert wagged the silenced .32 at Paso grimacing on the floor and Inman with his hands still raised, Bobby Tomes grounded and trying to sit up. Ozzie led Stucky to the door, helped him out and along the walkway. "Anybody wants to get knee-capped or cause me to shoot your friend here—" He pointed the .32 at them, then at Ozzie Decker. "—let me catch you following us."

The three entered the otherwise empty elevator. No one else stepped onto the elevator as it descended to the lobby. Delbert kept the silenced .32 concealed down along his thigh. He positioned Ozzie Decker in front of Stucky, keeping the hapless Lew Stucky's bloody face out of sight. In the late afternoon, foot traffic in and around the complex had fallen. Delbert looked all around as the three arrived at the Mercedes and Ozzie helped Stucky into the back seat.

"Can I go now?" Ozzie asked.

"I don't think so," said Delbert. "Check out your pals." Delbert directed his attention to Dennis Inman trying to stand out of sight near the lobby doors. Bobby Tomes had awakened and stood beside Inman with a towel against his swollen face.

"These sumbitches!" He looked at Delbert. "Mister, I'm not going to take a bullet for these meatheads. If I go with you, are you going to end up shooting me anyway?"

Delbert thought about it.

"It all depends," Delbert said, motioning him to the front passenger's seat. "Are you going to tell me what's gone on since I left Lambert?"

Ozzie looked him up and down, noting the silk shirt, the gabardine slacks, nice Italian loafers.

"I heard Joe Paso say you worked for Lambert?"

"That's right, I did," said Delbert. "Like I said, 'I *don't* anymore.'"

"I get that," Ozzie nodded. "I don't even work for Lambert. I work for Leone Morez. Do you know about him?"

"I do," said Delbert.

"I'm not as high up with Morez as you must've

been with Lambert," Ozzie said. "I doubt if I know anything you don't know already."

"Tell me about the big shipment I hear is coming in," said Delbert. "I don't see Lambert, or Trio, or even Old Bones hanging around. Instead I see more Morez men like yourself. I figure something's about to happen right?"

"Am I going to get in trouble telling you this?" Ozzie asked, still checking him out, trying to decide if Delbert Moss was some sort of boss.

"What do I look like, a cop?" Delbert asked, putting a little impatience in there.

"No, not really," said Ozzie. "Just being careful here." He paused, then said, "From what I get, it sounds like the big shipment everybody's waiting on has arrived. It's waiting out offshore."

"Yeah, that's what I'm thinking, too," Delbert said, playing it out like a couple of work pals talking shop.

Ozzie relaxed a little; he took a rolled-up bag of reefer from inside his shirt and took out a pack of rolling papers.

"You mind?" he asked.

"Help yourself," said Delbert with a slight shrug. "Don't forget the top is down."

Ozzie Decker looked all around.

"Yeah, I noticed," he said. "I've been wanting to ask you. What the hell happened to your ride, man? This thing looks really rough."

"I know it does," said Delbert. He nodded back at Charlie Betz in the rear seat. "This guy fired a rocket launcher in the garage, caused the roof to fall in."

"Bummer, man," said Ozzie.

In a boiling mid-day heat the flight from Grand Cayman touched down, landed smooth and easily on a runway with heat wavering up from it. The big jet coasted in close to one of many terminal walkways and stopped. A motorized mobile ramp rolled in and planted itself against the jet's door. In moments passengers filed down the ramp and followed the walkway through the simmering heat.

Leslie Wright carried her travel bag by its strap over her shoulder, her right hand lying loosely on top. In the bottom of the bag lay a stack of unsigned bearer bonds in the face value of two million and thirty thousand dollars. Beside her, less than a foot away, Eddie Vango carried a much larger black canvas luggage bag. Inside the large bag stacks of cash amounted to one million seven hundred thousand dollars.

Vango rolled the big bag alongside him on a fold-out baggage carrier provided by the airline. Inside the terminal as the two walked along toward the front entrance, Leslie called her home phone one more time trying to reach Delbert Moss. On the fifth ring she gave up and dropped the phone back into a pocket of her bag.

"I suppose we will take a taxi," she said, "unless you'd like to rent a car and drop it off in Jensen?"

Vango was looking away where six men walked along in twos, each of them moving along with a confident almost military demeanor.

"Eddie? Did you hear me?" she asked.

"I heard you," Vango said, catching up. "Yes, we'll take a rental from here to Jensen Beach." He looked at his large luggage bag. "Maybe even a van."

But as they walked out front and started to turn in

the direction of the car rental station, Vango gazed along the pickup lane.

"Oh, man!" he said. "Look what's coming here."

Leslie's gave a look of disbelief at her smoke-streaked, dented, rattling Mercedes ambling along lopsided in their direction. Other people stopped what they were doing long enough to give the car and its three ragged, mauled, bandaged passengers a dubious look as they passed by.

Leslie Wright spoke haltingly under her breath.

"Is that …? Is that … *my car?*" she managed to say.

"I'm afraid so," said Vango. He saw Delbert at the wheel. Behind the rear seat, a remnant of the hard-convertible top, battered and torn stuck up a foot from its storage space under the truck lid. "No wonder we haven't been able to reach Delbert. It looks like he's had his hands full."

In the rear seat, Ozzie Decker sat stoned, his head bobbing. Flanking him, Charlie Betz leaning slumped on one side, Stucky on the other, both of their bandaging looked much the same. The big cat stood on the edge of the front seat, his paws planted on the dash, supporting him. He stared forward through the spider-cracked windshield.

Vango and Leslie Wright stood in silence as if in awe as Delbert eased the Mercedes to a halt at the curbing in front of them. Delbert looked up at Leslie as if she would be the one he needed to talk to. She stood staring down at the car, the cat, the three disheveled semi-human passengers and Delbert Moss.

"What, happened, to my car, Delbert?" she said.

"Okay, I know it looks bad," Delbert said. "I mean it *is* bad, but—"

"What happened, Delbert?" she said again.

"I'm not going to sugarcoat it," Delbert said, looking back and forth between her and Vango. "A rocket launcher went off. It blew up your garage and tore up through your house. The garage roof fell on the car. It was a lot worse, but I straightened it up some."

"A rocket launcher," said the woman. "Okay now, Delbert, what really happened?"

"Lee," Vango said quietly, "I don't think he's joking. I left a rocket launcher in the trunk. They can be tricky."

"Boy I'll say," said Delbert.

"Is my house still standing?" Leslie asked. She looked at her ragged-out Mercedes. Her eyes got teary.

"Hey, take it easy, Lee," Vango said. He shook the baggage cart handle in his hand. "I will *buy* you a new Mercedes, Okay?"

Delbert saw him smile. He saw Leslie Wright smile too.

"Sorry, Eddie," she said. "I lost it for a second."

Watching the two of them, the big luggage bag on the luggage carrier, Delbert smiled.

"Uh-oh, it sounds like things went well," he said.

Vango looked at Ozzie Decker, Stucky and Charlie Betz in the rear seat, Stucky, knocked out cold on painkillers. Not taking any chance on being heard, he said quietly, "Let's get to the motel; he gestured a nod toward the trunk. "Have we got room in the trunk for these bags?" he asked.

"If we don't, we'll make room," Delbert said,

cutting the engine off and hitting the trunk lid switch. As he stepped out to help load the heavy bag, he said to Vango, "I'm sorry I didn't call you, Eddie. The Mercedes phone stopped working. Her hand-held phone wasn't connecting. I started showing up here yesterday every time a flight came in from the Cayman Island, hoping I'd be here—"

"Wait a minute, Delbert." Vango cut him off. "You have been here every flight to make sure you picked us up?"

"That's right," Delbert said. "I had a lot to tell you, but my call couldn't get through." He nodded at the rear seat where Stucky sat knocked out on painkillers. "I found Lew Stucky at Trio's condo. Some gunmen were going to kill him. So, I got him out of there. I brought one of the gunmen with us." He pointed at the back seat. "He's Ozzie Decker. He's been filling me in on things."

"Wow, Delbert, you really have been a busy guy," Vango said, adjusting the big bag into the trunk space.

Delbert asked, "What's in the bag? You didn't take a bag with you."

Vango looked all around then leaned in close even though there was no one in hearing distance. "Money, Delbert," he whispered. "Enough to last all three of us for the rest of our lives."

Delbert looked stunned.

Vango followed up, saying, "We got to get this to a bank, right away, set up some deposit boxes. Lee's, mine, and *yours.*"

Delbert didn't ask how much. He just said, "All right, Eddie, we're on our way."

PART III

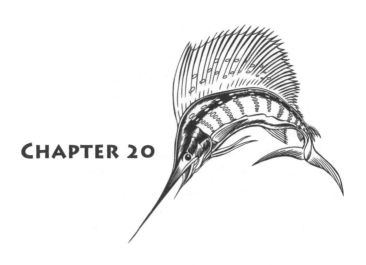

CHAPTER 20

Paulson Phillipe Burge looked down from his office window at a skiff of snow blowing across the city. He felt a great sense of relief from having stepped away from the big cocaine shipment due to change hands on a shipping dock tomorrow in Jensen Beach, Florida. The next worse thing than losing money on a large high-risk business venture was to only make a small profit on that high-risk venture. Only amateurs did business so poorly. He was not an amateur.

As soon as he suspected the Wright Way bearer bonds might be short, and the American deal going sour right before everyone's eyes, he acted quickly. He contacted his accountants, comptrollers, international attorneys, and yes, even his personal physic regarding what would be his best move. *And here's how it will go,* he recounted to himself, making sure every avenue of the deal was covered.

Of the forty-million-dollar investment the deal called for, only twelve million was his actual share. The rest had come from investors globally, some legitimate businessmen, some cutthroats and criminals. The legitimate investors, the people who'd had purchases of low rate junk bonds slipped into their portfolios through brokers working on commission, would bear the brunt of the loss.

How much? Who knew? He sure didn't. He smiled faintly, glad he will have dodged the bullet and walked away as everyone else scrambled to explain what had happened. En masse, these investors will lose the bulk of twenty million dollars, all on paper of course. Each investor would have to balance and recoup their losses as best they, or their investment wizards, could.

As for himself, Paulson Phllipe Burge would have the loss of his twelve million spread out over several other incorporated companies he owned, in part or in total. His money would be written on taxes as cost for updating properties, depreciating machinery, etc., etc. With taxes and property gains, instead of losing twelve million, his accountants had already calculated he would actually realize eighteen million—*not profit per se.* But *yes, profit* by any other name. His overall worth would be eighteen million dollars higher than it was before. He liked that. This cocaine business was changing fast. It was time he got out. The South Americans wanted this cocaine business so bad, let them have it. It made sense. After all they had the product in their own back yards.

He had considered, at first thought, that he might warn Morez and his six best men what was coming, but he decided against it. Let them find out on their own. Odds were, as soon as the South Americans took over, they would be hiring his men, those of them who lived through the transition. He couldn't risk telling Morez and his top men. What if they someday told their new employers what he'd done? No-no. *Must be prudent,* he cautioned himself. *Let them work it out.*

This was good, he decided. *A win win ....* The sort of business outcome he always enjoyed.

He relaxed for a moment watching the snow swirl on the wind, the stone-tiled walkway, the rows of plush evergreens along the property line. When the quiet soft ring of his private phone called him to his desk, he sighed and stepped over to it. *And now to business ....*

"Yes?" He said into the receiver.

"It's me," was all Morez said.

All Burge said in turn was, "Tomorrow. The same time as usual."

"All hands on deck, sir?" Morez inquired.

"Yes," said Burge. Then without another word, he hung up his phone.

Alright! Alright! Morez cheered to himself, pumping a victory fist in the air. Before even hanging up the receiver, he called Jill Wray on her business number and passed along the information. He read excitement and elation in her voice as relayed the information to her.

"Are we good?" he asked.

"Oh my, yes, Leone," she said. "We are good."

Now, who's your daddy ...?

Morez grinned to himself.

"Can we get together in an hour, hash everything out?" Jill Wray asked. "Maybe a few drinks?"

"Sure, we can do that," said Morez, keeping it brief the way Burge had handled his call only a moment ago. "Pick me up at Oceana. I'll be waiting at Wright Way."

"Okay, Leone, I'm coming," Jill said.

"Good, I'll be waiting for you," said Morez.

Jill immediately called Police Sergeant Dan Hicky on the telephone in his garage.

"Ten o'clock tomorrow, it's going down, Dan," she said secretively.

"Who is this?" Dan asked calmly.

"It's me, Jill Wray, Sergeant Dan," she said, surprised he didn't recognize her voice.

"Okay, sure, *Jilly*. Copy that," he said, seeming to catch up. "So, ten o'clock tomorrow it is. I'll be bringing Captain Hirsh with me. I think he wants to see his name on some big-drug paperwork."

"Okay!" she said. "The more the merrier on something this big." She waited a second then said, "I hope we won't have to deal with DEA on this one, will we?"

"I don't think DEA has a clue. I've played my hand close to my chest. I know you've done the same."

"Yes, I have," said Jill Wray. "I've got all of my people on a need-to-know basis. They will hear something about it today, but the details they won't hear about until first thing in the morning."

"Okay, good work, *Jilly*, thank you," said Hicky. "I'll fill my men in on it. They'll be able to wear their tactical gear. That's always good for morale."

They both hung up.

On the way to one of the larger banks along the Treasure Coast, Delbert pulled the battered suet-smeared Mercedes over into a Denny's Restaurant parking lot. He gave Ozzie Decker two fifty-dollar bills and sent him on his way. Charlie Betz, still unconscious, leaned slumped to the side.

"Sorry I couldn't be more help," Ozzie said. "Everybody is waiting on a big shipment, but nobody who knows anything is talking about it."

"I understand," said Delbert. Vango listened from the back seat, watching how Delbert Moss handled himself. As Ozzie got out and walked away, Vango moved from the back seat and sat up front in the passenger seat. Delbert let out a breath and shook his head. Behind them, in the Corsica they'd picked up from the hospital parking lot, Leslie Wright sat with the AC going full blast, the cat sitting beside her, his fur blowing back.

"Well, that's the bad news, Delbert," said Vango. "But here is the *good news.* We don't care!"

"We don't?" said Delbert.

"No," said Vango. He looked around at Charlie Betz and Lew Stucky sprawled in the back seat, gauze-covered. Lowering his voice Vango added, "As soon as we've got our money tucked away safe somewhere, as far as I'm concerned, we're done here."

"Yeah, I like that," Delbert said with a smile of satisfaction.

Leaving the restaurant parking lot, they traveled North along US 1 and pulled into the large, shaded parking lot of a South Eastern Savings & Trust Bank. Leslie pulled in beside them and kept the engine running, blowing cold air. The big cat stood up in her lap staring at them.

"Before we go in, Delbert," Vango said, "this is for you." He handed him a bound stack of cash—$10,000 dollars stamped on the band around it. Delbert took it, looked at it and almost laughed. But he caught himself.

"Wait!" His expression turned serious. "You're not

joking, are you?"

"No," said Vango. "You've stuck with us, we've done everything we needed to do. Now it's payday."

"Oh, man!" Delbert said. His face went pale and flushed. "I can't take this much, Eddie. I don't deserve it!"

"Delbert, look at me. Listen to me," Vango said, nodding at the stack of hundred-dollar bills. "The ten bucks is walk-around cash."

Delbert stared with curiously as Vango took a folded piece of paper from his shirt pocket, opened it and handed it to him.

"I want you to know how much you're getting before we take the bag into the bank."

Delbert stared down at the piece of paper.

"Is this … I mean does this mean?" He swallowed hard, tried again. "Am I reading this right? It's—"

"Two million bucks, Delbert," Vango finished for him.

"Oh *my God* ...." This time he whispered. He stared blank-faced at Vango. "Eddie, why?"

Why ...?

Vango stared at him for a moment. "It's Happy Birthday, Merry Christmas, and Trick or Treat, all at once, Delbert."

Delbert held the small piece of paper up to his side window for Leslie to see it from the Corsica. She smiled and nodded, with no idea what he was showing her. *That's okay,* Vango thought. He had told her how much he was giving Delbert. She volunteered paying half of it.

"Okay," said Vango, "let's go take care of business."

They helped Stucky and Betz move over into the

Corsica where the cat had hopped into the blowing AC and wasn't about to give up any of the cold breeze. Then they closed the car door and carrying the large luggage bag full of cash from the Mercedes' trunk, they walked across the smoldering parking lot and inside the bank.

When the three of them came out of the bank an hour later, they each had their own rented deposit box, stuffed with cash and bearer bonds, passbook account books, and a book of temporary checks for their brand-new checking accounts. Delbert carried a folded roll of cash in his trouser pocket and kept his hand on it. Halfway to the Corsica, Delbert stopped, took a deep breath and let it out slowly. He looked all around.

"That was easy as pie," he said. "I don't know how I thought I would feel," he said. "But now that I've got all this money, I can't say that I feel any different."

"You will, Delbert," said Vango. "Give it time."

Leslie Wright smiled, agreeing with Vango as they walked on, her hand resting on his forearm.

Inside the Corsica, Stucky stirred as the car door opened and closed. The big cat growled and refused to move out of the way.

"Where's the other guy?" Vango asked, seeing that Charlie Betz had left the car. "What's that smell?"

Stucky raised his bandaged face and spoke in a barely audible voice.

"He got out … left. Said he couldn't take anymore." He gestured his head at Bruiser.

Delbert made a sour face.

"Bruiser, did you do that?" Vango asked. The cat only stared at them.

"Aw-Man!" said Vango, rolling a window down quickly.

Delbert opened the driver's door and rolled down the other front window. Stucky managed to raise his head enough to look back and forth.

"What has the cat been eating?" Vango looked at Leslie Wright.

"He is not *my* cat, Eddie," she said defensively. "I don't know what he eats."

"I've got to … get out of here," Stucky said, coming around some. He turned and pushed himself up out of the car and leaned against its side.

"Take it easy, Lew," said Vango. He stepped out of the car and helped Stucky steady himself. "You've taken a hell of a beating."

"Ha," Stucky said, coming around more, "you should see the other guys." He looked bleary-eyed at Delbert who stepped out of the other front door and walked around to them. "Ain't that right, *Surfer Boy?"* he said, eying Delbert's other new silk shirt, one covered with surf boards and surfers on it.

Delbert didn't answer, but Vango could see he wasn't happy with Stucky's wisecracks.

"He's still drunk, Delbert," Vango said. "Don't sweat it."

"I don't," Delbert said.

"Drunk? Hell, I ain't drunk," Stucky said. "I've got a hell of a hangover, is all."

Vango took a patient breath.

"So, Lew, are you sober enough to fly home today?" he asked.

"Yep," Stucky said, "but I ain't going home until

get Stanley's money."

"Good news, Lew," Vango said, He raised a sealed manila envelope from behind his belt. "I got Stanley's thirty-bucks yesterday. All you've got to do is deliver it to him. Are you able to do that?"

"Are you kidding me? Hell yes," said Stucky. "You and *Surfer Boy* here get me on a plane. I'm out of here."

"Easy, Delbert," Vango said under his breath, seeing Delbert taking more than he should have to from a jerk like Stucky.

"I'm good, Eddie," Delbert said. Hearing him, Stucky looked him up and down.

"Who are you, *Surfer Boy?*" he asked.

"He's the man who kept Lambert's gunmen from turning you into a foot stool."

Stucky straightened up a little.

"All right, then," he said turning to Delbert. "I suppose I'll have to buy you a beer."

Delbert stayed patient. All he wanted to do was get this guy out of town. He looked at Vango and Leslie Wright, then said to Stucky, "Soon as I get to Chicago, I'll look you up, first thing."

"Do that," said Stucky. "The beer is all on me." Something dawned on him. "Say. What about my car?" he asked Vango.

"We'll send it up to you, Lew. Let's get you to the airport, take Stanley's money to him ...."

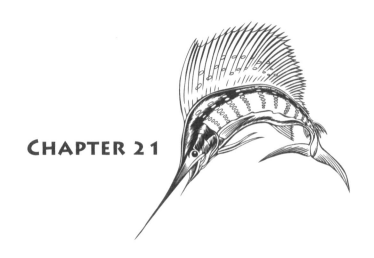

CHAPTER 21

After taking Lew Stucky to the airport, walking him to the departure lounge and watching him walk onto the boarding walkway, Vango stopped at a row of pay phones and called Stanley the Pole in Chicago on his private line. As he waited for Stanley to answer he watched Stucky's flight roll past the large observation window and move out of sight onto a runway.

"It's me," is all he said when the Pole picked up the receiver.

"I've been wondering what's keeping you guys," Stanley said, first thing. "I hope you've picked up my package for me?"

"I've got your package, just like you wanted," Vango said. "I just put Lew on a jet with it." Before Stanley could ask anything else, Vango gave him a whole quick made-up rundown of events.

"Trio took off," Vango said. "Good thing is, he left your package with Lambert. Next thing, Lambert disappeared. But I got the package from a guy that works for them. When I saw Lew wasn't fit for travel, I turned the package into something safer to carry."

"You can talk, Eddie," Stanley said. "This line is clean here, for now anyway."

"Okay," said Vango, "I turned the money into bearer bonds. Lew had been eating pain pills, shooting vodka. I thought it might be safer than having him carry cash—"

"Yeah, good thinking," Stanley said.

Vango noted a light suspicion in his tone. "But why are you still there?"

"Okay, the thing is, I met a woman down here."

"I see," said Stanley. "So, you want to hang there a couple days longer?"

"Yes, at least," said Vango. "Unless there's something there that can't wait?"

"Naw, it's quiet here," said Stanley, "take all the time you want."

"Good," Vango said, "I'm going to do just that."

"You need any cash?" Stanley asked.

"I could use some later, maybe," Vango said, just to play everything down. "But I'm okay for now."

"So all right," Stanley said, recapping, "Lew's headed back, you collected the full thirty bucks. You're staying awhile to get your bells rang. That's it?"

"There it is." Vango smiled to himself.

"This thing didn't go as bad as I thought it might," Stanley said.

"Naw, nothing to it, Stan," Vango said. "Catch you on the replay."

"On the replay …," said Stanley the Pole.

Leaving the airport, Vango drove to the battered Mercedes to a car rental satellite office in Jensen Beach. Out front at the curbing Delbert, Leslie Wright, and Bruiser the cat waited out of the heat in a newly rented Midnight Blue Lincoln Town Car. The car had its engine running, its AC blowing strong. Before Vango could motion for them to follow him to the Wright's house as they had pre-planned. Delbert got out of the Lincoln and hurried to the driver's side of the Mercedes.

"Hunh-uh, Eddie," he said. "I've got this. How about you drive the Town Car, I'll follow you in this." He opened the stiff noisy door. "Let me drive this baby one more time before it goes to the scrap heap."

Vango said as he got out of the driver's seat, "You know you could afford to go buy yourself one these today, and pay cash, right?"

"I know," Delbert said. "But this one will always have a special memory for me."

"All right, you've got it," said Vango. He walked to the big Lincoln and slipped into the plush leather driver's seat.

"What's all that?" Leslie asked, sitting comfortably on the passenger's side, cool jazz easing from the stereo.

"Delbert digs your car," Vango said. He pulled from the curb and let Delbert follow all the way to the Wright's home where Leslie Wright saw the yellow caution tape strung back and forth all around the badly damaged structure.

"Oh, my goodness, Eddie!" Leslie said, ready to lose it. "Look at this beautiful house!"

"You mean *your* beautiful house, Lee," Vango said, correcting her.

"Yes," she said. *"My* beautiful house. Just look at it! What am I going to do?" As she spoke, Delbert pulled in beside them.

"First thing first," Vango said, he drove the big Lincoln back to the blown-out garage and stopped a few feet back from the missing doors. He got out and walked around and opened her door.

"It looks even worse up close," Leslie said, stepping out.

"I know you've got insurance, though," he said. "Even if you don't you can cover it."

"Yes, I forgot for a second," she said, settling some. "I know it will be all right. And yes, we do have insurance. I have our agent's card in my purse."

"I think you mean *you* have insurance, not *we.*"

"Yes, I have insurance," she said. "Everything's been happening so fast, I still haven't dealt with the question of insurance, either of the property—she gestured a hand at the damaged house—or his personal life insurance."

"Not trying to crowd you, Lee," Vango said, "But you really need to check these things out."

"I'll call our—I mean *my* agent today," she said, correcting herself. "I still need to get all the personal items out of here and store them somewhere—maybe rent a U-Haul or something."

Vango just stared at her for a second, then said, "Lee, please, call in a personal security company, and a moving company they recommend. They'll put everything in a storage unit and bring you the keys."

"Of course, they will," she said. She shook her head. "I'm just having a hard time catching up."

"I know," Vango said close to her ear. He slipped an arm around her waist. "I'll be here with you. We'll figure it all out as we go."

"Thanks, Eddie," she said, leaning her head over onto his shoulder. "I just want the two of us to be on an island somewhere, away from all this."

"Hold that thought," Vango said. "We'll get there."

Delbert got out of the Mercedes and walked into the garage with them. The firefighters had covered the large hole in the roof with a heavy-duty blue sheet of vinyl. The three looked up though the wide long ragged hole and the blue vinyl sheeting covering the top of it.

"I'm so sorry this happened," Delbert said. He stood looking down at the thick streak of burnt tire rubber on the wet concrete floor. The smell of burnt rubber still wafted in the garage.

"Forget about it, Delbert," Vango said, him and Leslie looking down with him. "You were lucky this roof didn't pin the car down when it fell."

The garage roof had been axed and chain-sawed into pieces and piled outside beside the driveway.

"Yeah, I have to admit," Delbert said, "I must've left a deep *butt-crease* in the driver's seat when the whole thing fell." He looked at Leslie and added, "If you'll pardon my language."

Vango heard the quick rack of a shotgun behind them. Instead of freezing, he spun around toward the sound. But too late. A dark-complexioned man stood with the shotgun to his shoulder, less than ten feet way, the gun aimed at Vango's chest. On either side, two men flanked him, each carrying an Uzi machine pistol aimed and ready. In a flash of memory Vango recognized the three as part of the six men he'd seen getting off a flight at the airport.

Delbert started to make a move, but Vango stopped him with a raised hand.

"Easy, everybody," Vango said, in a steady tone. He could see these men were a cut above the ragtag crew that Trio and Lambert had sent to bring him down. These guys struck him as pros. They'd slipped in cloaked in silence. The shotgun was only racked to draw his attention. The Uzis stood the right distance away, and apart. The shotgun held the middle where it would do the most damage.

Delbert settled, following Vango's order. Leslie stood, shaken, but managed to hold herself together.

"Okay, you've got us," Vango said calmly. "What do you want from us?"

"Hey, you're a smart *hombre,*" the shotgun holder said. He lowered the butt of the gun a little as he took a step forward. Vango knew what that meant. When the man smiled and took his time moving closer, Vango knew what that meant too. *This is going to hurt ...,* he told himself. He prepared himself, keeping his jaws tight, but his neck, head and shoulders loose and ready to move.

When the man snapped the gun butt around to his face, Vango managed to roll with it the same as a boxer would roll with a sharp punch, unable to stop or avoid it, but lessening it, minimizing the impact. Which he did, minimizing everything except for the pain.

Even as he fell onto the concrete floor, the blow staggering him, jumbling everything going on inside his head, he struggled to stay conscious—hoping the man wouldn't see it and hit him again, next time *harder.*

Delbert and Leslie Wright stood watching, the woman with her hands cupped over her mouth, Delbert looking all around for what move to make.

"Pull this bad boy up," The man with the shotgun said to the other two. Vango had quickly recovered from any damage the shotgun butt had done, but he was wisely playing it the other way. He staggered in place, letting the men raise him by his outstretched forearms.

"What's up?" Vango said in a feigned groggy voice. He kept his head lowered as they dragged him to his feet.

"What's *up?*" the man with the shotgun asked with a chuckle. He flashed a confident smile. "Everywhere I go I keep seeing the three of you." As he spoke, he reached around behind Vango and slipped his wallet from his hip pocket and flipped it open. He looked at the driver's license. "Now I've got all of you by the wings, I'm going to find out what you've got to do with things here, Mr. *Adams.*"

Vango caught a knowing look move across Delbert's and Leslie's face.

"I'm here to collect a gambling debt from Ian Lambert." He spit a trace of blood on the floor. His jaw hurt, but not too bad. The trace of blood was a good touch, he thought. "I know all you guys are up to something. I could care less."

"Yeah?" The man looked him up and down. "I heard some *gringo* clown with a sunburn is going around making threats about the Lamb. That must be you huh?" He looked closely for any sun damage.

"I had a sunburn," said Vango. "But I'm here to do a job—"

"A *sunburn ...,*" the man scoffed. He flipped Vango's wallet to him. Vango caught it and shoved in back into his pocket. Then the man looked away dismissively and checked out Leslie Wright.

"What about you, pretty mama?" he said. "What are you doing here?"

I'm here because I'm stupid," Leslie said, giving Vango a dirty look. "I've been sticking with this loser because I thought he had money. Now I'm finding out he's as broke as I am!"

"That is too bad," the man said. "A woman who looks like you do should never be with a loser."

Vango saw Delbert was ready to make a move on one of the Uzi holders. To stop Delbert he cut in, saying to the shotgun holder, "What do want with us?" he asked. "We don't have any money."

"I'm keeping you out of our way," the man said turning to Vango.

Vango gave a little shrug. He rubbed his jaw, which actually was sore.

"So, you're not going to kill us or anything?" he asked.

"Maybe," said the man with the shotgun. "We'll see." He looked all around then back at Vango. "We're going to take you with us, to keep you out of everybody's hair." He waved a manicured finger. "You see, I have heard enough and seen enough to know that you are troublemakers."

"We're not troublemakers, we're not in anybody's hair," Vango said. "We're minding our own business. Let us go. We'll head for Atlanta right now."

"In that big pretty Town Car?" the man said glancing at the shiny dark Lincoln. "For a loser with no money, you are driving way over your head."

Vango said, "It's a rental. As soon as they locate

me, they'll jerk it out from under me while I'm waiting for a light to change."

The man gave a little laugh, so did his two men.

"That's what I mean about troublemakers," the man said. "Anyway, they won't take the car away from you tonight," he said to Vango.

"Why's that?" Vango asked.

"Because the three of you are going to spend the night with us," the man said. "Won't that be fun?" He gave a wide toothy smile.

"Wait a minute," Vango said. He motioned toward Delbert and Leslie Wright. "You can let them go. Take me."

"No, I think we'll take all three of you with us," the man said. "If we decide to shoot you, we'll want to shoot all three. Does that make sense to you?"

"Not really," Vango said. He gave Delbert a look that could only mean, *wait until I give you a sign, then we'll take these jokers down.*

"By the way ..." the man said, gesturing Vango and the others out of the garage. As a warning, he said, "I've got more men standing outside."

"You know the good thing about this big Town Car?" said the shotgun carrier. He sat in the passenger seat beside Vango while Vango drove along Indian River Road. When Vango didn't answer the man smiled the Uzi carrier in the middle of the back seat and said to him, "Tell him, Big Dude."

"We can stuff all three of your dead asses in this trunk, we feel like it," the *Big Dude* replied in a deep bass voice.

Under the passenger seat, Vango heard Bruiser growl in a low tone. He tried picturing a cat Bruiser's size squeezing down under the seat but couldn't.

"The hell is that noise?" Big Dude asked. He tapped his toe hard against the back of the driver's seat. Bruiser growled louder.

"It's a cat," Vango said.

"A cat? You kidding me?" He kicked the seat a little harder.

"I wouldn't tease him—" Vango tried to say.

"Yeah, but I *would,*" the man said. "I hate cats." He tapped his toe against the seat again. "Come on out, kitty, kitty."

Jesus!

Vango glanced in the rear mirror, realizing this could go really bad if Bruiser decided to explode onto the scene and start attacking. The Big Dude sat in the back seat with his Uzi across his lap, the tip of the barrel resting on Delbert's thigh. In the car following close behind them, Leslie occupied the passenger seat. One of the gunmen drove. Two more men with Uzis sat in the back seat. If Bruiser blew up, and the Lincoln started weaving, the men would see it as an attempt to takeover. It might easily get Leslie Wright killed.

Easy Bruiser ..., he said to himself. Two malevolent eyes appeared and turned upwards from the front edge of the driver's seat.

"Leave the cat alone, Big Dude," the shotgun carrier said from the passenger seat. Bruiser rummaged around out of sight and in a moment fell silent. *How in hell did he get under there?*

Vango gave Delbert a look in the rearview mirror

that told him to keep cool. And they rode on, crossing a bridge onto the island and heading north in the direction of the Oceana Princess II complex. Without asking, Vango followed the shotgun holder's instructions and swung into the open gates of the parking lot and pulled in close to the main entrance. Behind them, he was relieved to see the car following them do the same. This was no time for the three of them to get separated.

They moved from the two cars as a group, the gunmen gathered close to Vango and his party of two. In the shadows of the afternoon they walked unnoticed into the lobby, onto an elevator and up to the fifteenth floor.

As the man carrying the shotgun opened the door with a key Morez had given him, everyone filed inside and stopped abruptly. They stood starting wide-eyed, hearing the sounds of steel crickets—gun safeties snapping off all around them. Across the room they saw no less than ten guns pointed at them in all size, shapes and calibers.

"Freeze, you sonsabitches!" Police Sergeant Dan Hicky shouted over a mouth full of deep heavily-topped pizza, from Dante's Oven across the street. Eddie Vango saw surprise on everybody's face.

Oh, sweet God …! A massacre in the making!

Vango threw his hands up. So did Leslie Wright, beside him. Behind them Delbert Moss did the same.

"Drop your guns!" shouted the man with the shotgun, his followers with their Uzis up, aimed and ready.

Vango eased his raised forearm against Leslie Wright and took a very cautious step backwards, coaxing her alongside him. Behind them Delbert didn't need to be told what to do. He backed slowly toward the wide-open door.

"Drop the guns!" the police sergeant shouted, his words badly muffled by three cheeses and four selected pizza toppings. His free hand had raised a big .45.

"No!" the man with the shotgun shouted in reply. "Your badges don't frighten us!"

Nice and easy ..., Vango told himself, taking another slow backward step, his two followers moving along with him.

The sergeant shouted another quick threat; the shotgun holder shouted one right back, just as quick. Vango could almost hear triggers being squeezed. Another step. Vango judged the open door to be close—close enough to leap for when bullets started flying. Was it time?

Yes, now ...!

He moved backwards fast, grabbing Leslie's forearm, pushing Delbert behind them.

"Where you going, cowboys, cowgirl!" A loud voice bellowed from the open door as more guns and gun holders spilled inside around Vango and his two followers. "Anybody don't want to die raise your hands!" the voice said, as if looking for a consensus.

Overwhelmed by the heavy surge of suits, tan and gray uniforms and SWAT gear that swept inside, Uzis, one shotgun and three pistols hit the floor. Vango glanced sidelong at Leslie Wright. They both let out a tight breath.

CHAPTER 22

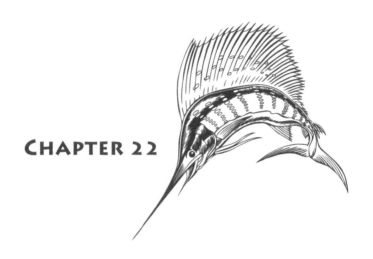

Vango saw the sergeant had a streak of red sauce on his chin. The captain and Jill Wray had escorted Vango into a bedroom that had been converted into Trio's and Lambert's office. On their way Vango looked down at men seated on the floor, many with their hands restrained with white plastic wrist bands. One whose hands were unrestrained was Charlie Betz.

Betz still wore an arm sling, a head bandage, and several bandaids here and there. He was the one Delbert said blew the hole in the Wright's residence. The one who'd later walked away from Lew Stucky and the Corsica because of Bruiser the cat passing gas. He looked away from Vango, until Vango walked out of sight into the other room and someone closed the door behind him. Inside the bedroom converted to an office, Sergeant Dan Hicky cold-stared Vango for a moment.

"I'm not going to waste any of my time with you, Mr. James Adams," he said finally, cocking his head sideways, consulting Vango's wallet he held spread open in his hand. "Either tell us what you're doing here or go to jail." He straightened and looked Vango up and down.

"Do we understand each other?"

"Yes, we do," said Vango. "I'm not going lie to you. I'm in town from Chicago, came down to collect a bad gambling debt." He gave a slight shrug. "That's it, plain and simple."

"And I suppose you know nothing about any shipment of cocaine on its way?" he asked in a sarcastic tone.

"Correct," Vango said firmly, "nothing at all."

The sergeant looked at Jill Wray for either confirmation or denial. She wagged a security tape in her hand.

"It's true as far as my people can determine," she said. "Here's everything we've videoed on him." She gave Vango an annoyed look as she continued speaking to the sergeant and the captain. "Some stupid gambling debt is all he's harped about everywhere he's gone—to Victor Trio, or Ian Lambert, to anybody else he runs into."

"Has your surveillance tape shown him or his cohorts handing, trafficking, or using any illicit drugs?"

"No," said Jill Wray, sounding disappointed. "So far none of them seem smart enough to be into the drug market. She shook her head and gave Vango a hard stare. "But given time …."

"You either have something on him, or you don't," the captain cut in. "Let's quit screwing around here. If this drug deal is coming down, we need to keep moving in on it!" He looked around the busy room. "Does everybody get that?"

"Got it, Captain," said Sergeant Hicky. He turned to Vango and shoved his wallet into his hand. "When we let you go, I don't want to see your face again, Adams," he said, "unless there's bars in front of it."

Vango took his time closing his wallet and slipping it into his back pocket. "So, I can go now?"

"Yes— No! Not just yet," said Sergeant Hicky.

"Then when?" Vango asked.

"Soon, maybe," Hicky said.

"What about my *cohorts?* Out there?" Vango asked skeptically. "When can they go?"

"He means the man and women he pals around with," Jill Wright said.

"I know who he means," Hicky said.

But Jill Wray went on, watching Vango's expression as she spoke.

"Her husband is the accountant for Lambert and Trio," she said. "It appears he's skipped town with Trio and Lambert." She nodded at the door in Leslie Wright's direction. "Adams here is sleeping with her any time he hears a door close."

"Hey!" said Vango, acting incensed. But Jill Wray smiled and went on.

"She's a dumb, rich slut—doesn't know squat about their drug business," she said. "But she's not involved with any of the drug business as far as we've determined. She's balling anybody who crosses her path. But that's—"

"Hey…!" Vango repeated, cutting her off in a stronger voice.

She paused, then changed the subject from Leslie Wright to Delbert Moss. "The guy Moss is a day laborer, shows up out front of the big box lawn and garden every morning. He tried working for Lambert a short while, couldn't cut it." She shook her head in contempt. "Too stupid for crime. *Hell,* he's too stupid for slip-on shoes."

Vango kept quiet. Let them think what they wanted to. Delbert didn't need to impress anybody here.

The captain looked at Sergeant Hicky.

"Wipe your mouth, sergeant!" he demanded. "You're supposed to eat the pizza, not wear it!"

Hicky scrambled awkwardly. "Sorry, Captain Carter," he said, embarrassed.

Jill Wray reached over atop the desktop, yanked up a tissue and handed it to him. He quickly wiped his mouth and chin and looked at Vango with violent eyes.

"Your cohorts are still being questioned," he said. "If they're not arrested, they'll be released."

"Arrested, for what?" Vango asked flatly. "For being kidnapped at gunpoint and brought here, against their will, like I was?"

"Tell us more about this *alleged* gambling debt, Adams," he said, ignoring Vango's question. "We'll turn your friends loose when we're damned good and ready!" he said. "What about the gambling debt?"

"Okay," Vango said, settling down. "A friend of mine made a bet with Victor Trio. Some ball game or something. Trio lost and hasn't paid him yet. I came here to remind him."

"Remind him, how?" said Hicky. "Remind him by breaking an arm, or a leg?"

Vango gave a short chuckle.

"Man-oh-man! Sergeant, you're either watching too much TV, or making your bets with the wrong kind of people."

"I don't gamble," Hicky was quick to point out, shooting the captain an innocent look. He gathered himself and said firmly to Vango, "Do I need to remind you that gambling is illegal in the state of Florida?"

"I had no idea it's illegal," Vango said, looking sincere.

"Oh, it is indeed," said Hicky. "In fact, it is punishable by up to—"

"Shut your *stupid mouth*, Sergeant!" Captain Carter shouted. "He's jamming you in the ass!" He gripped his holstered .38 special and stared hard at Vango. "Get him the *hell* out of my sight, Sergeant, before I shoot him in the foot!"

Vango shut up, but stood firm, staring at the captain, almost daring him to shoot.

"Wait a minute, Sergeant," the captain said eyeing Vango up and down, the nice clothes, the nice shoes, his cool overall demeanor. "What do you know about *Swordfish?*" he asked quickly, hoping to catch Vango off guard.

Vango shrugged, loose and easy. "It makes a nice sandwich?" Vango said. Seeing that wasn't the answer the captain was looking for, he added, "I know this Treasure Coast is the *sailfish* capital of the world?"

"I'm not asking about *sailfish,*" the captain said. I'm asking about *Swordfish*. They're two different fish altogether." He saw everyone's eyes on him. "And that's all you know about *Swordfish,* huh?" he asked Vango.

"Did I mention the sandwich?" Vango said. The two just stared at each other in a tight silence, until at length the silence was broken when a quiet knock resounded on the door.

"Come in, damn it to hell, *come in!*" the captain shouted.

Jill Wray tried to catch the door before it opened but was too late. Charlie Betz opened the door with his good hand and stepped inside. Vango stood staring at Betz as Betz clipped a shiny detective badge onto his belt before realizing Vango was still in the room.

"Holy shit!" the bandaged Betz said, trying to cover his badge.

"Hell, detective!" said Captain Carter. "It's too late to cover it now! Adams has seen your badge! You can kiss your undercover off-loader work goodbye."

"I haven't seen a thing," Vango said quickly, cutting his eyes away from the two of them staring at him.

"I thought he was gone," said the undercover officer. "You told me to come *in!*"

"Yes, I did, damn it!" said the captain. "Now that you're here, what the hell do you want?"

"Well, captain," said Detective Darren Gibson, heretofore known as Charlie Betz. "I just told this Delbert Moss I'd say something on his behalf. So, I want to make it known that he saved my life. Moss got me out of that collapsed garage when somebody accidently fired the launcher. Wasn't for him I'd be dead right now." He looked at Vango, wondering if Moss had told Vango who it was that fired the launcher, and was he going to keep his mouth shut about it.

"That's the kind of guy Delbert is," Vango said. "We're all just glad you're alive." He gave the bandaged detective a knowing look.

Officer Gibson looked relieved. "I also want to thank you. You could have abandoned me when I was in bad shape with my injuries, but you didn't. You and Delbert took care of me. I can't forget something like that."

"Like I said, we're just glad you made it," said Vango.

"So am I …," he nodded, looking all around. "Believe me, so am I."

Vango saw his good eye get watery.

"Yeah, well," said Captain Carter, looking back and forth between Gibson and Vango, "unless you two would like to get a room *and be alone for a while,* I'm still looking for a drug shipment going down somewhere along our coast!"

"Captain," Jill Wray said, "Leone Morez still insists it's going down tomorrow."

"I understand that," Captain Carter said. "And if it's tomorrow we'll be prepared for it by having gathered all our intel on it today!"

Detective Gibson interjected, "Half the men sitting out there are undercover agents, posing as gunmen and off-loaders waiting to know what to do. If anybody knows, they'd know. And they don't know diddly."

Jill Wray spoke to Sergeant Hicky under her breath.

"Screw all this," she rasped. "I can't take any more of this crap. I'm going to smoke a joint. You going?"

The sergeant looked all around, hesitant at first. Then he said, "What the hell. Yeah, let's go."

On their way to the balcony, Jill Wray and Sergeant Hicky stepped through the restrained gunmen still sitting on the hard tile floor. Past the gunmen they walked into a bedroom where Leone Morez lay cuffed to the iron post of a bed's headboard.

"What the living hell is this?" Leone Morez shouted, almost shrilly. He shook the cuff against the iron post. "What am I, some kind of frigging dog?"

"No, Leone," said Jill, walking over to him. "You're a man who is about to become very rich, if you can control yourself that is."

"Control myself? *Control myself!* Turn me loose! I will show you how I control myself." He screamed until Jill clamped a hand over his mouth, shutting him up.

She leaned near his ear and said, "Listen to me you little prick. How is your math?" She eased her hand from his mouth.

He settled down, lowered his voice.

"You're asking about my math? It's good! Why?"

"Tell me how many times you can step on top quality coke and still take it to the street," she said.

Morez got serious. He stared into her eyes.

"Seven times easily—" he grinned "—ten times probably. I've seen it stepped on more than that. Depends on who you sell it to and how bad the market needs it."

"So, tell me then," she asked, getting cagey, "how much is seven times *forty million?"*

Morez went blank, then came back.

"It's *uh,* let's see." He held up three fingers and looked intently at them. "Ten times one million, times two million." He spread the fingers as if that would help him find the answer. He shook his cuffed hand. "I can't count like this. I need my other hand!"

"I bet you do," Jill whispered close to his ear, the talk of big money warming her, making her tingle all over. "It's two … *hundred and eighty million dollars,* Leone."

Sergeant Hicky cocked his head in curiosity, wondering if that figure was true.

"Yeah, okay, I knew that already," Morez said, clearly bluffing. "So, what does all this mean?"

Sergeant Hicky stood stunned, listening.

"It means, I am working with two members in state legislature, one of them is on our drug task force. One holds the reins to federal drug funding subsidy." She gave him a minute to let it sink in. "They'd like support our bounty to be for the full street value of the drugs confiscated."

"Oh my God!" Sergeant Hicky said, moving in closer. *"Jilly*, that comes to—" He paused. Morez considered the figure and gave up, the figures swirling too high in his head.

"Don't hurt yourselves, guys," Jill Wray said with a sharp little grin. "It's too much money for one wagon to carry." She looked at them in turn. "Can we hold it together here long enough to make this thing fly?"

"And what if these lawmakers do not do as they say they will?" Morez asked.

Hicky gave a chuckle and said, "Oh, they'll do it. For the kind of money they'll be putting in their pockets, you can count on it! They'd kill their own grandmothers."

"Look, Leone," said Jill Wray, "Sergeant Hicky and I are going out on the balcony and burn a doobie. Want to go out there with us?"

"Yeah sure," he said. "I could use a doobie, straight up big time. Take these cuffs off me."

"That's not a good idea," Jill Wray said. "These guys on the floor out there see you walking around free as a bird, it could raise red flags, cause the deal tomorrow to get called off. Maybe moved somewhere we won't know about."

"Okay, so how do I smoke with you?" Morez asked.

"Like this." She reached up and unlocked the cuff from the iron bed post. Then she cuffed his hands together in front of him. "I march you out back right past these guys, maybe even give you a little shove.

"Hey, you're not setting me up for something, are you?" he asked as he stood up from the side of the bed, recalling what had happened to Ian Lambert on this same balcony.

"If I were setting you up. Leone," she said, "would I admit it?"

"No, you wouldn't," he said. "So, what does that mean? That you are, or you're not?"

"It means don't waste our time asking stupid questions," she said, her and Sergeant Hicky guiding him to the door between them. "There so much money to go around, nobody has to get setup. We'll all make out big on this."

Morez nodded as they walked him to the balcony.

"See how it is here," he said. "I love this country so much, sometimes I think I'll never go home."

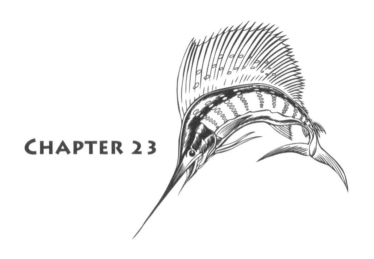

CHAPTER 23

Darkness had begun slowly closing around the Oceana Princess II as Vango stood outside of the lobby under the portico waiting for Leslie Wright and Delbert Moss to join him. First thing he'd done when he left the complex was go to where the big Town Car sat parked in the shade. Opening the driver's door and seeing the key hanging from the dash, he quickly started the engine and turned the AC dial to its coldest setting.

He looked around the floor and rear seat for the big cat, not finding him.

"Bruiser, come out," he coaxed. But then it came to him that the cat probably didn't realize that *Bruiser* was his new name. Without a name to call him by, Vango resorted to the old standby.

"Here, *kitty-kitty,*" he said, feeling foolish calling a monster feline like Bruiser a *kitty-kitty*. Still he got no response. But when he turned to step out of the car, he saw the big cat sitting three feet away staring up at him, meowing. His fangs looked too big and sharp to be asking anybody for anything.

"Hey, you had me worried," Vango said opening

the driver's door. Before the door fully opened the cat slipped through it like a streak of dark smoke, leapt up onto the rear seat, and sat staring at him. Vango reached a hand over the seat and rubbed his big head.

"As soon as they get here, we're taking you to McDonalds or somewhere." The big cat gave out a rattling purr and forced him to rub his head more.

"Okay, pal," said Vango, "I know we're not an easy crew to hang with."

"There he is," he heard Leslie Wright say, causing him to look up. He saw her and Delbert walking out of the building and over to the Lincoln. The woman carried two bottles of water in her hands. So did Delbert. Vango relaxed back in the driver's seat for a second. Then he got out and closed the door loosely, in case someone had planted a bug.

"Man, what a day," he said, but he said it with a smile. He saw a plastic cup perched atop one the bottles in Leslie's hand. He lifted it and filled it with water and turned and sat it inside on the Lincoln's floor. The cat went after it, lapping out loud. Vango closed the door, raised the rest of the bottle to his lips and drank.

"Have you been waiting long?" Leslie asked.

"Long enough to get real thirsty," Vango said. Looking at each of them he asked. "Did they get you to say anything you wish you hadn't?"

Leslie Wright shook her head and opened her own bottle of water. "If that's their idea of *questioning,* I can see why they never catch anybody."

Vango said, "I think they already had this thing laid out to suit them. They just wanted to gather any *additional* information we might be able to give them."

"Yeah," said Delbert, "they seemed dead set to move on this big deal if it ever comes down. That's all they wanted." He gave them his federally subsidized dental smile. "Our *captors* caught them by surprise." He paused, took a drink of cold water and said, "I have to say, I've never been treated so well in my life. I was prepared to take a few punches in the face." He gave a little laugh.

Leslie and Vango looked him up and down. Vango took note of his silk shirt, nice triple-pleated slacks, new Italian slippers.

"Clothes really do make the man," Vango said. "Look at you, Delbert."

Delbert spread his hands and looked himself over. His face reddened a little.

"Dang!" he said. "Who is this handsome devil?"

"I knew you'd be a cool player once you got steady on your feet," Vango said. He fished a brand-new plastic credit card from his pocket and handed it to him. "This is yours."

"What's this?" Delbert read his name on the card and looked confused.

"It's a prepaid credit card I had Lawrence Trange, the bank manager, issue to you. You take it to any motel, restaurant, whatever, and its treated just like a regular credit card. Except it's only good until the ten thousand runs out. Beats carrying so much cash around."

Delbert breathed deep and wagged the card between his fingers. "Eddie, how long you going to keep giving me stuff?"

"I haven't given you anything, Delbert, you've earned it all. But don't worry, I'm done," Vango said.

While they were standing there, three dark sedans and two black vans barreled through the entrance gates and circled and stopped under the portico roof.

"FBI?" Vango said quietly, watching men in suits spill out of the vehicles and rush inside the complex, long guns and pistols in hand.

"DEA …?" said Leslie.

"Both," Delbert said with quiet resolve.

One car circled around, left the others and sped the short distance to the Lincoln.

"Uh-oh …," Leslie said. "Here they come."

"Be cool," Vango said. "We're okay." He waited a second then said, "I think."

"You *think?"* she said.

"Are you holding anything?" he asked her sidelong.

"I'm good," she said. "I'm going clean." Seeing Vango raise his hands chest high, she did the same; so did Delbert Moss.

The sedan slid the last three feet to a halt; a very official-looking young man in a blue suit came bounded from behind the wheel and hurried to them, leaving his door hanging open. His badge swung on a chain he'd thrown around his neck. He held a hand on his holstered service automatic.

"Agent Arno, *DEA!"* he said, louder than he would have needed too. "Everybody, hands up!"

The three stared at him, each with their hands already raised, holding their water bottles. Vango wiggled his fingers a little, enlightening him.

"Oh! All right. Thank you." the young agent looked embarrassed. He took a badly needed breath. "Okay. Now take your hands down." He noted that the three stood close to the running automobile. "Set your bottles on the hood and step away from the car," he said with authority.

They did.

"What are you doing here?" Agent Arno asked all three in a stiff and serious tone.

"We're watering our cat," Vango answered calmly. Up the front of the tall complex people started forming along the balcony out front of their condos. They looked down with curious interest.

"Doing what?" The agent craned his neck a little, trying to see through the Lincoln's tinted windows.

"Watering our cat," Vango repeated.

"What cat?" the agent sounded agitated.

"Our cat." Vango shrugged. What else could he say?

"No, I mean *whose cat is it?"* the agent said.

Vango said very slowly, very clearly, "Our, cat."

"Okay, I get it," the agent said. "Let me see the cat."

"Why?" said Vango.

"Because I don't believe you have a cat," he said. As he spoke, he stepped over to the car door and clenched the door handle.

"Agent Arno!" Vango said. You don't want to open the—"

But Vango's warning came too late.

The unsuspecting Agent Arno swung the big door wide open. Bruiser shot out into his chest with all fours, letting out a deep, jungle-like snarl.

"Holy God!" Agent Arno screamed. He tried reaching his gun with one hand as he fought the cat back

with his other. But the gun fell from his hand and landed at his feet. His foot wildly kicked it under the car. The gun went off. The loud gunshot made the cat wilder. He had the agent's shirt torn almost completely off when Vango managed to get his arm around the battling animal and peel him from the agent's scratched-up stomach. On-lookers stood riveted in place along the high balcony railings.

"Oh, man!" Vango stooped down, cat in his arm, to find the gun.

"Don't touch that gun!" Arno shouted.

"No problem," said Vango. He stood up quickly, opened the car door, pulled the cat from around his arm and put it in the car. He closed the door. Another agent came running from the portico at the sound of the gunshot. He carried a shotgun. Leslie and Delbert stayed calm but backed a few steps away from the Lincoln.

"Everybody stand where you are, raise your hands!" the second agent shouted.

Vango, Leslie and Delbert all three raised their hands, again.

"I've got this, sir," said Agent Arno. He gestured a hand down his shredded shirt. "The cat jumped me."

"What cat?" the other agent asked looking all around.

"Here we go," Vango said quietly.

"What's that?" the agent said, "Speak up!"

But Arno cut in. "Sir, this was an accident. My gun is under the car. I need to get it."

"Who are you people?" the second agent, Arthur Snell demanded. "Are you with *Swordfish?* Were you upstairs?" As soon as he mentioned Swordfish, both agents gave each other a look. Vango could tell this one had let something slip.

"Yes, we've been upstairs," he said. "They saw we've got nothing to do with anything. They let us go." He looked back and forth between the two agents. "Otherwise we wouldn't be here." He smiled. He intentionally let the question of *Swordfish* go unanswered.

"Do we need to take you back up there and verify who you are? What you're doing here?"

Vango sighed, but before he could say they were watering their cat, a hand-held phone rang in the agent's pocket. He handed his shotgun to Agent Arno and answered it.

"Yes, sir," he said into the phone. "It was an accident. A cat caused it to fire." He stood nodding and sweating until he finally said, "Yes, sir, we're on our way."

"Let's go, Arno," he said. "They've got a whole string of traffickers cuffed and ready to go. Cops, community workers, and you name it! And it's just now starting."

Vango, Delbert and Leslie Wright stood looking away as if not hearing him.

"Folks, you're free to go," Snell said to Vango. "This is a joint FBI and DEA operation you've walked into. Our two agencies working together is something new we're trying. Your government will appreciate it if you keep quiet about it."

"You've got it," Vango said. He smiled and looked at Agent Arno who stood stuffing ragged strips of his shirt tails down into his slacks. "We'll just take our cat and water him somewhere else."

They watched in silence as the agents walk into the complex in the falling darkness.

"What is *Swordfish* all about?" Vango asked, not really expecting an answer.

Delbert shrugged.

"I know," said Leslie Wright. The two both looked at her.

"Operation *Swordfish* is a joint operation—a group of state and federal law enforcement agencies working together. It means they're out to catch the *big fish* in the drug market—getting rid of the offshore bearer bonds next year is just one part of it." She saw them staring at her and smiled. "Good thing we made our moves when we did, huh?" she said.

"Yes," said Vango. "But how do you know about a secret FBI-DIA joint operation?"

"Harold told me about it," she said. "He heard about it from a 'Big'—I mean 'really *Big*'—dealer in Amsterdam over a year ago. The big dealers know everything. Harold helped him set up some corporations he could file some big losses on when the time came to walk away. Which is now."

Sailfish .... He looked around at an area known as the sailfish capital of the world. Operation *Swordfish* in the *sailfish* capital. It just seemed strange, he thought. *Okay* .... What did he know?

He dismissed the matter and turned to Delbert.

"So, you're going to use Stucky's Pontiac for a couple of days while you find yourself a new pickup truck."

"Yep," said Delbert. "Maybe not a *brand-new* pickup. Maybe a nice clean—"

"Stop it, Delbert," Vango said. "Get a brand-new pickup. You can afford it. You can afford a new car too."

"I know," Delbert said. "And I will get a brand-new truck. This thing about having money just takes some getting used to."

"Good," said Vango. "And when you get your truck, you'll take Stucky's car to the car hauler I told you about and send it up the Lew Stucky in Chicago. Right?"

"Absolutely right," Delbert said. He looked at Leslie, then at Eddie Vango.

"I can't believe how much I'm going to miss you two," he said. "I hope I can see you both real soon."

"Any time, Delbert," said Vango, "you don't have to wait until visiting day." He shook his hand and gave him a short hug.

Delbert sniffled. "I like having friends like you two."

"Oh, Delbert," Leslie said, affectionately. She hugged him tight and kissed his cheek.

"And we want you to always be our friends," she said. Vango saw she was getting a little misty too.

"Okay then, kids," he said. "If Bruiser will let us back in the Lincoln, let's get out of here." He looked at Delbert and saw him touch his eyes. "—Drop you off at Stucky's Pontiac."

It was dark when they dropped Delbert off and watched him drive away in the big dark green Pontiac. Neither of them said anything for the next few miles, even though as soon as Delbert was out of sight, Leslie scooted over against Vango and squeezed his knee.

"Where would you like to spend the night?" he asked. "We can stay around here or drive down the coast."

"Let's stay around here tonight," she said. "Tomorrow I'll set things up with some contractors, get the house emptied out into storage, see what it takes to rebuild it." She sighed. "I don't know yet what the insurance is going to pay. Anyway, I don't think I'll want to live there anymore. Maybe I'll fix it up and sell it?"

"Sure, whatever suits you," Vango said. As they drove along, Bruiser hopped up on the seat and laid down beside her. She rubbed his head.

"I think he's might be hungry." Vango looked over at the big cat. "Let's pick him up something from a drive-though, a McDonalds or something?"

"Are you hungry, Eddie Vango?" she asked.

"I could eat," he said. But they drove on a little ways in silence, until she rubbed her hand up and down on his thigh.

"Eddie," she said, almost in a whisper, "Did I ever tell you how much I like sex?"

"You mentioned it," he said. "But I didn't know if you were serious or not."

She gave him a look in the shadowy light of the dash.

"Why would I not be serious?" she asked.

He shrugged. "I don't know, maybe I thought you were shining me on, looking around for a sugar daddy?"

She sat silent for a moment rubbing the cat slowly. Then she said, "Well, I don't need a sugar daddy now, do I?"

"No, Lee, I'm sure you don't," he said.

"Did I tell you I've quit shooting eight balls?" she asked.

"You did tell me," he replied. "I'm glad."

"The other night you told me you love me. Remember?" she asked.

"Yes, I remember," he said.

"Good," she said. "I want us to spend lots of time together, Eddie Vango," she said. "Are you good with that? I mean we could go anywhere we want, see the world together, spend nights watching sunsets, just the two of us—"

"Hey, Lee," he said, cutting her off gently, "that all sounds good to me. Everything you're saying, I'm in for it." He put his arm around her, drew her closer against him. The big cat purred easily, steadily. Cool jazz playing quietly on the FM cut away to local news. When something caught Vango's attention he turned up the volume.

They listened as the news announcer detailed the discovery of an unidentified body found in the swamplands west of the Treasure Coast. "Hope it's not someone we know," Vango said solemnly, checking Leslie out, wondering how she might react if it turned out to be Harold Wright.

Leslie smiled slightly, seeing what he was doing. She turned the volume down some more, not too much, but enough to talk comfortably.

"If it is, I can think of a half dozen other people it could be besides Harold. Including Victor Trio, Ian Lambert and three or maybe four gunmen—"

"Okay, I get it," said Vango.

She sighed and said, "I know I've got to deal with it all when the time comes, the life insurance, which I know is a large amount. There's properties, some here, some in Miami, Costa Rica, some other places."

Vango just looked at her. She wasn't joking.

"But until the time comes," she said. "I can think of any number of things I'd rather do than think about it."

"I hear you," Vango said. "I agree."

They drove on quietly, but only for a moment.

"There's a really nice motel up ahead," she said, looking at him with promise in her voice.

"Think they're cat friendly?" Vango asked, already slowing down, changing lanes.

"I don't know," she said. "If they're not we'll roll on, find another place."

"Or, we'll *buy* this place," Vango said. He clicked on the turn signal and glanced over at Bruiser. The big cat lay sprawled against Leslie's thigh, fully relaxed, yet with its eyes sharply focused, staring into the slow blinking turn signal.

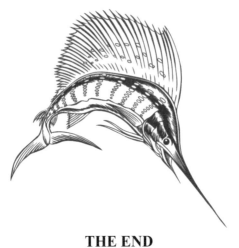

THE END

Previews –Books 1 & 2– Gun Culture Crime Series

FRIEND OF
A FRIEND

2015

Thank you, Readers. You have finished reading the third book in the Gun Culture Series: **Blowback: Treasure Coast,** by Ralph Cotton. Following *Blowback*, are previews of the first book, ***Friend Of A Friend,*** and the second, ***Season of the Wind.***

If you enjoyed *Blowback* but haven't read ***Friend of a Friend*** or ***Season of the Wind***, these previews will give you a little taste!

SEASON OF
THE WIND

2017

(HAPTER ONE

FRIEND OF A FRIEND

Chicago, Illinois:
Temperature 36 degrees:

Christmas music played from an overhead speaker in the grilled metal ceiling. Dylan gazed up from beneath his hat brim at the floor number lights above the stainless steel doors. The elevator climbed; he watched the digital floor numbers click higher, feeling the upward push of the carpet beneath his feet.

Here we go ....

He wore black-rimmed drugstore glasses with dark tinted lenses. A tangle of wild blonde hair bushed up under his hat brim covering his ears. He looked anonymous enough, easily unnoticed he liked to call it, yet the getup put him in mind of some street performer embarked on some sort of skit.

This was no skit.

Outside, a dusting of light snow had blown through the city overnight. Wind off the lake pulled the temperature down into the low thirties. Cold, but not unusually so for this time of year, he thought, remembering the brutal winters he'd survived here years ago. In front of him an elderly woman stood only inches from the closed elevator doors. She wore a heavy coat and a dark green feathered hat. She stared at the doors as if waiting for instructions. Two rolls of wrapping paper stood up from a shopping bag in her gloved hand.

A bell gave a soft single ring when the elevator whooshed to a halt. He watched the woman step out and walk away as the doors closed behind her. Alone now, he stared at the closed doors himself, holding gloved hands in the pockets of a black down-filled hooded jacket. He knew a security camera lay somewhere up in the grillwork overhead, but it wasn't working this morning. *Not this morning* ....

When the bell rang again, the elevator stopped at the top floor and opened its doors. He stepped off, started walking. At the end of a carpeted hallway he looked down at a small unoccupied desk where a morning paper laid spread open beside a half cup of coffee. He removed a gloved hand from his left pocket and opened the unlocked door. He stepped inside the penthouse suite and closed the door behind him without a sound. Then he moved quietly across the carpet, pulling a silenced .22 caliber pistol from inside his coat.

He seated himself in a high-backed chair and listened to a shower running in a bathroom down the hall. When the water stopped, he heard the far end of the apartment grow silent for a few minutes. Then he heard the bedroom door open and close. He waited, poised. A few seconds later an elderly man in a white terrycloth bathrobe walked into the room barefoot. The man crossed the carpet without seeing him and bent over a glass-topped coffee table.

He picked up a silver six-tube cigar case and a small aluminum emergency medicine container from atop the tinted glass. He straightened, opened the cigar case and started to drop the medicine container into his robe pocket. But he froze when his eyes went to the figure standing up quietly from the chair twelve feet away. A streak of surprise and outrage came over his face, but only for a second. It went away as a cool hardness set in. The man recollected himself and started to put his hand and medicine container down into his robe pocket.

Dylan shook his head slowly, stopping him.

"Hunh-uh, lay them on the table," he said in a low even tone.

Before doing as told, the man gestured toward the cigar case in his hand. With a nod from Dylan he took out a cigar, snapped the case shut and pitched it onto a small catchall tray sitting atop the table. He pitched the medicine container down on the tray with the cigar case and let out a breath.

"How did you get in?" he asked, his voice was gravely, but carried the same low even tone as the man who had come here to kill him. His stare had turned to cold gray granite.

Dylan only stared back at him.

The man glanced away toward the front door, then back. He shook his head as revelation set in.

"Figures," he murmured. "After all the money I

pay that son of a bitch ….” He let it go and looked Dylan up and down. He said, “What are you in that getup, some kind of street clown?” He eyed the hat, the large black-rimmed glasses, the curly hair. “You look like Harpo Marx for God sakes.”

Dylan didn’t answer.

“That’s a rug you’re wearing, right?”

Still no answer.

“Jesus, I hope it is,” the man said, getting in a dig even under the circumstances. “All you need is a handful of balloons.”

Letting the man work his situation out in his mind, Dylan only continued to stare—some quiet doctor here to deliver bad news.

“Is my son behind this?” The man stuck the fresh cigar between his teeth.

Dylan still gave no reply. Supposedly the room had been swept for sound and video surveillance, but you never knew. He stepped slowly over to the man, gun aimed and ready. Reaching down into the man’s bathrobe pocket, he pulled up a small shiny pistol and held it on his palm for the man to see.

“That? I’ve carried that for years. I can’t even tell you if it’s loaded.” He gave a half shrug and brushed the matter aside.

Dylan put the pistol into his coat pocket. He stepped back and motioned his gun barrel toward the sofa.

“What about money? Will cash do me any good?” the man asked quietly as he stepped around the coffee table and sat down. “I can lay a hundred thousand dollars in your hand this minute. You can walk out of here.”

Here came the negotiations. Dylan watched him

take the unlit cigar from his mouth and hold it forked between two manicured, arthritic fingers.

"What do you say?"

Instead of answering, Dylan took a syringe from inside his coat and laid it on the table in front of the man.

The man looked at the syringe, then back up at him.

"Go fuck yourself," he said.

Dylan understood. He took a calming breath and motioned his gun barrel toward a framed picture of a young boy in a baseball uniform, a bat propped over his shoulder. At various places in the room, Dylan had already seen other pictures of the same boy, several more pictures of a slightly older girl.

"Grandkids?" he asked quietly. He gestured toward the pictures.

The older man studied the pictures with him.

"What's it going do to them, you checking out this way?" Dylan queried.

"Leave them out of it," the old man said. "My *son of a bitch* son does this to me? Let him deal with it." He appeared to stiffen with resolve. "My own *son* for God sakes," he grumbled under his breath.

"It's not your son," Dylan said, still keeping his voice low and even.

The old man stared at him as if deciding whether or not to believe him.

"Who the hell else, then?" he asked, showing no sign of giving in. "He's the one who gains the most." He paused and said. "You do know who I am, don't you?"

Dylan only stared, waiting, studying the closed face. He wasn't going to answer—wasn't going to say he knew who he was, wasn't going to mention that he had in fact even worked for him twice over the years. He'd said all he needed to say here. He'd given the man a choice. After a silent moment, he said, "Have it your way …," and he leveled the gun an inch from the man's left eye.

"Wait," the man said sharply. "You're telling me he's not behind this?"

"What did I say?" said Dylan, his hand still poised, his finger ready to press back on the trigger.

The old man reminisced something in silence for a moment.

"Jesus, all my life it's been for him—" He caught himself and stopped and shook his head.

Dylan waited, watched. He was used to this, hearing how hard a guy like this had worked, always for his family. He'd never heard one admit in the end that they'd really been a greedy, self-serving prick. It was always about their sacrifice for the good of something, someone. Good family men these guys, they liked to claim. Dylan didn't judge.

"All right," the man said, still in a quiet tone. He flipped open the right bottom edge of his robe revealing a graveyard of needle marks a few inches above his knee, some older, some more recent.

Dylan backed up a step. His information on the man was right. Everything was going as it should. He stood watching the man pick up the syringe and uncap it. The man closed his eyes for a moment. When he opened them, without another second of hesitation he slid the thin needle into the patchwork of insulin marks and plunged the syringe's clear contents into his thigh. He removed the needle from his thigh and looked up at Dylan as he relaxed back and pitched the syringe back atop the glass coffee table.

"What now?" he asked.

Dylan didn't answer. He took a step farther back and stood relaxed, lowering the gun a little.

"Baseball, huh?" He nodded at the boy's picture.

"Yeah. The kid's always been good at everything," the old man said. "He's older now, going on seventeen— already getting offers. The girl's planning on law school."

"That's nice," Dylan said in a quiet tone.

"Yeah, real nice ...." The man gave a tired little smile, leaned his head back and closed his eyes. "Do me a favor? Don't tell my son what I said, even if he *did* do this," he half whispered.

"No problem," Dylan said almost soothingly. "Go to sleep now." He looked at his watch, took note of the time and let his gun slump a little more.

(HAPTER TWO

And that's how it's done ....

Dylan watched, listened as the man murmured final words to a white ceiling in the silent room. Then the man's head gave a single exit bow and he fell as silent as the room itself. His purple-veined foot had drawn up tight on the carpet, then twitched, relaxed, and slumped over on its side.

Good and quick, no mess, no fuss ..., Dylan told himself. Nothing like it used to be. He stood up, walked over and pressed two fingertips to the side of the old man's throat. No pulse. Okay. He looked all around the room, put his gun inside his coat and went to work, setting things up.

He picked up the syringe and capped it and put it in his coat pocket. He picked up the unlit cigar from the sofa where the old man had let it fall from his fingers and laid it on the glass tabletop. He pulled the old man forward at the waist and laid him face down on the thick smoke-colored glass beside the cigar. Standing back examining the scene as he set it up, he noted for the first time the heavy smoked glass rested on the palms of two dark metal mermaids. They gazed up at him through the dark smoky glass with brassy smiles, their bare breasts loosely covered by cascading ringlets of hair.

Mermaids ....

He picked up the aluminum medicine container, twisted the top off of it and shook out a few tiny white glycerin tablets atop the table near the dead man's face. He stopped short of placing one of the pills between the man's lips. He didn't need to go that far. He let the container fall from his hand to the floor and looked around again.

Everything looked good. The man was diabetic, had a bad liver, a bad heart, carried glycerin for emergencies. There it was. The man was alone. He'd walked in here feeling bad, sat down on the sofa, even tried to grab for his pills—never made it. End of story.

He pulled the dead man's gun out of his coat pocket and reached out to drop it into the man's bathrobe. But before he turned it loose he heard a sound of music and a shrill pulsing alarm spring to life down the hallway from the master bedroom. Loud, but not too loud.

He froze and listened and waited for a second. *All right. This would work* .... The alarm had gone off after the old man walked in here from the shower, sat down and died. It was believable; leave it alone. Walk away. He clicked back into motion.

But again he stopped short when he heard the music and the alarm suddenly cut off. This was getting worse; he pictured a hand reaching out from the bed, hitting an *off* button. He froze and listened. After a tense moment, he laid the dead man's gun on the glass tabletop above the two mermaids and straightened and looked down the hall. He glanced toward the front door, wanting to reach for the knob. But then he looked back down the hall. No, he had to check it out. Who was there, what had they seen, what did they know?

Taking out his gun from inside his coat, he crept down the hallway, staying close to the wall on his left, keeping his right hand ready, the gun raised. When he got to the half-opened door, he stopped and listened again. Nothing. He opened the door an inch farther, enough to peep in and look back and forth into the wide shadowy bedroom.

In a glow of morning sunlight seeping in from the edge of a drawn curtains he saw a naked young woman stretched out on her back, only the corner of a sheet drawn across her waist. She held a hand outreached to the side, resting on the nightstand near the radio. A thin gold chain bracelet hung from her wrist. Dylan studied her face for a moment, then looked around the room again in the silence. Was she asleep or feigning it? Only one way to know. He eased forward and stood over her and pointed the gun barrel down an inch from her eye.

Everything stayed the same, her breathing, her sleeping expression.

"I know you're awake," he whispered. His voice was barely audible, but loud enough to draw a response from anyone who knew they were about to die. He held his trigger finger poised and ready. But her eyes didn't open. Nothing changed. Not the slightest twitch of nerves, not the slightest change in her breathing. If she was faking, she was the best he'd ever seen. A pointed gun revealed more truth about nerves and breathing than any polygraph.

He backed away.

A few feet away he saw a purse resting on a leather ottoman. He stepped over, picked up the purse and backed away through the door. He closed the door without a sound and went back to the living room.

He rummaged through the purse and pulled out a pearl-blue lady's wallet and opened it. He pulled out a driver's license from inside the soft leather and looked at it. *No harm done,* he told himself. She hadn't heard him, hadn't seen him. In a few minutes the alarm would go off again. She'd find the old man here dead. *Good enough* .... Everything still moving along like it should. He compared the face on the driver's license to the sleeping woman in the bedroom.

It was her. *Jill Markley,* he told himself, reading the woman's name and the address of an apartment complex over in Oak Park. He committed the information to memory, shut the wallet and slipped it back down into the purse.

He pictured the place an hour from now, provided she didn't find the man dead and slip out of here. There would be uniformed police in and out, a detective or two. Lots of questions for her, a coroner. *Enjoy your day, Jill Markley ...,* he said to himself.

He left the apartment and boarded the elevator without looking around. The desk outside the apartment door would remain unoccupied for another few minutes. *Plenty of time ....*

Outside in the chilled morning air, he walked a block and turned off the street into an alley. He stuffed the hat down into a full dumpster, dropped the small syringe into some debris on the ground and crushed it underfoot. He took off the wig and carried it inside his coat. He walked back out and along the sidewalk going over what had happened.

The girl being there wasn't his fault. The old man was supposed to be there alone. Whoever had set this up would have to explain how they'd overlooked the woman. For his part, he'd handled it the right way, he thought, still walking. Nobody had died who wasn't supposed to die. That meant a lot.

Three blocks farther, he dumped the wig and he pulled a knit skull cap from his coat and put it on. Another block, he stood in another alley, unscrewed the silencer from the gun barrel and dropped both pieces onto a sewer grate at the edge of a curbing. He actually could have kept the gun and silencer, since he hadn't used them. *But no ....* He scooted them both into the sewer with the toe of his shoe.

That part's over ....

He took a deep breath and walked a block farther, to where he'd left the car. He got in the late model Ford, started it and drove away. Two miles along the parkway, he pulled off and drove down an exit ramp. A moment later he pulled into a sprawling motel parking lot where he left the Ford with the key lying under the front seat. He left the parking lot in a black Lexus he'd rented in Atlanta under an assumed name. At no time did he look up at the cameras mounted on the edge of the brick building. Cameras were everywhere these days. You had to live with them, give them as little as you could.

Pulling away from the lot he took off his gloves and shoved them back under his seat. He would leave them there until he crossed water somewhere. The lake, the canal. He didn't care. He'd pitch them out without stopping, not even slowing down. He was done here.

Next stop Atlanta ..., he told himself, then south in his own car, back down to the Gulf. Back home— *Get out of this cold ....* He relaxed behind the wheel and headed south out of town.

(HAPTER THREE

Two days later:
Hernando Beach, Florida:
Temperature 81 degrees:

On Sami Bloom's lanai, overlooking the Gulf of Mexico, Sami and Ray Dylan watched a red sun sink into the gulf. They lay half-entwined in a rope lounge hammock drinking vodka tonics, Ray with his eyes half-closed, still a little weary from the road.

"Welcome home, Ray," Sami whispered, even though he'd been there with her most of the afternoon. Much of that afternoon they'd spent in her bedroom just inside the sliding doors behind them. She lay with her head on his chest.

"Um-hmm," Dylan nodded. "Good to be back. Anything going on around here?"

"No, not really," Sami said. Then she said, "Oh, Henry Silky, my pool man scared the bejesus out of me the other day. He was here cleaning the pool, 5:30 in the morning. It was still dark out. I heard a noise, went to see about it—walked into him coming around the side of the house before I saw his truck back there."

"What were you doing up at 5:30?" Dylan asked.

"I just told you, I heard a noise," Sami said. "Anyway, he told me he thought I was out of town, like that made it okay." She shook her head. "Poor Henry, I know he's old, and he needs the business. But sometimes …." She let her words trail for interpretation.

Dylan smiled.

"I've heard this one," he said. "You can't get rid of him, because he and Sidney had an exclusive agreement for years."

"It's true. Silky Pool Service wouldn't exist if it hadn't been for Sidney. Henry's been coming here for years, like clockwork." She breathed out a sigh of resolve and changed the subject.

"So, how was Sarasota?" She asked. He'd told her he was driving down to Sarasota to check on the sale of a property he owned there. The less she knew about his work the better.

"Warm and busy," he said.

"How do you like the new agent?" she asked.

"He's okay."

"He …?" Sami looked at him. "I thought you said the agent's a woman."

"I meant she," Dylan corrected. "She's okay. Very efficient, seems like. She and her husband work together—both brokers, that's why I said he."

"Do they have names?"

Dylan detected a tone.

"Diane and Max Foster," he came back quickly. "She's the listing agent. Her husband brought in the buyer."

"What're they like, the Fosters?" Sami asked.

"Max is easygoing, a quiet guy," said Dylan. "His wife is all real estate. Long nails, big rings and coffee jitters. Pushy."

"But she brought you an offer fairly quick."

"That she did. I'm happy," Dylan said.

"So, the place sold and you're through dealing with it?" Sami said.

"Yes, I should be." Then he said, "I might have to go back for the closing in a couple of weeks. Depends on how things go." He let his eyes close more. "Did you miss me?"

"Yes," Sami said. "I've gotten used to us being together."

"Me too, I like it." Dylan smiled a little. "I thought about you, about back when you were a mermaid."

"You realize I wasn't *really* a mermaid, right?"

"No kidding?" He gave a faint smile.

"Really though, I'm flattered," Sami said. "Thank you for thinking of me."

"My pleasure," Dylan said, his eyes closed now.

A quiet moment passed while Sami drew little circles on his chest. Dylan's chest was still a little damp from earlier in the pool, and from the shower moments ago.

"I've been thinking, Ray …." She let her words trail. There was more coming; he waited for it. "Will you teach me to shoot a gun?" she asked.

Dylan cocked his head a little.

"That depends. Who are you going to shoot, Henry Silky some morning?" he asked.

"I'm serious." She gave him a friendly little slap

on his chest. "Will you? It's something I think I should know how to do, the way things are these days. What could I do if someone forced their way in here?"

"Call me …?" Dylan smiled, still playing it light. "I'll come over and shoot them for you?"

"It's not a joke, Ray," Sami persisted. "What if that wasn't Henry the other day, but some creep? What if you're *out of town?*"

There it was. Ray liked the slightest pout she put in her tone. It was something about him not asking her along on his made-up trip to Sarasota, he told himself.

"If I'd asked you to go with me, would you have gone?"

"No, probably not," said Sami. "But it's always nice to be invited."

"Next time then, I promise," Dylan said.

"Anyway, we could go to the gun range out off nineteen," she went on. "You could teach me. We could go tomorrow, make a day of it. I mean if you're rested up."

He considered it. She wasn't going to let up.

"You mean it …?" He looked at her, swirled his glass of Ketel One, ice and tonic.

"Yes, of course I *mean it."* She gave a push on his side. "Why would I say it if I didn't mean it?"

"Sorry," he said. He collected himself. "Sure, I'll teach you how to *fire a gun.* But you know they'll have instructors there who do that sort of thing—"

"No, I want you to teach me," she said, cutting him off. "I trust you, somebody I know. I don't want some stranger behind me, up against me. I've seen how they do."

"On television?" he said.

283

She smiled.

"Golf lessons, years ago. But that's what these *instructors* do, isn't it? Always trying to cop a feel, as they say?"

Cop a feel ...?

"I don't know, I've never *instructed* anybody," Dylan said. "But maybe I should. You make it sound interesting."

"Anyway, I'd rather you teach me," she said. "I know you carry a gun."

"Everybody in Florida carries a gun," Ray said wryly. "It's a state law."

"Sidney once told me you were in law enforcement a long time ago. Said you were some kind of undercover cop?"

Undercover cop ... He gave it a thought before answering.

"No," he said, "I was nothing like that. Sidney was mistaken."

Sami pondered the matter for a moment, a finger to her lip. "Of course, he once told me he thought you were a hit man."

Dylan stared at her, bemused.

"Jesus, Sidney said that? About me?"

"He did," Sami said. But then she played it off. "Later he took it back. He said he shouldn't have told me. Said he didn't know why he'd ever thought it in the first place."

"Man ...." Dylan shook his head. Then he said, "Okay, I spent some time in *law enforcement* a long time ago. I wasn't cut out for it. I never talked much about it back then." He smiled a little. "Who cares anyway?"

"I do," she said. "I can understand you didn't talk about it back then, if you worked undercover," she said. "But you can talk about it now, can't you?"

"I'd as soon not," he said, liking the way he was handling this, neither confirming nor denying a thing.

"You *did* carry a gun, though, all those years back then?" She kept at it.

"I did carry a gun back then." Dylan answered as if admitting to something pressed upon him. "I still keep one in the car."

Sami smiled coyly.

"You still know how to point it, aim it, and all that?"

"Yes, I can do all that," he said. Again he relaxed, sipped his vodka.

"Wow, that was like pulling teeth for you, Ray," she quipped. She returned his smile. "Can we do it then? Tomorrow, if you've got nothing else planned?"

Dylan thought about it again, gave a slight shrug.

"We'd have to get you some ear plugs, a gun to use—maybe a range rental."

He figured the next thing, she was going ask to use his gun. She'd seen the big .45 semiautomatic once when she'd opened the console in his Buick. He was ready for her: The .45 was too much gun for her, too big for her hand, too heavy, had too much recoil ….

But Sami didn't ask.

"I've bought one, a brand new one," she said, sounding excited at the prospect. "I picked it up the other day at the gun store on Cortez. Want to see it?" She was up from the hammock swinging a gauzy beach robe around her before Dylan could answer. "Don't move," she said, "I'll be right back." She walked away into the shadowy house, evening sunlight turning her loose.

Dylan stood up and slipped into his trousers and sat down in a cushioned aluminum chair and raked his fingers back through his hair. He hiked the chair around from facing out onto the gulf and sat half-facing the lanai sliders as she came walking back, a black and gray gun case in her hands.

She laid the case in front of him on the glass tabletop and opened it.

"Nice," he said. He looked at a compact two-tone stainless and black Sig Sauer .380, lying in a hard foam rubber bed. An extra stainless steel magazine lay beside it. "But you didn't have to go buy a gun."

"You mean I could have used yours?" she said, as if she'd read his thoughts. "I was afraid it might be too much gun for me to handle, starting out."

He just looked at her.

"Anyway," she went on, "You said it's nice. *Nice,* how?" She stood with a hand parked lightly on her hip.

"What do you mean, *nice how?*" Dylan countered. He picked up the gun, dropped its empty magazine clip into his hand and racked the slide, pinned it back and checked it. The gun chamber wasn't loaded; it appeared to have never been fired.

"I mean is it nice and *chic?* Nice and *accurate?* What?" she asked. "Did I do well, choosing it?"

"A Sig Sauer is a good choice. A little expensive maybe. As far as *accurate,* you won't know until you've shot it." Dylan said. "As far as it being *chic,* I've never heard anybody describe a gun that way." He smiled a little.

He turned the compact .380 on his palm, inspecting

it, hefting it, judging its weight. It was a handsome gun, he had to admit—a little small for his hand, about right for hers, and a nice backup either way. "How does it feel to you?" He looked up at her.

"It's a good fit," she said. "It feels comfortable." She held her hand out and he laid the pistol in it. She gripped it a little tight, then loosely; but she kept her finger on the trigger.

Dylan said, "It's a good habit to keep your finger off the trigger unless you're getting ready to fire."

"Why?" she asked. "It's not loaded, is it?"

Jesus ....

He gave her a look. "You have to ask?"

"Oh—" She got it. She smiled and took her finger out of the trigger guard and let the gun lay on her palm, the tip of the barrel pointed loosely at him. He reached out turned the barrel away from him.

"Well, anyway," she shrugged, "it's just the two of us here."

"Right," Dylan said, "so odds are if you accidently shot somebody it would only be me ... or yourself."

She sighed a little and handed him the gun.

"See? I do need someone to teach me."

"We'll go tomorrow, if you want," Dylan said. He shoved the empty magazine back into the .380. He laid the pistol inside the case down in its hard rubber bed and closed the lid.

Sami slipped into a chair beside him.

"Is it the right caliber? The fellow at the store said for personal protection, it is."

"It'll do," Dylan said. "It doesn't have the knock-down power of a .40 or a .45 caliber, but I wouldn't want to get shot with it."

"Ted said some cops carry the .380 for backup," Sami said.

"*Ted ...?*" said Dylan.

"Ted, the fellow at the gun store," Sami said.

"Ted." Dylan nodded; he considered it and said, "He's right, some cops probably do." He gestured at the Sig Sauer. "But this would be an expensive backup. "For less money, you can get a compact .40 caliber that gives a harder punch. Cops like .40s."

"If you were a cop today, what would you carry?" Sami asked.

"A cop *today?*" Dylan said. "I'd carry a flame-thrower, maybe hand grenades."

"I mean it, Ray," she said. "I'm trying to understand all this. I want to be able to take care of myself—in case I ever need to."

"I know," Dylan said, getting more serious. "Police need something that can take a person down, quick. A backup for emergencies, in case something happens to their regular sidearm." He stopped and looked at her, and said, "Sami, is everything all right?"

"Yes, of course," she said, "why wouldn't it be?"

Dylan let it go.

"No reason," he said. "We'll go to the range tomorrow, see how it goes. Florida has some rules you need to know if you're going to go heeled. Keep you out of trouble."

"*Heeled ...?*" she smiled. "Now there's an old term I haven't heard in a long while. Anyway, I'm not going to go *heeled.* I just want to keep a gun around the house. Know how to protect myself."

"Got it," Dylan said. "I've been watching too many Turner Classics," he said. "Still, if you're going to own a gun you need to know the Florida gun laws—to protect yourself." He looked at her again. "Are you sure everything's all right?"

"Everything's *fine*, Ray, I promise," she said; but he wasn't convinced. Women like Sami Bloom weren't usually interested in guns. *Unless something happened that caused them to be,* he told himself.

He'd see.

PROLOGUE

SEASON OF THE WIND

Here they come ....

Ray Dylan watched the cabin cruiser arrive ahead of the coming storm, the dark storm hanging low in the southeastern sky, grumbling and gathering like an angry crowd. When the captain cut the engine and let the boat sidle in and brush up alongside the dock, Dylan stretched out prone on his stomach, the rifle butt to his shoulder. He spread his legs comfortably and flattened the sides of his battered Red Wing boots against the platform deck— grounded himself down good and solid. He ran his arm through the leather rifle sling, made a wrap around his wrist and held the rifle scope tilted down toward the dock along the water's edge.

He kept his right eye close to the scope for now, using it to scan the three men standing on the cruiser's deck. Two of them held pistols partially hidden down close to their thigh. They looked all around at the shoreline. The captain of the private charter cruiser stayed at the console, hand on the wheel, as if to distance himself from the transaction. When one of the three men stepped off onto the dock and wrapped a line around a cleat, the captain turned his gaze straight ahead across the water.

Dylan moved his scope from face to face. *Russian spooks, the three of them ....* He saw Randall Parks step away a few feet, keeping an eye on everything, the submachine gun across his abdomen.

The man who tied off the boat reached his free hand out to assist the oldest of the three men out onto the dock. But his help was ignored. As soon as they were off the boat, Dylan scoped onto the captain, the console, articles on the boat's deck, the open door to the cuddy cabin. He moved his circle of vision back onto the dock and watched Leonid Volkov—aka The Professor—unlock the handcuff from his wrist and hold the leather case out to the older man. Thunder gave a low threatening growl in the Southeastern distance.

Dylan watched, seeing a trace of a smile on each man's face. He saw soundless words form on their lips— like watching a silent movie. The other two men from the boat closed around them, their pistols held low but ready. Dylan saw the older man hold out a thick manila envelope in exchange for the leather case. On the dock, Volkov brought up the loose handcuff and clasped it shut around the older man's wrist. Then he gave the man a tight smile and shook his free hand.

"The keys to the cuff and the case are on the way to Vancouver even now, Doctor," he said. "They will be there waiting for you. As always it is pleasure to do business with you."

"On behalf of our homelands," said the older man, nodding at the leather case in his hand. He gave the merest semblance of a bow and raised the case up against his chest. "*Auf wiedersehen, mein Freund.* Until we meet again."

"*Auf wiedersehen,*" said Volkov in the older man's native tongue. But to himself he said, *Again indeed ... this slimy East German prick.* He continued to smile as he took a step back. The envelope disappeared up under his loose shirt.

Randall Parks and the Russian stood motionless and watched as one of the men loosened the boat's line from the dock cleat and stepped onboard behind the older man. The third man followed. When the boat had swung away from the dock and started to make a wide circle out onto the bay, Volkov took a deep breath of satisfaction.

Moving in closer beside him, Parks lowered the sub machine gun a little and said, "Ready when you are, Professor."

On the moving boat the three men stood looking back at them, growing smaller, moving out farther across the water. Without turning his words to Parks, Volkov said sidelong, "Yes, Randall, proceed." As he spoke his right hand made a fist around a small black item in his pocket. He gave a smile and a wave to the departing cruiser, then backed away a few feet. A few seconds passed as the boat put more distance between itself and the dock.

From his perch atop the watchtower, Dylan saw the professor move back off the dock. But he didn't try to follow him with the scope. Instead, he kept his circle of attention on Parks, watching, waiting, mindful of the boat moving farther away as every second passed. He kept a running tab on the widening distance starting with a hundred yards at the water's edge. Now it was a hundred and twenty-five yards. Now a hundred and fifty—a hundred and seventy-five. He kept his breathing calm and even.

When he saw Parks' hand go to the handkerchief sticking up from his back pocket, he slid his face an inch farther back from the scope. *Ready ....* The instant Parks shook out the handkerchief and removed his glasses, Dylan moved the scope from the dock, out onto the cruiser. He locked himself down and settled in on his first target—the older man with the leather case cuffed to his wrist.

CHAPTER 1

This had all started with half of a torn dollar bill arriving in the mail. Ray Dylan knew what it meant, and he knew what to do. He was ready for it—ready and willing. More than willing.

The next morning at exactly 10:00 a.m. he took a call from Chicago in a designated phone booth over on McGregor Avenue. Keeping an eye on the street around him, he'd gone over the particulars with his contact man, Stan Delipello, finding out from him who to meet, where to meet, and how much *front-end money* he would be picking up. Dylan listened extra closely to Delipello. Usually, payment for a job was handled *in* Chicago, *by* Chicago. This was something new, Dylan picking up his own pay. He knew the Outfit had already been paid for brokering the deal. Their money always came first. *Always* … That's how the world worked—this world anyway.

"If the money's not straight, you walk, right then," Delipello said, "no ifs and buts about it."

"Sure," Dylan said. No one had to tell him that.

"Oh, another thing, listen up. You're military trained, if anybody asks."

"Got it," said Dylan. He wouldn't be lying. He'd served a hitch in the army.

"You were a marine, okay?" Delipello said.

"A marine …?" That boosted his curiosity.

"Yeah, don't ask me why," said Delipello. "Maybe this guy's got a thing for marines." A dark little chuckle, then it turned serious. "I'm only saying it in case it comes up." He paused for a half-second. "Any questions?"

A marine … what was this?

Dylan hesitated, just long enough for Delipello to realize he did have a question or two. Collecting his own pay seemed odd, for one. Now this *marine thing* was another.

"Your money is going to be larger than usual," Delipello said, as if hearing what was going through Dylan's mind, and getting out front of it. "We're talking twice as large." He let Dylan consider that for a moment. "You hearing me?" he asked.

"I hear you," Dylan said, the figure of thirty thousand dollars coming to mind. He wanted to ask why so much. But decided it wasn't a good idea. In fact this was not the time for questions of any kind. Questions had a way of answering themselves if he kept his eyes open and his mouth shut. *Let it lay*, he told himself.

"But listen to me, Kid," Delipello said. "These are Russians. They're heavy players. You watch yourself …." He paused, making sure Dylan got it. "Now, I'm going to tell you a little about them," he added.

Still calling me Kid …. But Dylan considered it a good thing. He lightened up; he started to say he always *watched himself.* But instead he said, "All right, I'm listening." He decided this was something bigger than what ordinarily came his way. Maybe this was why he would be collecting his own pay this time. Had Delipello been told by someone higher up to keep an extra wide distance from this thing? Yes, he believed so. Could this thing possibly be a bump up for him? Yes, he believed that too....

Three days later Dylan met with the two Soviet spooks Delipello told him about, the Russian, Leonid *The Professor* Volkov, and his Cuban-American henchman, Randall Parks. The three stood beneath a Tiki shelter out of a blowing rain, thunder rumbling in the distance. Dylan wore faded Levis, a dark polo shirt, and a pair of battered Red Wing 877 work boots—ironworker boots. The men scrutinized him. Dylan stopped a few feet away and looked them up and down in response. Then he stepped in closer.

"I believe you have something for us?" the Russian said. He spoke with only the slightest trace of a Russian accent.

Without answering, Dylan took the torn half of a dollar bill from his shirt pocket and handed it over to the Cuban, then watched, along with the Russian as the Cuban fitted the torn half to another torn half he'd produced from his trouser pocket. All three leaned in close over the torn halves, heads bowed as if in prayer and checked the fit, the torn serial number, how well the two halves fit together.

"I'm satisfied, are you?" the Russian asked Dylan after a moment.

Dylan gave a short nod.

"Good," said the Russian. He nodded in turn at the Cuban who put both halves in his pocket and stood staring at Dylan. If the Cuban was supposed to be intimidating him it wasn't working. He just looked big and awkward, with pasty skin. *A junkie ...? Maybe.* Dylan sized him up. He wore thick-lens glasses, their black frame held together across the bridge of his nose by a wrap of soiled white tape. His eyes looked huge, looming behind the thick glass. His stare continued as he produced a thick manila envelope from under his shirt and handed it over.

Dylan opened the envelope and reached a thumb and two fingers into it. The two watched him start to raise the cash from the envelope.

"So then, what do we call you?" the Russian asked.

Call him...? Dylan stopped what he was doing and looked at him. *What was this ...?*

Seeing the flat expression on the young American's face the Russian offered the slightest shrug. A cheesy smile flickered. His teeth were small and beady, with a grayish tint to them. "I like to know what to call the man I am working with," he said. "We are civilized human beings after all." Again the slight shrug.

Okay....

Dylan looked back and forth at the two. Then he'd stopped and held the cash just above the top edge of the envelope.

"Call me *Mr. Green*," he said, gesturing at the money in his hand. He tucked the cash back into the envelope and shoved the envelope down behind his belt. *Mr. Green...?* The two men glanced at each other, but let it go. And that was that.

He spent most of the next three days in his hotel room, the envelope of money laying open on the nightstand beside his unmade bed. He'd thought about his two clients. From the details Delipello had given him they were part of a KGB spook operation working out of South Florida. But that was all right. Florida was rife with spook operations. He'd worked for them before, probably more times than he realized. When Chicago set up a job for him he took it, no questions asked. KGB? Sure, sometimes. He didn't know. Anyway, they paid well, and for the most part they only killed their own, rogue KBG agents, Cuban contract agents, smugglers, counterfeiters they no longer needed —anybody who had served their purpose and might now get in the way.

He checked the clock beside the bed: 3:14 p.m., and sipped the last of his coffee from the Styrofoam cup. Randall Parks was on his way. They would look like two guys riding to work together, second shift somewhere. He sat the empty cup down and scoped up the envelope. *Time to go….* If spooks wanted their own people killed, what did he care? He stuffed the envelope behind his belt. Besides, there was something almost patriotic about killing *commies* for a living—*commies, spies*. Whatever.

Now and then everybody in the intelligence community needed somebody killed. He'd heard it referred to as clipping weeds from their gardens. When clipping time came both the KGB and the CIA contacted the Chicago Outfit. He picked up the rifle case and looked around the room. He wouldn't be coming back here.

"You're driving," Parks told him, stepping from the battered topless Jeep as soon as he'd pulled up out front of the hotel. There were no doors on the vehicle, no top. Dylan stepped up inside and stowed his rifle case on edge between the two front seats.

"Where to?" he asked, settling in, his hand resting atop the tall floor shift knob. The street was still wet and steamy from a hard windy rain that had swept through earlier then stopped as suddenly as it had started. Thunder still grumbled far off.

"I'll tell you as we go," Parks said, his voice sounding a little tense.

All right….

Dylan pulled the shift back into first gear and put the Jeep forward into the afternoon traffic along palm-lined McGregor Avenue, following the Caloosahatchee River through the heart of town.

CHAPTER 2

A half an hour later they traveled through the outskirts of the city, their surroundings turning gradually into weed and sand. Palm and swampland tightened around them. Dylan drove on, guiding the Jeep along a secluded two lane road that appeared to be headed nowhere. Randall Parks rode shotgun beside him. At a wide turn in the crumbling asphalt Parks said, "Stop here," and motioned for him to pull off onto a sand trail leading into a tangle of swamp bracken and wild cabbage palm. Snakes crawled away from the side of the trail, out the sight and sound from the encroaching engine.

Dylan braked the Jeep to a halt, his right hand resting atop the gear shift. As he looked at Parks, he saw the big man pull up an FMK submachine gun from the opposite side of his seat. He seemed to make a point of letting Dylan see him rack a round into the gun's chamber.

"I'll be carrying this from here on in, *Mr. Green*," he said.

Dylan saw a trace of a smug grin turned stiff by a

swollen cold sore on Parks' lower lip. Parks' hand rested on the gun, his big thumb under the safety switch. Dylan sat watching stone-faced, not about to give him whatever reaction he was looking for.

"Does the machinegun make you nervous, *Mr. Green?*" Parks asked.

"No," Dylan came back, "do I look nervous to you?" He stared at Parks with ice in his eyes. The big Cuban was being way too confident for his own good. Dylan considered grabbing the machinegun barrel with one hand, drawing his .45 from the back of his belt with his other and batting him across the face with it. *Take it easy,* he cautioned himself, *you've got money riding on this….*

"Oh, I forgot," Parks said. He jiggled the machinegun a little. "Being a big tough marine, this doesn't bother you, does it?" He paused then said, "You are a marine, eh?"

"No, I'm not," Dylan said flatly. He let the word hang for a moment and saw a strange look come over Parks' face. Then he added, "I was once. Did a four year tour."

"Okay." Parks looked relieved. "You know what they say, 'Once a marine always a marine.'" He offered a cold-sore twisted grin.

"I suppose so," Dylan replied. "Why did you ask?"

Parks only nodded without answering, but Dylan thought he saw him breathe a little easier. *Just checking him out.*

Dylan was right, the FMK was for show, like wearing a sign that read, *Don't fuck with me, I've got a machinegun.*

"Are we ready to go?" he asked Parks, the Jeep idling, the transmission in first gear. "Or have you got some more bullshit questions for me?"

Parks ignored the sharp attitude. He stared at him a moment longer, as if he had things he wanted to ask but wasn't sure how to go about it. Finally he turned forward and nodded at the overgrown trail lying before them. *Yep, a junkie …*, Dylan assured himself. A screwball junkie at that.

"Yes," Parks said, "we're ready." He nodded along the overgrown trail. "We going to go to a—"

"Hang on," Dylan said, cutting Parks short. Revving the Jeep's engine as he popped the clutch, he sent the vehicle bolting forward. The force sent Parks jerking back in his seat, then thrust him forward in his seat toward the windshield. He threw a hand up and grasped the overhead roll bar, bracing himself. The FMK spilled forward off his lap. He grappled with it and managed to get it back onto his knee.

"Now where are we going?" Dylan asked with more iron in his tone.

"To a lookout station up ahead," Parks replied.

Dylan gazed straight ahead, knowing he could have taken the big guy apart in those past few seconds. But he was here for the money, nothing else. Do the work, take the rest of his pay and roll on.

Any other games in mind …? He gave Parks a sidelong glance. Parks wouldn't face him. The Jeep bounced and swayed over potholes, sand mounds and past fleeing reptiles. He saw Parks hold onto the roll bar with both hands, clamping the FMK between his thighs, watching the trail through his thick glasses.

Moments before the killing started, Leonid *The Professor* Volkov had arrived and stood out of sight among wild palm at the edge of a clearing near the docks. He mopped his wet face with a handkerchief and cursed the damp scalding heat in Russian. Though he kept his voice low, and though the land surrounding him lay vacant, he instinctively glanced around as if to see if he'd been heard. A few miles behind him the city of Fort Myers Beach lay in surrender to the afternoon heat. Even if there had been someone within hearing range, here on the narrow strip of sand and mangrove swampland, Volkov doubted they would have recognized his language. And if they had, what of it? Americans seldom paid attention to what went on around them. They wouldn't know what language he was speaking. He could be speaking Russian, or Zulu, or *Martian*. Whatever. These ignorant mongrels wouldn't know. They would likely bat their eyes and laugh, and offer him a beer.

Fucking Americans ….

This time he cursed to himself in English, as good as any English he'd heard during his tenure in this sweltering pigsty. He looked around again, in contempt, loathing this scalding inferno, this primordial bacterial *swamp*. He hated Florida even worse than he hated Cuba, if such a thing was possible. Although not by much, he had to admit. True, he found both places equally repulsive, the heat, the insistent sweat, the stench of sewerage improperly treated. Fortunately the Cubans had learned from *his people* not to mix their natural odor with that of some sickening sweet western cologne. His nose crooked a little at the thought of it.

At least in the austere barrio that all of Havana

had become there was no one out to kill him—he smiled faintly—no one he knew of, that is. He took a deep breath, knowing that his status there might change quickly after today.

He stepped over to the water's edge and watched as the boat grew larger, moving toward him from the direction of Sanibel Island. The cruiser bobbed slightly, its bow tilted up, not rising up onto plane or even attempting to. Volkov shook his head and watched it for a few seconds longer. He turned at the sound of Parks walking through the foliage and bracken behind him, holding the submachine gun across his waist.

"Do you have our *hired help* squared away?" Volkov asked, liking the sound of his English, not realizing there remained a slight hint of an accent in it.

"He's waiting for my signal," Parks said, his English also good, even with a shadow of Urban Cuban Spanish behind the vowel sounds. Two men well spoken, from opposite sides of the planet, each driven to master the language of a people they would destroy without hesitancy.

"He appears to be well prepared," Parks said. If he could keep from it, he wasn't going to admit that he'd learned very little about the young American in the scuffed up work boots. He nodded in agreement with himself. "I think we'll like the job he does here." He looked out at the approaching boat. "Although, I have to say, my teenage sister could do this."

"Oh?" Volkov appraised him up and down cynically. "Is your sister a military trained American assassin? Is she proficient with a sniper rifle?" His hard stare demanded an answer, no matter how obvious. "Is she a hired killer, like our fellow here?"

"No, of course not, comrade," Parks said. "I apologize"

"Then she certainly would *not* be proficient in doing this," Volkov snapped, turning his face away. He looked out at the cruiser, then back at Parks with a sharp stare and said, "Did you learn any more about him. Does the assassin I *received* fit the assassin I *ordered?*"

"No more than he told us the other day," Parks had to concede. "He does not say much, comrade."

Volkov glared at him and said, "Please dare to call me *comrade* again, *imbecile*! So I can take pleasure in examining your eye on the palm of my hand." He held his palm out as if Parks' eye was already in it.

Parks swallowed a dry knot in his throat. He'd seen enough out of Professor Leonid Volkov to know that his threat should be taken seriously.

"His rifle and scope are the kind Marine snipers use. They are difficult for civilians to acquire—especially the scope."

"But you did not find out if he is a marine, did you?" Volkov pressed.

"He said he was a marine for four years, com— I mean, *Professor* Volkov," Parks corrected quickly. "I tried to find out more about him, but he doesn't say much." He paused then added, "He doesn't appear to like people."

Doesn't like people ….

Volkov grumbled under his breath and shook his head. As the sound of the approaching boat became audible he turned toward a patch of thick foliage and gave barely noticeable hand sign. Parks looked surprised as a large man carrying an Uzi stepped from behind a cabbage palm and moved forward a little and went back out of sight.

"I didn't know you were bringing Gilbert Haas," Parks said.

"That's because I chose not to tell you," Volkov said in a crisp tone. "I also brought Thomas Moon. I want dependable backup." Dismissing the matter, he bent down and picked up the small leather case at his feet. As he straightened he saw Parks searching the foliage for the other man Volkov had mentioned.

"Be ready, Randall," he said in a tone of warning, drawing Parks' attention back to him. "Our futures are at stake."

Parks stiffened his stance. He watched Volkov snap a handcuff onto his own wrist and snap the other cuff on the case's handle. Volkov smiled a little and wiggled his cuffed hand at Parks.

"Image is everything, here in this land of simpletons and psychotics," he said with wry contempt. He held the case at his side. "Now, let us complete our mission." The two stepped onto a weathered dock and walked out and waited as the boat slowed and idled in toward them.

CHAPTER 3

On the boat, the captain jerked his hands back from the wheel when thick blood and matter dashed across the instrument panel. He saw the man with the leather case handcuffed to him fall to the deck. "*Good God!*" He caught a glimpse of blood splatter on the console and the door of the cuddy cabin to his left. He felt the slap of warm blood on the back of his neck. The sound of the shot followed a second behind the damage it produced. When he'd seen the older man fall, it took only a fraction of a second for realization to set in. "*Good God!*" he said again. He shoved the throttle forward, wide open. The other two men had turned to their fallen comrade, but the sudden thrust of the boat plunged them backwards, off balance. They grabbed the safety rail atop the rear gunwale and hung on.

On the watchtower, Dylan slid the rifle bolt forward and down with a sideward flick of his finger. His position never wavered. His right eye stayed riveted on the two figures trapped inside the dark circle of death. In the short seconds it took the two targets to regain their balance, fate had stood them side-by-side. *Good position....* They clung to the rail, looking around at the dead man on deck.

Knowing the two wouldn't stay there long, Dylan drew his aim to the one on his right as the boat sped farther away. Instead of trying to follow the rise and fall of the boat among the waves, he locked down and held his breath. *Let it come up to you ....* He watched the target go down almost completely out of his sight—out of his scope circle. He held steady. *Time it ....* As the target reached the lowest point of the boat's fall, Dylan made the shot. Then, without breathing, without releasing his eye, he watched the boat's up-surge raise the target into the bullet's path, as if in slow motion.

Confident in his shot, Dylan slipped the bolt back and forth again expertly, and drew his aim on the third man just as the second target slammed down onto the deck. But the third man had seen enough. He leaped over the two bodies on deck and sprang toward the cuddy cabin door, covered with blood splatter and gore. Dylan's third shot sent a bullet striking him high between his shoulders as he ducked out of sight. Dylan watched him suddenly take flight, the bullet launching him into the cabin. His right shoe flipped into the air behind him.

And that's that ....

Contract completed, Dylan relaxed and breathed deep. He moved the scope across the boat and saw that the captain had abandoned the helm. He had slipped over behind a gear locker leaving the boat to steer itself. Left to its own resource, the boat had set about a wide meandering turn on the open bay.

What now ...?

Dylan watched for a second, speculating. He

309

lowered the rifle and looked down at Parks standing alone on the dock—his Russian comrade having slipped away into the nearby foliage, Dylan supposed. He saw Parks turn and look up in his direction. Then they both turned their attention back out to the boat where Dylan saw the captain had stepped back behind his console and re-taken the helm. He'd righted the boat and made a beeline across the bay.

Good enough. You're done here …, Dylan told himself.

He gathered the three warm empty shell casings and laid the rifle over beside him. Still, he had to wonder why the Russian was leaving the captain alive. *A living witness.* The man had seen the Russian's face—had seen Parks' face as well. Under the circumstances, it would seem only practical—

His thoughts cut short. A powerful blast out on the water shook the watchtower, the ground beneath it, the foliage surrounding it. Dylan ducked in tight reflex, but still managed to look out onto the middle of the bay. The boat was gone. In its place, black smoke, debris and broken pieces of the cruiser's hull still spinning upwards in a roiling ball of fire. He watched as the fireball reached its apex and started raining back down. Whatever was left of the boat, its captain, its cargo, splashed in a ragged fifty yard circle out there under a darkening evening sky.

End of discussion, time to go ….

He gathered his gear. Now that the question of a living witness was off the board, he had another question. If the Russian's plan was to blow the boat up, why pay him to first take out the three targets?

Good question …, he told himself, *now forget it.*

He hurriedly rolled up the straw mat.

It was something he'd ask about if he had time, but he had no time. He opened the case and laid the mat in its spot. He capped both ends of the scope and laid the rifle in its foam rubber bed. His eyes went to the binoculars and the steady-bag that were there when he'd arrived. Something troubled him about the items. He left them where they stood. Nobody had ever left something like that for him. He hadn't known how to take it. At any rate, they weren't his; they weren't leaving here with him. He would mention the items to Parks—let him deal with it. Now that the job was finished, all Dylan had left to do was collect the other half of his money and he was out of here ....

Other Books by Ralph Cotton

The Gun Culture Series

1. Friend of a Friend	*2015*
2. Season of the Wind	*2017*
3. Blowback: Treasure Coast	*2020*

Western Classics

The Life and Times of Jeston Nash

1. While Angels Dance*	*1994*
2. Powder River	*1995*
3. Price of a Horse	*1996*
4. Cost of a Killing	*1996*
5. Killers of Man	*1997*
6. Trick of the Trade	*1997*

** **While Angels Dance** was a candidate for the **Pulitzer Prize** in fiction in 1994. This entire **Western Classic** series has been released and is available from Amazon.com and other retailers, as well as Kindle and other ebook formats.*

Dead or Alive Trilogy

1. Hangman's Choice	*2000*
2. Devil's Due	*2001*
3. Blood Money	*2002*

*The **Dead or Alive Trilogy** is available from Amazon.com and other retailers, as well as Kindle and other ebook formats, as part of **Ralph Cotton's Western Classics.***

Other Books by Ralph Cotton

Danny Duggin (Written for the Estate of Ralph Compton)

1. The Shadow of a Noose		2000
2. Riders of Judgement		2001
3. Death Along the Cimarron		2003

Gunman's Reputation (Lawrence Shaw)

1. Gunman's Song		2004
2. Between Hell and Texas		2004
3. The Law in Somos Santos		2005
4. Bad Day at Willow Creek		2006
5. Fast Guns Out of Texas		2007
6. Ride to Hell's Gate		2008
7.Gunmen of the Desert Sands		2008
8. Crossing Fire River		2009
9. Escape From Fire River		2009
10. Gun Country		2010
11. City of Bad Men		2011

Spin-Off Novels

1. Webb's Posse		2003
2. Fighting Men (Sherman Dahl)		2010
3. Gun Law (Sherman Dahl)		2011
4. Summer's Horses (Will Summers)		2011
5. Incident at Gunn Point (Will Summers)		2012
6. Midnight Rider (Will Summers)		2012

Other Books by Ralph Cotton

Ranger Sam Burrack (Big Iron Series)

1. Montana Red	*1998*
2. The Badlands	*1998*
3. Justice	*1999*
4. Border Dogs	*1999*
5. Blue Star Tattoo	*2000*
6. Blood Rock	*2001*
7. Jurisdiction	*2002*
8. Vengeance	*2003*
9. Sabre's Edge	*2003*
10. Hell's Riders	*2004*
11. Showdown at Rio Sagrado	*2004*
12. Dead Man's Canyon	*2004*
13. Killing Plain	*2005*
14. Black Mesa	*2005*
15. Trouble Creek	*2006*
16. Gunfight at Cold Devil	*2006*
17. Sabio's Redemption	*2007*
18. Killing Texas Bob	*2007*
19. Nightfall at Little Aces	*2008*
20. Ambush at Shadow Valley	*2008*
21. Showdown at Hole-In-The-Wall	*2009*
22. Riders from Long Pines	*2009*
23. A Hanging in Wild Wind	*2010*
24. Black Valley Riders	*2010*
25. Lawman from Nogales	*2011*
26. Wildfire	*2012*
27. Lookout Hill	*2012*

Other Books by Ralph Cotton

Ranger Sam Burrack (Big Iron Series), *cont.*

Stand Alone Novels

Author Ralph Cotton

Ralph Cotton is a *Best Selling Author* with over *Seventy* books to his credit and millions of books in print. Ralph's books are top sellers in the Western and Civil War/Western genres, and in 2015 he debuted his new ***Gun Culture Crime Series*** with ***Friend of a Friend***. Known for fast-paced narrative and wry dark humor, Ralph's introduction to the Florida crime fiction genre has been well received.

Blowback Treasure Coast is the 3rd novel in the ***Gun Culture Crime series***, written and published in 2020,

Ralph lives on the Florida coast with his wife Mary Lynn. He writes prodigiously, but also enjoys painting, photography, sailing and playing guitar.